Barbed Wire
and Brumbies

Alicia Hitchcock

ISBN: 978-0-6483578-5-8

For my Mum,
who instilled in me a love of reading
and the belief that I can follow my dreams.

Chapter 1
Margaret
April 1943

When shadows covered the page, Maggie looked up and found the sun had almost reached the horizon. Snapping her book shut, she ran through the paddocks and inside the homestead, rushing into the dining room just as her father finished saying grace. George opened his eyes and glared at her.

"Tardy again, I see." Maggie bit her bottom lip and mumbled an apology before taking her seat next to her brother, James. Their older brother Richard and his wife Joan were seated across from them while their mother and father sat at opposite ends. George began carving the large roast chicken while Elizabeth lifted the lid on the bowls filled with roasted vegetables. There was more than enough to feed the family thanks to their efforts in the expansive kitchen garden at the side of the homestead.

As they ate, George and Richard regaled the group with an anecdote about their neighbour Old Watto falling face-first in mud while trying to chase after a sheep attempting to make a run for freedom. Elizabeth, Joan, and Maggie discussed the upcoming CWA meeting and the planning for the next dance to be held at the Colton town hall. Maggie felt a companionable warmth spread through her and she relaxed back in her seat. Family was everything and these Sunday night dinners were the highlight of her week. As the youngest child and only daughter, she often felt unseen, but not on nights like this. James broke her reverie and the cheery mood in one fell swoop.

"It irks me that we're at war with those bloody Jerrys, Eyeties, and Nips. Our men are fighting and dying over there while their families are struggling to keep their farms going back here. The sooner this war is over, the better," James pointed his fork towards Richard, "but they need men who are willing to fight. Conscripting men who don't want to be there isn't the answer." Elizabeth closed her eyes, and Joan studied the tablecloth while Richard and Maggie looked from James to their father. Please don't argue again. Not now, Maggie thought. George put down his cutlery and wiped his mouth with a napkin before responding. "James, I will not have that kind of language used in this house. As for the war efforts, all we can do is continue to work this farm and provide what we can for our community." James opened his mouth to protest, but George raised a hand to silence him. "This discussion will not continue. Nobody in this room will be going to war if I have anything to do with it, and that's final. I don't want to hear another word about it." James scowled but refrained himself. The only sound to fill the room after that was the clattering of cutlery as they finished the meal in silence. Maggie took the last bite of her roast potato and snuck a look at James. His brow furrowed, and he shoved the food into his mouth with his fork. Why did he have to ruin their dinner with talk of war? I just wanted to forget about it, even if only for a moment.

Maggie, Elizabeth, and Joan cleared the table, and George declared he was too tired for a nightcap. Maggie glared at James and opened her mouth, but Elizabeth coughed and drew her lips into a thin line. Now was not the time.

They all moved to the verandah to bid farewell to Richard and Joan, who lived in a small home on the neighbouring farm. James retreated to his bedroom, George retired to his study, and Maggie and Elizabeth finished cleaning up.

"Why did he have to do that?" Maggie asked. Elizabeth shook her head and sighed.

"He's filled with the passion of youth. So many young men are the same. I just hope he doesn't disobey your father." Elizabeth stood over the sink, looking down at her hands still in the water. Maggie put the last of the dishes away and hung the teatowel over a chair before bidding her mother goodnight and walking down the hallway. Passing George's study, she saw him sitting at his desk with his head in his hands. James's patriotism was creating a rift in their tightknit family.

***

Maggie sat on the front lawn with her back against the trunk of the willow tree as the warm autumn sun filtered through its leaves. Her mother would scold her if she found her reading the new novel by Simone de Beauvoir that she'd borrowed from Patty, so she propped the book behind her knees and kept an eye on the front door. Elizabeth and Joan were inside baking a new biscuit recipe that Elizabeth had seen in the Women's Weekly. The novel's world drew Maggie in until the spell of the words was broken by the sound of hooves galloping along the driveway. James dismounted and ran inside, calling out for George. Maggie's stomach knotted and her chest tightened. She raced to the kitchen and stood next to Joan, panting and holding her chest.

"James? What's wrong?" Elizabeth asked. James ignored her and paced the floor. He turned as George pulled open the screen door and stormed in.

"What's all this about?" George demanded. James stood with his arms at his sides and his hands in fists.

"Those bastards are winning this war and I will not stand back any longer. I've enlisted. You can't stop me," James shouted his revelation, pointing at George. The women in the room let out an unmistakable gasp. Maggie looked from one man to the other. She could see the rising anger in the throbbing vein in her father's neck.

She knew this day was coming. They all did. James had been discussing the war at every opportunity, and his prejudice against the Germans, Italians, and Japanese was bubbling closer to the surface with each passing day. But that didn't make this any easier. George took a deep breath and squared his shoulders.

"This war was not of our making. Men are dying over there every day and you want to join them? You're needed here. I forbid you to go."

"It's too late, Dad. I've made my decision. You can't stop me from fighting for what I believe in," he said as he thumped his fist on the table.

"But James, what if something happens to you? What about Kathleen? We need you here. Your place is with us," Elizabeth cried out as she moved towards him and took his hand in hers. James's eyes betrayed the pain of his decision, but there was purpose in the set of his mouth. Maggie knew there was nothing anyone could say that would change his mind. James had always been headstrong. A Sleeman family trait.

"I'm sorry, Mum. What's done is done. I've talked it over with Kathleen, and she understands. I'll be leaving for New Guinea next Monday." He freed his hand and headed back through the house towards the front door.

"If you go, you'll not be welcome back here." George's voice boomed and his chest rose and fell in deep breaths as the anger grew. He let the kitchen door slam behind him and he stalked towards the shed. The three women stood rooted to the spot for what seemed like an eternity. Their family would never be the same. James's decision had changed everything. What if he was injured? Or worse, what if he was killed? Maggie cursed his stubbornness. Elizabeth dusted her hands, took off her apron, and left the room. There was nothing Joan or Maggie could do or say to make the situation any better.

"I want to tell you it'll be all right, but I can't," Joan said as she gathered her belongings. Maggie knew she was right. Nobody knew what was going to happen from one day to the next. This war had made life even more precarious. As she waved Joan off, Maggie recognised that this tension in their home was far from over.

***

"Maggie dear, are you ready yet? We need to be there before 10," Elizabeth called out. Maggie reluctantly finished dressing, quickly braided her long blonde hair into a messy plait, and hurried into the hallway just in time to catch Elizabeth as she exited through the front door. Maggie knew she'd be furious that they were late, but the thought of sitting through another afternoon tea with the ladies of the Colton branch of the Country Women's Association wasn't all that enticing. Every week was the same old routine. At least, that's how Maggie viewed it. The women would sit and discuss their husbands and children, the war effort, or their current craft project. Meanwhile, the Younger Set mingled in the next room, discussing the latest fashionable item or which eligible bachelors were left in the district. Maggie found it all tiresome. Why couldn't they discuss novels or art or grand ideas about the world?

Elizabeth jerked on the handbrake as she parked their dark-coloured Ford next to an identical car. They walked through the immaculate rose gardens toward the imposing two-storey home, and the sound of high-pitched laughter rang out. Maggie harrumphed and trailed behind her mother. Elizabeth headed for the sitting room, where the natter of five voices, all trying to be heard at once, rang out through the rest of the house. The voice of esteemed branch president Mrs Fulton pierced through the rumble as she regained control of the room. Elizabeth clicked her tongue and glared at Maggie. Then she walked in, leaving Maggie to find her way to where the Younger Set congregated. She stepped into the dining room to a perceptible silence. The eyes of the young women were on her. She felt like a mouse in the grips of a standoff with a cat. She knew what they wanted—a reaction to James's enlistment. Straightening her back, she surveyed the room. The outer edge was ringed with women sitting in high-backed chairs, and the large mahogany dining table was covered with biscuits, scones, slices, and cakes. She spotted Joan and

Mary sitting by the window overlooking the garden and made her way to the vacant chair next to Joan. The chatter resumed, and she leaned forward as she strained to hear them over the cacophony.

"I don't know how we'll manage now. Oh, Harry!" Mary sobbed into her crumpled handkerchief. Joan looked at Maggie, her mouth turned down at the corners, and she patted her friend on the arm.

"I'm so sorry, Mary. Harry was a lovely lad. He always had a story to tell." Joan cleared her throat. "I would offer to send Richard over to help, but with him tending to our farm, as well as his father's, he's feeling a little overworked lately. The drifters come through, but they don't stay long enough to make a real dent in the workload. This awful war is taking its toll on so many people." Comprehension dawned on Maggie. She knew Mary's younger brother, Harry. A few months ago, he won the unfortunate lottery and was conscripted. He must have been killed in action. Her thoughts turned to James. He'd been gone for five weeks, and the family hadn't had word from him. They didn't know where he was or if he was still alive.

The air in the room seemed suffocating, and Maggie looked for a way out. She strode to the back garden and stood near the rose bushes. She looked up at the grey clouds rolling in and hoped they didn't bring bad news as well as much-needed rain.

"There you are." Patricia's voice broke through Maggie's thoughts, and she turned to see her best friend, holding a plate full of cherry slice and chocolate cake. Patricia was a head taller and slightly broader than Maggie, dark-haired to Maggie's light. They were the opposite of each other in many ways. Patricia was outgoing and always up for some mischief. In contrast, Maggie was reserved and always followed the rules. Lately, Maggie had been consumed by an almost desperate desire to experience more of the world. They'd been best friends since they met as five-year-olds at church one Sunday, not long after Patricia's family moved to Colton. "I heard about James. Kathleen's garnering the sympathy of anyone who'll listen, of course. How did your dad take it? I bet your mum was a mess. Larry Obermeer did the same thing last week, and I swear I could hear his parents yelling from across the paddock. Did I tell you I'm going to be a nurse?" Maggie smiled. Patricia always talked a mile a minute, and it was just what she needed.

"Really?" she asked, grabbing some cake from the proffered plate. Patricia nodded and stuffed a large piece of cherry slice into her mouth.

"I'll get to travel and meet lots of people. I can't wait. Dad's proud as punch, but Mum thinks I'm not ready to leave Colton. I'm 21, for goodness sake. You should become one too. We could get stationed together. We might even meet some handsome soldiers." She winked, and Maggie laughed. Patty made it sound like a fabulous adventure, but as much as she'd like to go, she knew she couldn't leave the farm just yet.

"I think I'd better stay here for now. I know you'll have a swell time though. When do you leave?"

"I sent my application last week, but once it's accepted, I'll be off to Perth for training and then who knows where. It's exciting to think in a few months, I could be in a whole different country." She raised one shoulder and head cocked to the side. "It would be even better if we were doing it together." Maggie finished her cake and considered Patricia's proposition. She could sign up as a nurse and Patty would find a way to make it fun. But her parents would not be happy about having another child so close to the war. She let out a sigh. Jarrah Downs was her home, and it was the right place to be for the moment. Her father had worked hard to build their large stone and weatherboard homestead surrounded by paddocks filled with cattle and draught horses. He'd bought neighbouring properties and expanded the operations. Now, it was almost 1000 acres and one of the largest farms in the district. Running it was an enormous job and with James gone, all the work had fallen on George and Richard. "I can't. I'm needed here. But don't forget about little old me while you're gallivanting around the world," Maggie said as she linked her arm through Patricia's and they strolled back towards the Fulton's house.

***

The days were sunny, but the nights had started to chill. Maggie heard the fire crackling in her father's study. She imagined he was working through the agenda for the town council meeting next week. George had been a councillor for years, and as an eminent business owner, he was well respected among the local community. She knocked on the door and entered when she heard a mumble. He sat behind his large oak desk while the family's black and white kelpie, Max, lay curled on the mat near the fireplace. Maggie walked over, kneeled and stroked the dog's soft ears. She turned and looked at her father and then back at the fire.

"What is it, Maggie? I know you have something on your mind." Maggie sighed and moved to the chair in front of his desk. He knew her too well. He often joked that her inquisitive nature would get her into trouble one day. Maggie steeled herself and looked him in the eyes.

"Will we be able to keep the farm? I know you don't think I can help, but I can do almost anything that James could." Her words tumbled out quickly before her resolve softened. After they'd returned from the CWA meeting, Maggie had spent the afternoon by the river pondering Patricia's news and thinking about what some families in the district were going through. With many of the men away, the women often found themselves trying to work their farms and raise their families on their own. She knew that her family was in a better financial position than most, but this war was seeping its way into every aspect of their way of life. George swirled his whisky and took a sip. He ran a hand down his face and over his mouth and greying beard, resting it on his chin.

"We are by no means losing this farm. Richard and I can manage just fine." He came to stand by her side and lifted her up gently by the arm so that they stood facing each other. "I know things are changing for our neighbours, but this farm has been in our family for two generations. I'll be damned if we lose it on my watch." He looked down at the fire and then at Maggie. "You, young lady, need to stop fussing with your books, and the local gossip, and concentrate on helping your mother and Joan." His reply left her angry and deflated all at once, but she knew there was no arguing with him. She kissed him on the cheek, then bent and ruffled Max on the head before making her way to her room. Standing by the window, she lifted her gaze towards the stars. She should have known that the conversation would not go the way she had planned. If he wasn't so stubborn, she could help make things easier for him. She thought back to when she'd seen him earlier that day struggling to manoeuvre the wheel off the tractor; his maimed left leg didn't help the situation. She puffed the air out of her cheeks and folded her arms. If he could be stubborn, then so could she.

***

Maggie inclined her head and held the piece of paper closer, then moved it back, repeating the process several times before shaking her head and dropping the note on her desk. At times, Doctor Mosely's scrawl was a challenge to decipher, and she had to ask him to take a look. Often, he couldn't even read his own handwriting, so he never berated her for not being able to do it. He was in with a patient, so she tidied up the files that appeared to pile up perpetually on her desk.

"Rightio, you're all set, Mrs Winkler. See you next week," Doctor Mosely said to the older woman as he opened his office door. She briefly nodded to them both before tugging the surgery door open with a low grunt. The bell jingled as the door shut behind her.

"Doctor Mosely, would you mind helping me with this one?" Maggie handed him the note and he squinted at it. Recognition crossed his features.

"This one's for me. It's supposed to read 'research penicillin'. There's some movement in medical circles about this new wonder drug, so I'm keen to learn more about it. I guess I'll have to work on my handwriting, too." He looked up from the paper. "How's things at home? I hear young James has created a bit of a stir." Maggie wasn't surprised that Doctor Mosely already knew about James leaving. That was the way a small town like Colton worked. "He certainly has." She hesitated for a moment before continuing. "I might need to help at home a bit more. I mean, with James gone, there's more to do, and you know my father shouldn't overdo it." Maggie held her breath. Doctor Mosely ran his hand through what was left of salt-and-pepper hair before he answered. "I think with Patricia leaving us, we might require more assistance here. But I also think you should do what you need to do." Maggie tried to decode the meaning behind his words. Was he saying she could take some time off to help around the farm or not? She'd been working part-time as a receptionist at the surgery for almost two years. She delighted in organising the paperwork and Doctor Mosely had given her free rein to decorate the surgery how she liked. She found it enjoyable enough but often thought Doctor Mosely was subtly, and sometimes not so subtly, guiding her in the direction of a nursing career.

"Thank you. I'd better get back to this," Maggie gestured towards the filing. Doctor Mosely nodded and retreated to his office. Alphabetising the files gave her the time she needed to figure out what he meant and decide how she was going to help her family.

***

The air outside was warm, so Maggie wound down the window and stuck her hand out, waving her arm up and down in the balmy breeze. Elizabeth loved to drive the Ford into town to fetch their weekly rations, and Maggie had decided to tag along.

"Maggie dear, can you stop that, please?" She wound the window up, folded her arms, and angled her legs away from her mother. Why must she always treat me like a child? She glanced out the passenger window as the town came into view. Established in the late 1800s, Colton was a progressive town located amid a rural landscape filled with farms and forests, only four hours' drive from Perth. Maggie watched as they passed the post office, police station, and the town hall; all constructed from local limestone and wood. Flowers filled the window boxes and the wide streets accommodated horses, carts, and cars.

Elizabeth parked outside the two-storey building that housed Williams' General Store on the bottom level and the Williams family on the top. Maggie pushed open the heavy door and the bell dinged. The scent of fresh produce filled her nostrils as she looked around the shop. It had changed a great deal since the war began. The shelves, crates, and barrels that had always been fully stocked weren't as full, and all the products were now labelled with how many coupons from the government-issued ration books it took to purchase them. Maggie looked at the large signs posted on the walls, each showing women in various forms of domestic duties: "Grow your own vegetables", "Help win the war on the kitchen front" and "Make do and mend". She walked over the wooden floorboards towards a large barrel in the centre of the store and picked up the reddest apple she'd ever seen. "You can have that if you like. No charge." She looked up to find Thomas Williams standing on the other side of the barrel. He moved closer and touched her forearm. "I heard James left to fight. Are you all right?" Her cheeks blushed as red as the apple in her hand.

"I'm fine," she mumbled. Why did she suddenly become so shy? She'd known Thomas her whole life. At 25, he was four years her senior and had been in the same year as Richard in school. His family had owned the general store for as long as she could remember. She perceived his stare, and her mind raced, struggling to find words to say.

"As long as my number doesn't come up, I plan on staying right here. I have to help my dad with the shop." Maggie nodded and detected in her peripheral vision that her mother and Mr Williams were watching the two of them. Thomas bent to pick up a box of tea, and she couldn't help but notice his short blond hair, muscular arms, and well-manicured hands. He had grown into quite a handsome lad.

"Come along, Maggie dear," Elizabeth called and jolted Maggie from her musing. Thomas stood and turned towards her.

"Well, it was nice talking to you. I hope I'll see you again soon."

Striding to catch up to her mother, she almost bumped into a stack of cans and felt herself turning crimson for the second time that morning. She couldn't get out of the door quick enough.

"Thomas is such a nice boy, isn't he?" Elizabeth said during the drive home, her eyes firmly fixed on the road ahead.

"Yes, I suppose he is." Maggie was still thinking about their brief exchange, and her embarrassing exit, when Elizabeth continued. "He's still a bachelor, you know. And, he's quite a handsome young man, with a solid future. Perhaps we should invite him over for dinner one day. What do you think?" Maggie drew her lips over her teeth. That I know what you're up to, she thought. Elizabeth had been married 2 years already when she was Maggie's age, and she'd been hinting about Maggie's future ever since Richard and Joan had married the previous year. Maggie had given a lot of thought to marriage and concluded that she didn't want to settle down and live the same monotonous existence as so many other women she knew. She wanted more from her life than to be stuck here in Colton, but she also felt obligated by her duty to her family.

Chapter 2
Giuseppe
1943

The Ruys docked in the Port of Fremantle in early 1943. The weary men packed the deck when land was just a speck on the horizon so that they could get their first glimpse of Australia. Giuseppe jostled for space at the front of the crowd. Holding the rail, he gazed across the water at the pale sand-coloured buildings and the busyness of the port town. Then he looked around him at the exhausted men he'd spent the last five months with. Their capture in Italy, the months spent in the primitive staging camp in Egypt, and their transportation to Western Australia had taken their toll. They were drained and done in. Conditions on board the troopship had been appalling. The ship's hull and partitions were often so hot to the touch that they seared skin. The food was bland and the tea was scalding, and it felt as if it was coming through their pores. The stench of sweat filled the cabins, and dirt seemed to be etched into the crevices of skin.

After disembarking, the men gathered together, waiting to hear news of the final leg of their journey. Giuseppe looked up at the sky full of bulbous grey clouds, praying for them to open up and drench him. Egypt had been hot, dry, and dusty. Some days, it felt as if sand coated the back of his throat. He looked over to his right as a disembodied voice boomed orders, and felt himself moving with the jostling mob towards the trucks lined near the dock. He knew that most of the men spoke little to no English, so the officer's words didn't resonate. He translated the officer's commands to the men closest to him and watched as it rippled through the crowd. When he reached the truck, an officer handed him a pannikin and overcoat; he hesitated and looked around. The two men standing on either side of the truck grabbed him and pushed him into the back before closing the canvas and shouting to the driver. He sat on the hard floor and let his eyes adjust to the darkness. He could almost smell the fear in the air, mingled with the scent of unwashed bodies.

"Don't bother trying to escape," a low voice snarled, and he felt the butt of a rifle prod him in the side. He looked up into the eyes of an army officer. The man with short grey hair and a wrinkled forehead sat on the bench close to the rear of the truck. His eyes pierced Giuseppe's until he sneered and turned away. It was clear that this man hated him. But for what? For being dragged into a war he didn't believe in? For fighting on the other side? Giuseppe shook his head and looked at the floor. The truck started up, and he moved to the bench across from the officer.

"*Sono con te, compagno*," whispered a familiar voice. Relief washed over him as he briefly closed his eyes and nodded at Luigi. Wherever I'm going, he thought, at least I have a friend with me.

Giuseppe looked from the frayed edges of the cards in his hand to Luigi's face before placing one on the bench next to him.

"Book?" he asked.

"*Libro.* Newspaper?" Luigi replied.

"*Giornale.*" They had created this game on their voyage from

Egypt. It helped them to pass the time, but the real reward was the improvement in their English with each round. Giuseppe felt fortunate to have been placed in the same cabin as Naples-born Luigi. The two young men were so similar - dark hair, brown eyes, medium build and strong working hands - that they were often mistaken for brothers. Although Giuseppe was the older of the two, Luigi was more street-smart.

"*Io vinco*. I win. Good game, amico," Luigi said. Giuseppe conceded his defeat with his hands in the air. "Another round?" Luigi asked. Giuseppe shook his head and leaned back against the canvas. The truck's movement, combined with the arduous journey, had helped many of the men doze off. Giuseppe looked at the sleeping man sitting across from him. He was wearing a dirty *Regio Esercito* uniform, much like Giuseppe's own. He closed his eyes and prayed that wherever they were headed was better than where they had been.

After a few hours, the truck came to a halt, and the men stretched as best they could in the cramped space. The officer with the grudge jumped down and ushered everyone out. The sky had cleared, and the sun shone down through the trees. They were standing near a large clearing with a few buildings, surrounded by a high barbed wire covered fence. Beyond that was dense bushland in all directions. At least this is better than the desert, Giuseppe thought as he looked around. He noticed theirs wasn't the only truck pulling up. By his quick calculation, at least 200 men milled in the centre of the sizable compound.

An older man with a stern expression, crewcut hair, and a neatly pressed uniform moved to the front and shouted directions at the officers. Giuseppe looked for Luigi as the officers forced the prisoners into haphazard rows. They stood next to each other and waited. The older man stood on a wooden crate, so the men in the back could see him, and cleared his throat as he surveyed the crowd.

"I'm Major Browning, and this is my camp. Marrinup number 16 Prisoner of War camp. By order of the Australian Government under the National Security Act 1939, you will be held here until such time as the government sees fit to release you." Giuseppe could see the shock and disbelief that he felt reflected on Luigi's face and the faces of every other man he looked at. They were all going to be held here until the war ended, however long that might be. He looked at the ground, then brought himself to full height. This wasn't the time or place to show weakness.

Further along their row, a man fell to his knees, protesting in Italian. He was trying to explain that he was just a farmer who'd been caught up in the war, but the language barrier was a hindrance. Major Browning jumped off the crate and marched toward him. "Get up!" He pulled the man to his feet and pushed him back into position. Then he looked up and down the formation before relaunching into his prepared speech as he made his way back to the crate.

"This is your new home and we need to establish clear rules." He gestured around him. "As you can see, there's a lot of work to be done here. Every one of you will help build this camp. Each man will also be assessed as to his nationality, religion, political affiliations, and suitability for work," he paused and looked among the crowd for any dissension, "Prisoners will rise at 6 am, have breakfast at 6.45 am, and start work at 7.30 am. There will be an hour's break for lunch before you return to work until 3 pm. 'Lights out' is at 10 pm. No exceptions." With his speech delivered, he jumped down and stalked to one of the buildings, leaving the men standing in disbelief. Was this going to be their life now? How could they do this to them?

Giuseppe pivoted to examine the so-called camp. High fences with triple concertina wire surrounded 6 main watch towers made from large trees, topped with floodlights. The whole compound appeared to be separated into three sections. A few weatherboard buildings topped with corrugated iron stood in each section, with more situated outside the fenced area. He assumed those were for the guards. The work needed to make this camp livable for hundreds of people was immense. Giuseppe concluded that the Australians expected the prisoners to be in that camp for a considerable amount of time.

"Line up!" A guard called out as he gestured to four nearby huts. The prisoners formed long queues and trudged inside one by one. Waiting in line, Giuseppe felt his body relax in the afternoon heat. He could smell the rich earthiness of the surrounding bushland and hear unfamiliar birdsong. When his turn arrived, he walked into the sparsely furnished hut to find one man sitting at a wide table and another standing by the open window, holding a camera.

"Do you speak English?" The man at the desk asked. Giuseppe nodded. "Good. What's your name and where are you from?"

"Giuseppe Russo. Rimissa, Italy." Giuseppe replied. The man filled in a Prisoner of War Identity Card with Giuseppe's details, including his religion and political associations.

"Right. Put your thumb on here, stamp it there, then stand over near the wall and face the camera." Giuseppe did as he was told. The entire ordeal only took a matter of moments, but it left Giuseppe feeling like a criminal. He leaned against the wall and kicked at the dirt while he waited outside the hut for Luigi. They were quiet as they walked along the rows of huts. They wanted to choose a well-positioned hut to be their home for the foreseeable future. They decided on one towards the end of the last row. Inside were 3 wooden bunk beds, each with a thin mattress, a couple of woollen blankets, and a lumpy pillow. There was a long, narrow window along the back wall that could be shielded from the outside in inclement weather. Shelving and lockers covered the front wall to house the few personal effects they had.

Giuseppe sat on the bottom bunk furthest from the door and Luigi lay on the bottom of the middle bunk.

"*Ciao*," called a voice from above. Giuseppe peered up and saw a broad smile and kind eyes on a lined face. Three men walked into the hut and claimed the last few bunks. With all the beds taken, the group turned to introductions. Eugenio, the man who had said hello from the top bunk, was from Rome and had a wife and two grown daughters. Giovanni and Domenico were brothers from a small town near Naples. Enemy bombs had destroyed the port where they had been working, forcing them into the war. Carlo was a sheep farmer from a small town in Lombardy, not far from where Giuseppe's aunty and uncle lived.

Giuseppe sat back against the wall, knees bent, hands behind his head.

"This is not what I expected," he admitted.

"It's better than the staging camp in Egypt. Hot winds, sand everywhere, and nothing to do. At least here we have beautiful trees, *no*?" Carlo said.

"I guess we'll just have to wait and see what happens. With any luck, the war will end soon, and they'll have to send us home again," Domenico said. Giuseppe and the others nodded in agreement. Later that night, as he fell asleep on the thin mattress listening to the chirps and croaks of animals he'd never seen, his thoughts returned to the green trees and hills of home.

***

The monotony of building the camp and the routine of its schedule made each day feel the same as the one before. Days turned into weeks and then months, with the change in weather being one of the few discernable ways to distinguish the passage of time. Giuseppe and the other prisoners spent their days building foundations out of concrete and aggregate that were later used for shower blocks, latrines, and mess halls for each section of the camp.

Each section had a leader and for Giuseppe, that was Domenico Cambino, who had been in the armed forces before the war broke out. Despite their very different backgrounds, Giuseppe felt he was a fair leader. Cambino understood that most of the men under his watch were farmers and stoneworkers, not soldiers. It didn't matter how any of them got there. To the guards, all that mattered was that they worked.

Their first winter in Australia had been cold, and frost often covered the rocky ground. Giuseppe would sometimes wake to what he thought was gunfire, only to find it was the heavy rain battering against the iron roof. When spring arrived, he welcomed the warmer weather. Standing in the sun near the mess, he took his hat off and wiped the beads of sweat from his brow. His ears picked up the rumble of trucks approaching.

"Looks like we're getting some new arrivals," he said to Luigi, as he threw the shovel down so hard that it stood in the dirt. The two men watched as the trucks entered the compound, and the guards started unloading men. Giuseppe guessed there were around 300 of them by the time the last truck had rattled through the gates. The guards who had been overseeing their work left to monitor the crowd.

"Must be *Tedeschi*," Giuseppe commented.

"Ha! Of course, they come when the work is nearly done," Luigi scoffed.

The guards lined the Germans up just as they had done with the Italians on their first day. Major Browning gave his customary speech, and the men were moved off into groups to get processed and settled into the German section of the camp. Giuseppe nudged Luigi on the arm and nodded towards the fence. They made their way over and stood, watching the men scramble to find the best hut. They didn't appear to have the same look of shock and disbelief that the Italian men had when they first arrived. Giuseppe whistled to get the attention of a tall man standing by the door of the nearest hut. He ambled over and looked the two Italians up and down.

"*Sprichst du Englisch*?" The man asked. Giuseppe nodded, recognising the last word.

"Where have you come from?" he asked the blonde-haired man. "A camp in Victoria. Some men have been in Australia for many months. Some were on the Kormoran when it sank in '41. And you?" he said in his strong, stilted accent. Giuseppe told him their story, and they shook hands through the fence. "It is nice here," Hans said as he looked around, "but I think the guards will be just as tough here as they were in Victoria." Giuseppe shrugged and offered him a cigarette, which he took with both hands. Hans was from a small village in southern Germany. He'd had to participate in the Hitler Youth and when the war broke out, there was no other choice for him except to join the Wehrmacht.

"Move away from the fence!" an older guard with short black hair and a scar across his cheek shouted as he marched towards them. They put their hands in the air and backed away, giving each other a quick nod. Luigi and Giuseppe walked back over to the drain, picked up the shovels, and resumed digging.

"They are going to catch more heat than us. Did you notice how many guards shot over there when the trucks pulled up?" Giuseppe said, as he pushed his shovel into the hard dirt and tossed it onto the heap.

"*Si*. They are the bigger threat, though, aren't they?" Luigi was right. Mussolini was overthrown, and Italy had surrendered. The Australians didn't need to worry about the Italians as much.

Giuseppe woke after a fitful sleep with an aching back and a thumping head. He stood and stretched gingerly before glancing at Luigi in the bed next to his. He was sound asleep despite the Reveille blasting.

"Wake up, *amico*," he said as he shoved at his friend's mass.

"*Ah, fanculo!*" came the muffled reply. Giuseppe laughed as he ambled out the door and over to the mess for breakfast. He sat at the long wooden table with a bowl full of sloppy porridge and a cup of lukewarm coffee and looked towards the guards' table at the front of the hall. Major Browning was holding court with Captain Marsh and Officers Johnson and Harris. They were frowning and speaking in hushed voices. Had there been another escape attempt last night? Giorgio Bertolini had tried it a few weeks ago and ended up getting caught and put in the cooler. Giuseppe shuddered at the thought of spending weeks holed up in a cold, concrete cell that wasn't even long enough for him to lie straight in.

Major Browning stood and headed outside to the central courtyard, followed by his companions. The siren sounded just as Giuseppe handed his bowl and cup to the kitchenhand on duty. He joined the men streaming out of the double doors, caught sight of Luigi coming out of the latrines, and whistled to get his attention. Row upon row of men, some in their military uniforms, others wearing the maroon shirt and pants issued at camp, stood facing the officers. Major Browning paced up and down the rows before stopping front and centre.

"The Australian Government has created the Rural Employment without Guards Scheme to ease labour shortages as a result of our men heading off to fight. You now have the opportunity to work on local farms or as part of the timber-cutting industry. For this work, you will receive payment in the form of tokens, which can be exchanged through the canteen for certain luxuries. Those who do not wish to participate in this new scheme may be moved to another camp." Giuseppe looked at Luigi.

"Farm work," they said in unison. It made sense. Giuseppe had spent his life working on his family's farm. When Officer Johnson called for volunteers, they raised their hands. Johnson moved down the rows, asking each man about their experience, scribbling notes in a ledger.

"What's happening there?" Giuseppe asked, pointing to where the officers were segregating the Italians from the Germans. Johnson looked over.

"The Germans are going to do the timber cutting. Your lot will work as farmhands," he said. Giuseppe would have taken either job, anything to avoid the hard labour of building the camp, but he was glad the work would be something he was familiar with.

The new work arrangements weren't to start for another week and the announcement didn't stop the day's labour. Giuseppe and four other men had been working on building the pumping station. It was a big job, but with the camp now housing over 1300 POWs and guards, it was a necessary one. When the siren rang to signal the end of the workday, everyone cheered, downed tools and headed to their huts.

"What do you think about this farm work?" Eugenio asked the group while they got cleaned up for dinner. Carlo and Domenico shrugged.

"I think anything is better than being locked up in a cage all day," Luigi said.

"But what if the boss is worse than the guards?" Carlo asked.

"Well, he can't be any worse than Browning," Domenico said, lifting a shoulder.

"We should think of it as an adventure, or at least, a break from this prison of ours," Giovanni said as he finished brushing his hair and turned towards the door. "Now, who's up for a game of cards in the hall?"

***

The morning was brisk and the sun hadn't quite reached the point where it came through the high window in their hut, but most of the men inside were awake. Giuseppe turned to see Luigi and was greeted with a crisply made bed. Surprised, he got dressed and headed to the mess. He sat next to Luigi, who was already on his second cup of coffee.

"Today's the day. I can't wait to get out of this place," he said while Giuseppe downed his own porridge in record time. "Where do you think they'll send us?" Giuseppe shrugged. Luigi's leg bounced up and down, and he wrung his hands together.

"We'll be ok, *amico*. The war will be over before you know it, and we'll be back in Italy." He coughed to hide the crack in his voice when he spoke of home, but Luigi was too riled up to notice. It seemed like a lifetime ago that he was milking cows and picking juicy tomatoes with his father and brother. He remembered how contented, safe, and secure he'd felt and wondered how long it would be before he felt like that again.

The siren sounded, and they lined up in the centre of the compound. The officers called out names and the men walked over to the waiting trucks. Officer Johnson shouted Luigi's name. Luigi turned and patted Giuseppe on the shoulder before walking to the back of the truck. Giuseppe felt a shudder pass through him. Wherever we're going, we aren't going together this time.

Giuseppe climbed into the back of his assigned truck and noticed that it was relatively empty. Only 3 other men were waiting to see what fate was going to hand them. The truck rattled into gear, passed through the front gates and turned right down the gravel road riddled with potholes. The officers hadn't been forthcoming with the details, so none of the prisoners knew where they were going. Giuseppe's mind spun with questions. What type of farm will it be? How far is it from camp? What will the boss be like? Fifteen minutes after they'd set off, the truck came to a halt. Officer Grady opened the canvas flap.

"Russo, this is your stop," Grady said, looking at his notes. "Jarrah Downs. Horse and cattle farm. Owned by George Sleeman." Grady looked up at Giuseppe with a furrowed brow, lifted chin and pursed lips. "We'll be back at 5 pm sharp. Be here." Giuseppe nodded and started walking up the long, winding driveway towards the homestead in the distance. He stopped, closed his eyes, and breathed in this moment of freedom between the cage in the bush and the wide open space of the farm.

Two men approached from a large shed as he neared the clearing at the end of the driveway. The resemblance between them was unmistakable. The older of the two walked with a slight limp, but he reached Giuseppe first.
"You must be Giuseppe Russo," he said, as he held out a hand in greeting. "Do you speak English? If not, I imagine this is going to be a bit difficult to navigate."
"I speak English, but there are many words I do not know yet." George nodded.
"Have you done much farm work before?" Richard asked as he shook his hand.
"Yes, sir. My family owns cattle. We also grow fruit and vegetables."
"Excellent. Sounds like you'll fit in well. And just call me Richard, but he'd probably prefer Mr Sleeman." Richard said as he pointed to his father. George nodded.
"You call me Joe if that's easier."
"That's settled then. Let's talk a walk, and we'll show you what you're in for," Richard said with a smile.

The trio followed a well-worn track and spent the next hour touring the property and deciding what Giuseppe would help with over the coming months. When they neared the homestead again, George left the younger men to it. They walked over to the paddock closest to the shed and leaned on the wooden gate.

"We need to get these ones broken in so we can sell them. You reckon you can handle it?" Richard asked. Giuseppe felt his stomach tighten. He'd never broken in a horse before, but he wasn't about to let that stop him from showing the Sleeman's that it was worth having him there. He nodded, jumped over the fence and grabbed the rope before making his way over to the nearest brumby.

Chapter 3
Margaret
Mid-1943

The winter sun was streaming through her curtains, but Maggie wanted to stay curled up in bed, reading, for as long as possible. She'd just turned the page when her mother knocked and came in before she could answer. Elizabeth walked to the window and opened the curtains wider before turning back to Maggie and folding her arms across her chest.

"You know that with James away, your father and Richard have been having some difficulty keeping up with the demands of the farm." Maggie sighed and closed her book. "Well, your father has signed on for a new scheme the government has introduced. An Italian prisoner of war from Marrinup will help us. He's starting today. Please be friendly, but remember to keep your distance, young lady. We don't know how much about this man." It took Maggie a few moments to digest the news. She sat up and threw back the covers.

"But I could have helped with the farm duties. I told Dad as much." Maggie felt her breath coming faster and clenched her fists. She stood and faced her mother. "But he chooses to bring a stranger into our home instead. This man could have killed people for all we know." Elizabeth dropped her hands to her sides.

"I know you wanted to help, but there are some things that are better left to the men." Maggie rolled her eyes, and Elizabeth tutted and walked out without closing the door. Maggie groaned as she jumped back into bed and pulled the covers up. She stayed that way until the scent of toast wafted into her room. She pulled on a pair of slacks and a blouse and put her hair up in a bun. Elizabeth was about to set the tea and toast on the dining table when Maggie entered. She buttered a piece of toast before popping it into her mouth, hearing a satisfying crunch. Elizabeth sat opposite her and drank from her china cup, waiting.

"Why didn't Dad just let me help?" Maggie asked. "He didn't need to bring a stranger here." Elizabeth glanced at her with a weary expression.

"You've got your work with Doctor Mosely, Maggie dear. Why can't you be satisfied with that?" Maggie sighed. This was supposed to be her opportunity to show her family that she was just as capable as her brothers. Her father had completely ignored her and now an outsider was going to help instead. It should have been her. She chomped through the rest of her toast and fled the dining room, eager to be anywhere else.

With her shift not starting until later that morning, Maggie decided to spend some time by the river. Even in winter, it was teeming with life. Crickets chirped, frogs croaked, and birds cooed and called to each other. It was the perfect place to ponder how she could get her parents to listen to her and treat her like the adult she was. Intent on her destination, Maggie left the house and glimpsed the intruder in the paddock with the horses. It looked like he was trying to break in one of the wild brumbies that her father and Richard had caught in the bushland that backed onto their property, but he wasn't having much luck. She hesitated on the verandah for a few minutes. She'd watched Richard and her

father break in brumbies so often. Should she help him? Her mother had told her to keep her distance. I'll show them all, she thought. Ignoring Elizabeth's warning, she walked the 50 yards to the paddock, leaned on the wooden gate and watched the man approach the horse. He had almost reached him when the horse reared and the man fell back onto the ground with a loud thud. He muttered "*fanculo*" and she stifled a laugh. She didn't need to speak Italian to understand what he meant. She looked back towards the house and then climbed into the paddock and offered her hand as she approached. He looked up at her with a smile that reached his eyes, and Maggie felt her heart skip a beat. "Thank you. *Grazie*," he said as he wiped his muddy hands on his pants. "I'm having no luck with this one." He pointed in the horse's direction, who snorted and walked away. She couldn't help but laugh as the man lifted his eyebrows, looking offended.
"Maybe he needs a more gentle approach," she said as she bent and picked the rope up off the ground. "I'm Maggie, by the way," she said over her shoulder before strolling over to the horse, willing him to stay still. "Easy there," she whispered as she edged closer, her body tense. Standing inches away from the horse's face, she could see his black eyes trying to decide whether she was friend or foe. "Easy boy. That's it." She moved closer. Her heart was racing, but she kept her breathing even. She carefully reached up and patted the side of his head with her right hand while she lifted the rope up and over his head. It slid down the horse's neck, and she slowly moved her left hand up to pat him. As her palm touched the coarse hair, she took a deep breath and felt relief wash over her. She turned back to the man who was still

standing near the gate. "See, it's not that hard," she said with a grin. He laughed as he made his way over.

"You have a magic touch." He winked. "I'm Giuseppe. People here call me Joe." He offered his hand and Maggie shook it firmly, trying to hide her nerves. He stood a head taller than her, with dark hair, tanned skin, and broad shoulders that pushed against his maroon-coloured shirt. He didn't look like a soldier. He looked like a regular man. A handsome one at that. A loud bang shook her from her musing. She looked around and saw Richard coming through the gate towards them.

"I see you got this one sorted," he said, pointing to the horse, "and you've met Maggie." Richard took the rope from her hands. "I think Mum wants some help with her sewing. We'll take it from here." Maggie raised her eyebrows and pursed her lips. Why does everyone in this family treat me like a child? She looked at Joe, who averted his eyes by trying to wipe more mud from his hands. "Fine." Maggie huffed, then turned and stalked to the house without looking back. Frustration and embarrassment rose to her flushed face in equal measure.

***

The next few weeks passed quickly. Maggie noticed that her father's leg didn't seem to give him as much trouble, and Richard's mood was lighter than it had been in months. Reluctantly, she had to admit that having an extra pair of hands around the farm was making a difference. She contemplated the situation as she pulled weeds from the vegetable garden, enjoying the satisfaction of unearthing a particularly stubborn dandelion. She hadn't spoken to Joe since his first day. The way he looked down after Richard came over had irked her. He obviously doesn't want to know me, so I am certainly not going to go out of my way to talk to him, she thought and yanked another weed from its home in the soil. If Dad and Richard think they can do without my help, then I'll just have to concentrate my efforts elsewhere. Maybe I should join Patricia. She seems to be having a good time.

"I think we might have too much cauliflower and broccoli here. Would you be a dear and take some over to Joan and Richard's?" Elizabeth said, jolting Maggie back to the present. She sat back on her haunches and rubbed the dirt from her hands.

"Of course. I'm sure Lily would like to go for a trot." Between work and helping her mother around the house, she felt like she hadn't seen Joan for an age. She put some vegetables into a cloth bag and walked to the shed to get the saddle for her chestnut thoroughbred, Lily. Standing near the entrance, she let her eyes adjust to the dimness. She could see Joe in Lily's stall. He moved the brush up and down as he groomed her mane. He looked deep in thought, so she took the opportunity to observe him uninterrupted. He was wearing the same clothes he had been when they first met. They must be prison-issued, she thought. His hair was cut short and there was stubble on his chin. The lines around his eyes showed that he smiled often, or at least used to. He seemed to have a way with Lily. She rarely liked strange men going near her, but she seemed relaxed. Maggie coughed and startled them both. Joe turned in her direction, and a smile lit up his face. Maggie couldn't help but return it before quickly composing herself. She wasn't about to let him think he could smile at her, and all was forgiven.

"I'm going to Richard and Joan's to drop these off." She held the bag aloft. "I'll need Lily."

"Of course. Let me help you." Joe moved to get the saddle.

"I'm quite capable. Thank you," Maggie said, despite her slight struggle as the saddle caught on its hook. She felt Joe's presence behind her.

"Have I done something wrong?" Maggie hesitated. Their first meeting had often played out in her mind over the last few weeks. Was she just being silly? Had she read too much into his actions?

"I helped you. You thanked me. I thought we were getting along. But when Richard came, you just ignored me." His jaw dropped and his eyebrows shot up.

"It was not like that. I did not know if I was allowed to talk to you. And when Richard told you to go inside, I felt embarrassed for you." She hauled the saddle off the railing and climbed the step to put it on Lily's back, giving herself time to think. Perhaps she'd read the situation all wrong. "The way you handled that brumby...you seemed like a strong woman. My mother is a strong woman, too, so I know these things. But I saw how Richard's words made you feel. I didn't want you to see my thoughts." She let Joe help her saddle Lily, and then she mounted while he tied the bag onto the back. Her mind raced, but all she could manage to say was a simple thank you. Joe nodded as she moved off, and she left the shed without looking back. Galloping down the long driveway, the wind rushed through her hair, and the fresh air filled her nostrils. She couldn't shake the feeling that Joe had somehow reached right to her core without them having said more than a few words to one another.

Richard and Joan's small homestead was on a neighbouring property on the other side of the river. The farm was about a quarter the size of Jarrah Downs. The two-bedroom jarrah weatherboard homestead set among the trees was more of a cottage, but Richard and Joan had worked to put their own touches on it. Richard had added a wraparound verandah, and inside, Joan had used the space wisely to make the rooms seem bigger. Maggie dismounted and let Lily loose in the paddock nearest the house. The horse galloped away through the tall grass towards the river as Maggie approached the front door. Following the sounds of the Glenn Miller Orchestra, she found Joan in the kitchen, preparing for dinner. She deposited the vegetables on the bench and hummed along. Then Joan grabbed Maggie's hand, and the two women danced around the kitchen table, in fits of laughter.

"You seem quite pleased with the vegetables,"

"It's not just the cauli's, Maggie. I've got big news, but I probably shouldn't tell you just yet," Joan replied with a sly grin.

"Whatever it is, you can tell me. I won't tell anyone." Maggie said, hand on heart. She didn't think Joan's smile could get any wider, but it seemed to increase as she relented.

"All right then. But you can't tell anyone, especially your mother." Maggie had an inkling of what it might be, and she could hardly contain her excitement.

"Richard and I are going to have a baby." They hugged and squealed with delight.

"That's wonderful news. You're going to be the best parents. I'm going to be an Aunty!" They danced around the room a few more times before collapsing onto chairs. Their family needed some good news. This war, and James's departure, had brought so much sadness, but a new arrival would give them all something to look forward to. Maggie stayed to help Joan prepare dinner. Peeling the potatoes, she mentioned that Richard had been in good spirits lately.

"The new farmhand seems to be working out," Joan commented. Maggie blushed. "I saw that. What's going on?" she asked as she took the knife from Maggie's hand and laid it on the chopping board. Maggie's mouth twitched, and she looked out the window. Their first encounter had been so brief, but the conversation they'd just had changed everything. She gave Joan the details but didn't mention how it had made her feel. She didn't have to.

"I see," Joan said with a smirk and wisdom way beyond her 25 years. The back door opened and Richard walked in, cutting their conversation short.

"Hi, sweetheart. How was your day?" he said and bent to kiss Joan's cheek. He straightened, then turned to Maggie and said, "Mum wants you home." Maggie sighed and gathered her things. Joan followed her out and over to the paddock.

"Ignore him. You know he feels like he has to be your father's shadow."

"Yes, but he doesn't have to be like that when Mum and Dad aren't around." Joan shrugged, then put a hand on Maggie's arm. "Maggie, be careful...with Joe, I mean. We don't know much about him."

"I know. I'll be all right," Maggie assured her. She rode the long way home. Perhaps she'd been wrong about Joe after all. Maybe he wasn't ignoring her. He seemed nice enough, and he was certainly handsome. But he was a foreigner. James had voiced his concerns about the Italians and Germans on many occasions. Yet, when she thought more about it, she felt like there was just something about him. She shook her head. Nothing could come of it. He was a prisoner of war, and she was supposed to marry a local boy and settle down just as her mother had, just as Joan had. But she couldn't shake a niggling feeling that was hard to define.

***

The news of the impending arrival seemed to buoy everyone's spirits and make the months fly by. With the due date drawing nearer, Maggie decided to host a celebratory afternoon tea in Joan's honour. The invitations were sent to friends and neighbours and every member of the Colton CWA branch. Maggie and Elizabeth spent weeks leading up to the event giving the homestead a thorough clean and making sure the gardens were looking their best. On the morning of the party, Maggie helped Elizabeth bake scones before hanging the paper bunting around the eaves of the verandah. The aroma of freshly baked cakes and slices filled the house. As the guests arrived, Maggie ushered everyone to the back verandah, where she had set up several tables with food and drinks. When the last guest arrived, she took a seat near her mother, Mrs Fulton, Joan, and a few of the older members of the CWA. They were discussing the last dance at the town hall, but as with most conversations, they inevitably turned to the future. With the war still raging in Europe and the battles on the islands closer to home, everyone felt as if the fighting would go on forever.

"It appears as though your family are doing quite well though, Elizabeth," Mrs Fulton remarked as she looked around the verandah and across the back paddocks where the cattle and horses were grazing. Maggie noted the slight shift in her mother's expression before she gave her reply.
"Thank you, Emma. With James leaving to do his duty, we wondered how we'd manage, but we are getting through it." Mrs Fulton pursed her lips. Clearly, Elizabeth's response was what she'd hoped for. She sat up straighter and squared her shoulders.
"Yes. It appears as though bringing a foreigner, a prisoner of war, onto your property has worked out for you. I don't imagine that my Barnaby would allow that sort of thing at our home." There was an audible gasp from those close enough to hear the conversation. Everyone knew there was no love lost between Elizabeth and Mrs Fulton, and it seemed that this was too good an opportunity for Mrs Fulton to pass up. Maggie's back stiffened, and she brought a hand to her chest to compose herself. She'd always hated the way Mrs Fulton acted as if she was better than everyone else, and her snide remark had hit a nerve.
"Well, Mrs Fulton, since our farm is producing a lot more than yours, even in these hard times, I'd imagine you wouldn't need any help to manage yours anyway." Maggie cocked her head to the side with a smile plastered on her face. She knew Elizabeth would reproach her for it later, but seeing the shocked expression on the older woman's face was worth it. Maggie stood and

sauntered along the table, muttering about how much lovely food there was. Mrs Fulton mumbled and excused herself to use the bathroom. Maggie looked back at the women and caught a smile from Joan before she saw her turn and ask the women about their pregnancies, keen to move on to safer topics.

Later, as Maggie, Elizabeth, and Joan cleared the verandah, Maggie waited for her mother to bring up the incident, but it was Joan who raised the subject.

"I thought Mrs Fulton's remark was quite rude. The nerve of that woman," she said, shaking her head as she collected and stacked the plates.

"I'd say she's downright arrogant. Who does she think she is? Talking about our situation as if we were poor. And her remark about Joe. She really has no idea," Maggie said before moving the small table back into position near the door. Elizabeth bent to pick up some bunting that had fallen, then stood and glared at the younger women.

"You're both right, but the fact is she's the queen bee in the branch and, dare I say it, the district. If I don't appease her, she could start a lot of trouble for us." She turned to Maggie. "Even though what you said was the truth, the way in which you said it definitely caused offence." Maggie shrugged a shoulder. She didn't care whether Mrs Fulton was offended. "Look, I know how much our farm has come along since Joe started with us, but I'm also mindful that there are families around Colton who are not as accommodating as we are."

"That's true. I was speaking with Mary last week. They got a man from Marrinup to help too, and their neighbour old Mrs Potts, you know the one, she kicked up such a fuss that they ended up sending the poor man back to the camp," Joan said, shaking her head. Maggie knew Elizabeth was right, but it didn't quell her annoyance at the small-mindedness of some of the locals.

***

Doctor Mosely was unlocking the doors just as Maggie arrived. He bid her good morning and held the door open as she stepped inside.

"I hear you recently had a slight altercation with one Mrs Emma Fulton," he said with arched eyebrows. Maggie shifted her weight from one foot to the other and nodded. "Well, apparently, Mrs Fulton told her husband what happened, no doubt embellishing the truth. Now he's told some of the other husbands that he's going to keep a closer watch on your family." Maggie's shoulders slumped. "Can I suggest that in the future you keep your head down, do what needs to be done, and don't bother with the likes of old busybodies like Emma Fulton?" Maggie nodded and was eternally grateful when she saw little Samuel Smith running up the path with his exhausted-looking mother in tow. She hurried to her desk and got herself settled. She could worry about Doctor Mosely's warning later.

The surgery had been busy all day, and as the last patient hobbled out the door, Maggie sighed with relief. Just as she was almost finished tidying the waiting area, Doctor Mosely walked in. "Good. You're still here. I wanted to talk to you."

"With all due respect, Doctor Mosely, it's been a long day, and I'd like to be getting home."

"This won't take a minute," he said as he walked to the filing cabinet and pulled out an envelope. He handed it to her and gestured for her to open it. Maggie tore the envelope open and pulled out the sheets of paper. She read the first few lines. "What is this?"

"It's an application to begin your nursing studies. I've filled in my part. You just need to fill in yours, and I'll send it off." Maggie's mouth opened and closed. Was this what he'd meant about doing what needs to be done? Did she even want to be a nurse? She enjoyed working in the surgery, and she knew Patricia loved being a nurse, but she wasn't sure if it was something she wanted to pursue.

"Doctor Mosely, I appreciate the effort, but can I think about this?" She waved the application.

"By all means, but don't think too long. Enrolments close next week."

Chapter 4
Giuseppe
Late 1943

Giuseppe's saving grace at Marrinup was Luigi. During his first day on the Sleeman farm, he'd wondered if Luigi would be at the camp when he returned. He'd sent a silent prayer up when he walked into their hut and saw Luigi lying on his bed with a cigarette hanging out of his mouth. He'd plonked onto his bunk and held his hand out for a cigarette. Luigi threw him the packet and matches.

"Looks like I can't get rid of you," Giuseppe said.

"You're as stuck with me as I am with you," Luigi said and tossed his pillow at him. Luigi had also been posted locally, but the farm he worked on was in the opposite direction from the Sleeman's. Giovanni and Domenico had been placed a few miles further east, while Carlo and Eugenio were still awaiting their assignments. They had all agreed that, so far, they were the lucky ones. Some men they'd voyaged from Egypt with had spent that first day driving to farms hundreds of miles away. They knew they'd never see them again.

The Italian prisoners worked on local farms tending cattle, mending fences, sheering sheep, picking fruits and vegetables— anything that the boss asked them to do, they did it. The Germans spent their days logging the surrounding bushland, and the results were often sent to warm the houses of residents of Perth.

"What's the boss like?" Luigi had asked. Giuseppe had taken a drag of his cigarette and considered his answer. His first impression of George Sleeman was that he seemed to be a fair man. It appeared as though Luigi's boss had a stricter approach. "Boss man's son sits around and watches me do all the work. He thinks he's clever, calling me a bloody eyetie." Luigi had puffed out a breath. "You think I care what this kid says? My old man called me every name under the sun." He had sat up and looked around the hut. "*Amicos*, we just need to knuckle down, collect our tokens, and pray for the war to end." The men had nodded. Giuseppe knew he was right, but that didn't make it any easier.

***

Giuseppe and Mario, a man from Sicily who was staying in a hut one row back from Giuseppe's, stood in the kitchen of the mess hall washing the dishes they'd used to prepare dinner. Giuseppe didn't mind being on kitchen duty. It was something to do, and it broke up the monotony of camp life. He listened as Mario told him a story about working on a fishing boat back home and how he'd almost been taken under with a net.

"I have nothing as exciting as that to tell. I live and work on my family's farm, and I hope to have my own farm one day. I'm a simple man."

"Sometimes, the simple life is the best life," Mario said, wiping the towel over the bench. "We're almost done. I'll finish up here." Giuseppe gratefully accepted his offer and went to find Luigi. Aware of his fondness for socialising, he checked in a hut a few doors up from theirs. Nobody had seen Luigi. When he reached the hut nearest the German compound, Dom called out to him. "You looking for Luigi?" Giuseppe nodded. "Check by the powerhouse. He's been going out that way a lot lately." Giuseppe thanked him and walked the length of the fence and through the front gates, acknowledging Officers Parson and Grady as he walked past.

Following the narrow pathway through the guard's quarters, he found Luigi on his knees, laying a rock border around a freshly dug garden bed. The orange rocks of all shapes and sizes were scattered all over Marrinup and the surrounding bushland. Giuseppe snuck up, knelt nearby, and threw a gum nut in Luigi's direction, missing him by an inch. Luigi jumped in shock and looked around.

"*Fanculo*! You scared me."

"What are you doing?" Giuseppe asked. He sat next to Luigi and picked up a handful of gum nuts and threw them towards the closest guard hut. They hit the tin roof with a satisfying ping.

"What does it look like?" Giuseppe shrugged and looked around. The thick bush surrounding the camp was full of trees and shrubs that he hadn't yet learned the names of. Some were beginning to blossom with large yellow and white flowers, but the stark concrete and tin of the buildings looked out of place in the natural landscape. Giuseppe stood and tilted his head to the side as he took in the layout of the four garden beds - a diamond, heart, spade, and club. He chuckled at Luigi's clever reference to his fondness for cards. The man was a dab hand at rummy, but sometimes his wins were questionable.

A whistle came through the trees, and they both turned to find Officer Parson walking up the path to the garden beds.

"Alberti. Russo," he nodded at them and surveyed the ground before him. "It looks like Major Browning's beautification project is coming along nicely. Well done, lads." Giuseppe held both hands up.

"I wish I could claim the credit, but this was all Luigi's handiwork."

"Right. Well, I'll leave you to it. Just be back in that yard before the dinner siren."

"Beautification project?" Giuseppe asked after Parson had walked back towards the guards' buildings.

"*Si*. Browning wants to make Marrinup *bellisima* for everyone. We are making these garden beds, and he's got the *Tedeschi* making a fish pond." Hans had already made a start on the foundations of the fish pond over by the powerhouse a few yards away. The location Browning chose for the garden beds just happened to be close to his office. At least he'll have a pleasant view, Giuseppe thought.

"Why are you helping him with it?"

"Why not? We have to make this place better somehow, *si*?" Maybe he was right. He watched Luigi work for a while longer and thought of his family in Italy, of his father, Pietro, and his prized grape vines, and of his mother, Rosa, tending her proliferous vegetable garden. He longed to be back home on the farm with them. He shivered as a sobering thought struck him. Marrinup was his home, at least for now. He grabbed a shovel and started turning over the rich soil, ready for planting. The two men spent the next few evenings planting jonquil and daffodil bulbs, all the while hoping that they wouldn't still be at Marrinup when the flowers bloomed.

***

It was a warm morning, and even though he had to attend Mass, Giuseppe was in no rush to get out of bed. He lay on his back with his arms under his head, remembering the dream he'd had about Maggie. He closed his eyes, and a smile crept across his face. Over the last few weeks, they'd had more opportunities to talk, always ensuring that Richard and George weren't around. She'd told him about her work with a local doctor, of her brother who had left to fight, and of her best friend, who was a nurse stationed in Papua. He'd told her about the camp and shared stories about his life before the war. The more time he spent with her, the more he found himself looking for her as he went about his work.

"What are you smiling about?" Luigi's voice broke through his thoughts. "You've been daydreaming for weeks. It's got to be a...how they say...shiela, *si*? The wife? No. The daughter?" Giuseppe rolled over and faced the wall. "Aha! It's the daughter!" Luigi said, shoving Giuseppe with his foot.

"It's nothing," Giuseppe replied, then pushed the blankets back and sat up, swinging his legs onto the floor.

"You can't fool an old Romeo like me," Luigi said with a twinkle in his eye and a smirk on his face. "Listen up, *amicos*, our little Giuseppe is in love." He made kissing sounds, and the hut filled with a mixture of groans and praises from the other men. Carlo reached across and punched Giuseppe's arm with a loud "Hey, hey." Giuseppe rolled his eyes, grabbed his toiletries, and walked out the door. He could hear their laughter all the way to the shower block.

The recreation hall transformed into a makeshift church every Sunday. The guards tried to accommodate the different religions of the interned men; each had to worship in succession throughout the day. The Catholic priest followed the time-honoured traditions of Holy Mass, but the body and blood of Christ were not the usual fare. As with a lot of things at Marrinup, the men made do with what they had, but as long as they could worship, they were satisfied. Giuseppe knelt on the hardwood floor, closed his eyes, and raised his hands to his chin in prayer. He prayed that his family was alive and well, that they'd received his letters, and that they knew he was all right. He prayed for the war to end and for the strength to endure until it did.

When the last amen was spoken and the service was over, Giuseppe followed the crowd out into the sunshine and mingled with the other prisoners. There was something about attending church that made him feel hopeful, so when someone suggested going to the oval, he asked Officer Parson.
"Yes, all right. We'll head down around one," came the reply. He thanked him before running back to his hut, where he found Luigi, Domenico, and Giovanni sitting in the shade of a gum tree.
"Wristball on the oval at one. Spread the word." He headed over to the fence that separated the Italian and German compounds. The Germans were always up for a game. He flagged down Gunter and let him know. By 12:30 pm, there was a crowd of men waiting near the front gates. The oval was about a mile away from camp along a winding gravel road. Giuseppe jogged to catch up

with Luigi and the others.

"So, are you going to tell us about your sweetheart?" teased Giovanni. The men laughed as Giuseppe blushed and tried to hide his face by bending to pick up a stick.

"Come on, *amico*. Tell us," Luigi encouraged. They would not give up. And what harm would it do? He threw the stick into the bush and spent the rest of the walk to the oval telling them about Maggie, omitting his blunder during their first meeting.

"Ah, you're in trouble, *amico*. She's already got your heart. I can tell. Good luck with her *padre*." Luigi laughed. The others echoed his amusement, and Giuseppe felt his cheeks redden. Maggie filled his thoughts for the rest of the walk. She was feisty and smart. He could tell that she didn't seem to be happy with her lot in life. He could also tell that he was falling for her.

The oval was nothing more than an oversized patch of grass surrounded by tall trees and bushy shrubs. When they arrived, the spectators headed for the shade on either side of the field to watch the game. The Germans had won the last two matches, so the Italians knew they had to secure a victory this time around to stay in the competition. The prize was a pack of cigarettes each, and with a cost of 5 tokens, they weren't about to lose this game without a fight.

Gunter, the indispensable German forward, who had to promise that he wouldn't escape before being allowed to leave the camp, was right on the ball the entire game. There was a scrum of arms and legs, and Domenico managed to get hold of the ball, dodge the flash of bodies in his path and make it to the goal. The Italian spectators erupted in excitement, shouting, dancing and hugging each other. Many of them put their fingers under their chins and moved them in a quick forward motion. It was a slight that the Germans hated, and some of the Italian men loved to provoke them. The Germans weren't as emotional when their team was winning. Only the occasional *"Wunderbar!"* was heard with a goal from their side.

The game was 2-2 and had under a minute left when Giovanni barrelled through and snatched the ball from Hans. He moved with lightning speed towards the goal. The German team raced after him. The crowds on both sides of the oval were going wild. He kicked the ball and slid along the ground. It flew up into the air and straight past the goalie just as Officer Parson blew the whistle. The whole oval erupted. The Italian spectators ran onto the field and crowded the team, jumping and cheering.
"I'll take my packet tonight," Giovanni called to Fritz. The Italians burst into a fit of laughter and the tall German grunted and turned towards his dejected teammates.

As they made the long walk back through the bush to camp, Domenico started singing *Il Canto degli Italiani* in his baritone voice. Within seconds, the rest of the Italian men had joined in. Giuseppe couldn't wipe the smile off his face as he sang his national anthem with pride and gusto. When they reached the administrative buildings on the outskirts of the camp, the Germans fell in and silently trooped past. The Italians sauntered past, still singing their hearts out. They continued the celebrations for the rest of the afternoon. It was a win that they weren't about to let anyone forget anytime soon.

***

Giuseppe returned to camp bone-weary, having spent the better part of the day rounding up and branding cattle. He showered and walked over to the mess for dinner. As soon as he entered the hall, his nostrils flared at a familiar smell. In an instant, he felt like he'd been transported home. He imagined his mother, Rosa, and younger sister, Caterina, in the kitchen, and his father, Pietro, and brother, Lorenzo, in the field. He pictured his mother calling from the back door, and the men walking into the kitchen to find the table filled with an enormous bowl of spaghetti Bolognese. The block of parmesan they'd made and cured the year before sat on the table, ready to serve. He could almost taste it. A moment later, the vision cleared, and he was back standing in the long line of men, eagerly awaiting their dinner in the mess. He thanked the kitchenhand and moved to his usual spot at the long table closest to the wall. He leaned down to take a long sniff of his food, and as he looked up, he saw Eugenio slurp his first mouthful.
"How is it?" Giuseppe asked.
"It tastes like home," replied Eugenio with his eyes closed.
Giuseppe took a mouthful and licked his lips, savouring every morsel.

Everyone's spirits were high after enjoying a taste of the old country when Cambino walked in with Officer Harris and Officer Grady in tow. The chatter quieted, and all eyes moved to the men standing at the front of the mess with their arms full of small books.

"If you've already been assigned to a farm, raise your hand," called Cambino. Forty men raised their hands in unison. The three men walked up and down the tables, handing a book to each of them. Giuseppe picked his up and scanned the cover— "Pidgin English for Italian Prisoners of War published by the Department of Army." Giuseppe looked at the confusion on some of the men's faces. Among the hundreds of Italian prisoners, there were less than fifty men who spoke English well. Luigi looked at his book, then tossed it back on the table.

"At least they're doing something to help," Giuseppe said. Luigi rolled his eyes.

"They could help by letting us go home," Luigi said.

"You know that's not going to happen until the war ends. With this, the others might find it easier here and out on the farms."

"This is true." Luigi conceded, then picked up his book and flicked through it. Giuseppe grabbed his book and walked back to his hut. Eugenio was lying on his bed. The poor fellow had found it hard to adjust to life in Australia. He'd been sent back from two farms already and was in the guards' bad books. Despite Giuseppe's best efforts, he had only been able to teach him a few words of English. Giuseppe handed him the book, and Eugenio read the Italian description on the inside cover. His mouth dropped open and his eyebrows shot up.

"*Questo è per me?*" he asked, holding the book up.

"*Si. Impari l'inglese,*" Giuseppe replied, flopping onto his bunk. He sat with his head resting on his pillow, propped against the wall, reading the day-old, heavily censored newspaper. He glanced over the top of the page and watched as Eugenio mouthed the words, an idea forming in his mind.

***

Giuseppe pulled the cloth cover off the salad sandwiches that Elizabeth had left in the shed for him and took a huge bite out of one. The sound of galloping rang out as Maggie pulled Lily to a stop just outside the doors. He swallowed his mouthful with a loud gulp and coughed as it went down the wrong way.

"Are you all right?" Maggie asked, leading Lily into the stall and working the buckle to undo the saddle. Giuseppe could only nod as he guzzled water, then took a few heavy breaths and walked over to her. She was standing so close he could almost touch her.

"I'm all right now. How was your ride?"

"Good. I needed to think about something." He took the saddle from her and hung it up on the hook. He'd learned that Maggie often filled in the silence when they were alone. "Doctor Mosely has asked if I want to study to become a nurse." Giuseppe didn't understand why she looked worried.

"This is good, *si*?"

"Well, yes, and no. Nursing is a wonderful role, but I'm not sure if it's right for me. Besides, if I do it, I might have to go to Perth for some of the training." Recognition dawned, and he handed her the brush.

"Can you tell him in the New Year?" he asked. She shook her head.

"He wants to know as soon as possible. What do you think?"

Giuseppe bit his bottom lip. If it was his choice, he'd say no, but he knew that was only for selfish reasons. He felt her eyes boring into him.

"I think you should choose whatever will make you happy." She clicked her tongue.

"Well, that doesn't help me at all. I don't know what will make me happy." It took all his willpower not to tell her she made him happy.

***

At dusk three nights later, Giuseppe was walking the perimeter track when he saw Officer Harris coming towards him. Harris had fought in the First World War and never left the army. He took his position seriously. The second Giuseppe spotted his furrowed brow and straight mouth, his stomach tightened and his mind spun. He'd not had any part in the recent escape attempt. He diligently completed his work on the farm, he made his bed every day, and he always did his rostered duties when required. He couldn't think of any reason for Harris to have a problem with him.

"Giuseppe Russo, come with me."

"What is this about?" Giuseppe asked, but Harris remained tightlipped and led Giuseppe back to his hut. Giuseppe gasped when he saw the room. The room was a mess, with rugs and mattresses pulled from bunks, and the possessions of all the occupants lying in a heap on the floor.

"Did you give this to Eugenio Marzano?" Harris asked, holding a copy of the Pidgin English book up in the air. Giuseppe looked across the room at Eugenio, and as the younger man bowed his head, he glimpsed the shame in his eyes. He looked back at Harris and nodded. He knew there was no point denying it. "This

55

was only issued to those on farm duty. By giving it to Marzano, you're in breach of the rules. I've been ordered to put you in the cooler for the night." Giuseppe's mouth dropped open and Eugenio's head shot up.

"What? No! This isn't right," Giuseppe said, shaking his head.

"It's my orders," Harris said. Eugenio stood and went to stand in front of them but was pushed back onto his bed as Officer Harris shoved Giuseppe out the door, ordering him to walk ahead. Giuseppe knew where to go. Everybody knew that the detention cells were outside the perimeter of the main camp, close to the guards' sleeping quarters. Sometimes, when there was no wind and the camp was quiet, sobbing could be heard coming from the cells. Other prisoners paused their activities to observe as Giuseppe was silently escorted through the camp. When they reached the Italian side of the cells, Harris opened the heavy steel door and nudged Giuseppe inside. It was dim. Giuseppe felt for the wall on his right and followed it around the sides of the space. The cell was barely long enough for a man to lie down and not wide enough to stretch out. It was designed with misery in mind. He sat against the cold, hard wall. Harris had said he'd been ordered to do this and there was only one person in charge—Major Browning. Over the last few months, Browning had increasingly grown into a hard taskmaster. There were rumours that his only son had died fighting in France. This retaliation obviously came from a place of grief, but it didn't make things any easier for Giuseppe.

Dusk turned to night, the birds stopped calling, the camp

quietened, and the only sound he could hear was the wind whispering through the trees. Lying in the cell, he was thankful for the heat of the summer night, although it felt like it would never end. He rolled onto his side and put his arm under his head. He thought about how awful this war was, how unfair it was that he couldn't help a man better himself, and how much he wanted to go home. Then his thoughts turned to Maggie. Her silky golden hair and penetrating blue eyes flashed into his mind, and he wondered if she felt anything for him. She was always friendly. She even seemed to flirt with him at times, but was that just wishful thinking?

Chapter 5

Margaret
Early 1944

Maggie froze as the bedpan fell to the floor with a loud clang. Matron Drysdale clicked her tongue.

"You need to be more careful, Margaret. Perhaps you should just observe for today." Maggie inwardly sighed but followed the older woman to the next cubicle. She glanced at the patient—a young boy suffering from fever and stiffness in his legs. With the polio epidemic not too distant in their collective memory, Matron Drysdale and the other senior staff were keeping a close eye on him. While Matron Drysdale read through his notes, Maggie picked the boy's toy off the floor and handed it to him with the biggest smile she could muster. She had been at the hospital for a month now, and the learning curve had been steep. It was a stark contrast to the paperwork and minor tasks Doctor Mosely had set for her. Some days, she considered whether she'd made the right decision, but on days when she looked at a child with a bandaged hand or a grateful mother with tears in her eyes, she felt a tug on her heart. Today was the former, and that afternoon, she was glad to pass through the gates of Jarrah Downs. She plonked into one of the chairs on the verandah, and Max put his paws on her lap. Elizabeth came out through the front door and handed her an envelope.

"This arrived for you today," Elizabeth said. Seeing Patricia's name on the back, Maggie tore it open, almost ripping the contents.

Dear Maggie,

I hope you're well. This nursing caper is just as exciting as I thought it would be. I've met women from all over Australia. They're good sorts. We have plenty of laughs. They've got us stationed at the hospital in Buna, Papua. It's as different from Colton as you can imagine. It rains all the time, but it's sweltering too. I don't think I've had a day off since I arrived. Just yesterday, we received a load of soldiers who had been evacuated from New Guinea.

It's not all bad though. I've met a lad named Larry. Would you believe he's from Perth? What are the odds of that? He's lost a couple of toes to gangrene, and he's being sent home soon. He's promised to keep in touch.

Would you mind looking in on Mum and Dad for me? Mum seemed a little blue in her last letter. I suppose she misses me. Who wouldn't, hey?

Anyway, I must dash. We're putting on a little concert for the patients in ward B. Between you and me, they won't be with us much longer, so I thought we could brighten their spirits with a singalong.

Yours,

Patty

Maggie let the letter rest in her lap and sat back in her chair, one hand stroking Max's soft fur. She felt ashamed at feeling sorry for herself. Patricia and James were dealing with life and death situations and she was upset because she'd had a bad day. She heard whistling and looked up to see Joe ambling across the driveway towards the shed. Max's ears pricked up, and he ran over to Joe. She walked over to greet him. How can he be so happy when he's a prisoner?

"*Salve*. How was your day?" he asked with a smile. She fell into step with him.

"It's getting better." He nodded as if he knew why. "Joe, can I ask you something?" He stopped and looked at her. "How do you manage? How do you not get blue?"

"Some days it is not easy." He got a faraway look in his eyes, then he blinked and looked back at her. "But I have hope, and I look for the things that make my day better. Like sitting by the river on a warm day, playing a game of cards, and seeing you, of course." He winked, and she blushed. A truck horn blasted from the end of the driveway. "I have to go. *Arrivederci*." She waved him off and stood in the driveway watching the sun set. I can look for the things that make my day better too, she thought.

***

A new year brings renewed hope and the one thing the Sleeman family was all sincerely hoping for was an end to the war. Despite the hard times, or perhaps because of them, Maggie found herself looking forward to the annual New Year's Eve Ball more this year. Taking place at the Colton Town Hall, it promised to be a splendid affair attended by many people from the surrounding districts. Elizabeth, Joan, and Maggie had spent weeks cutting and sewing new dresses for themselves and assisting the CWA ladies with making hats for the attendees.

Elizabeth berated George as they stood outside the hall. The family was fashionably late thanks to a runaway calf that George managed to grab before it bolted out onto the road.

"I'm sorry, sweetheart. Have I mentioned how lovely you look tonight? Both my girls look beautiful." George said, grinning at them both. Elizabeth placed a hand on her hip and glared at him for a moment before leaning forward and kissing him on the cheek. She wore a blue full-length silk dress with black kitten heels. Maggie was dressed in a soft pink knee-length silk gown with capped sleeves. It was pinched at the waist and adorned with a delicate ribbon bow on the bodice. The dress was beautiful, but she felt self-conscious as she entered the hall. It seemed as though every pair of eyes was on their family. She scanned the large, high-ceilinged hall, taking in the banners across the stage at the front and the ribbons that weaved around the covered tables and chairs dotted along the sides. She spotted Joan and Mary sitting on the left, close to where the food was laid out on long trestle tables, and walked as quickly as she could without drawing any further attention to herself. The band was playing renditions of popular songs, and plenty of couples were already flouncing their way around the dance floor.

"You look gorgeous," Mary said. Maggie smiled and returned the compliment as she sat down.

"I think someone's making a beeline for you." Joan nudged her in the ribs. Maggie glanced over and then spun back to Mary and Joan, her eyes wide. In the last few months, she'd seen Thomas several times at the store and once at the hospital when he'd brought his father in with pains in his chest. Thankfully, it had turned out to be indigestion. Maggie's hand went to her stomach. She wondered if she was suffering a little indigestion, too. Her eyes shifted from Joan and Mary, who were both hiding smiles behind their hands. She scowled at them and discreetly wiped her sweaty palms on a napkin and handed it to Joan just as Thomas reached them.

"Would you do me the honour of this dance?" He asked, holding out a hand. She looked up into his eyes and her throat dried up. She couldn't dance with him. What if she stepped on his toes? He waited until she placed her hand in his, then led her onto the dance floor. She held his hands and hoped that he wouldn't feel how clammy they were. They waltzed their way around the dimly lit room. She looked over his shoulder for her parents, but they were both engaged in conversation. The room spun, and so did her thoughts. She could feel his hand creep down to the small of her back, and the sensation made her stumble.

"Sorry. I'm so clumsy tonight," she said, looking at the floor and willing her feet not to step on Thomas's for the fourth time.

"It's all right. Nothing to worry about. You look beautiful, by the way." A flutter of warmth ran through her body, and she couldn't bring herself to look at his face. "Have you heard from James?" She nodded. "How's the farm?" She shrugged and he sighed. She knew she wasn't making this easy for him, but she couldn't help it. Her nerves seemed to have taken her ability to hold a proper conversation. The song ended, and she dropped her hands to her sides. "Care for another twirl?" he asked. Her stomach was in knots, her hands were sweaty, and her mind felt like mush. There was no way she could endure more dancing without some sort of disaster.

"Thank you, but... I think I might keep Joan and Mary company for a while," she said and took a step backwards. He eyed her for a moment, and she was unsure how he was going to react.

"All right then. I hope you'll grant me another dance before the night is over, though." He turned and headed back to the group of young men congregating near the stage while Maggie made her way back to the waiting women. She suddenly felt flushed and had to sit down.

"Are you all right?" Mary offered her a glass of water, and Maggie gulped it down. Her skin cooled, and her head cleared a little.

"It looks like someone's a little hot under the collar," Joan remarked with a wink.

"I think I need some fresh air," she announced as she dashed out of the hall, almost bumping into Mr Sykes and his wife.

Standing outside in the dim light coming from the opening, she looked up at the full moon and took a few deep breaths. She felt her body relaxing, but her mind wouldn't quiet its constant chatter. I hope nobody saw that exit. Why did Thomas have to ask me to dance? I'm such a terrible dancer. Crossing her arms against the slight breeze, she turned and saw Doctor Mosely and his wife, Charlotte, exiting the hall.

"Are you leaving already?" Maggie called out. The couple walked over, and Doctor Mosely shook his head.

"I've left part of my costume in the car. But I'm glad I caught you. The surgery's been so busy lately that I've hardly had time for anything else. How's the training going? Matron Drysdale isn't being too harsh on you, is she?" Maggie shook her head. She couldn't tell him she was having doubts when he had gone out of his way to recommend her.

"I'm enjoying it. Matron Drysdale certainly doesn't put up with any nonsense from the nurses, or the patients for that matter, but I'm glad about the opportunity."

"Well, I miss you at the surgery. You're welcome back anytime." Doctor Mosely tipped his head, and he and Charlotte walked towards the row of cars. Maggie took the opportunity to go back inside and join the celebrations.

Just before midnight, a bell rang out. Maggie looked around as some of the town's more well-known men, including Doctor Mosely and some of the local councillors, left the dancefloor. A few moments later, the crowd erupted with laughter when the men appeared on stage in costumes. George was dressed as Father Time, and his voice boomed throughout the hall as he narrated the play. Maggie hadn't seen her father this animated in a long time. He deserved to have some fun. They all did.

The clock struck 12, and the hall erupted in a haphazard rendition of Auld Lang Syne. When the last note played, Thomas was by Maggie's side, and she found herself drawn back onto the dance floor. They danced the foxtrot, mambo, and waltz. Zipping around the dancefloor, Maggie found that her earlier concerns had disappeared with the ringing in of the New Year.

"Thank you for a wonderful evening, Maggie," Thomas said as they followed the parting crowd towards the open double doors. Maggie thanked him and was about to turn away when he added: "May I call on you?" She stopped abruptly, momentarily puzzled by his request. He was staring at her, waiting for a response. Without the time to contemplate the request properly, she felt compelled to nod in agreement before walking over to her parents, who were waiting at the door. Sitting in the back seat of her parents' car on the way home, Maggie replayed the evening in her mind. It had been a wonderful night. With a beginning like that, 1944 was surely going to be a glorious year.

***

The summer felt endless. The grass was long dead; the heat was blistering, and the water tanks were nearly empty. Despite all that, George was in a good mood and had decided to end the day's work early. George and Richard rested on chairs while Joe sat on the back step. They were discussing what was to come in the weeks ahead. Elizabeth placed the apple tea cake she'd made earlier on the table. Maggie was constantly surprised at her mother's ingenuity, given the lack of access to some of their regular food supplies. Maggie carried three bottles of beer in the crook of her right arm and a jug of lemonade in her left hand. She set the jug down and handed a bottle to George and Richard before walking across the verandah to give one to Joe. He smiled up at her and she felt herself blush. She noticed Richard was watching their exchange, so she walked back to the table, using the time to compose herself. Elizabeth poured two glasses of lemonade and they all sat quietly for a few moments, enjoying the slight breeze, before Richard broke the silence.
"Hey Joe, do you get summers as hot as this where you're from?" Joe looked across the back of the property towards the dam before answering.

"Not as hot. No," he replied, taking a swig of his beer. Richard nodded and then began discussing the rising price of cattle with George. Joe looked down at the bottle in his hand, his expression contemplative. Maggie sat on the steps, ensuring that she had left enough room between herself and Joe.

"Do you miss your home?" she asked and then instantly regretted it as a look passed across Joe's face.

"*Si*. I miss my family too," he replied. Maggie put a hand to her chest, struck with a sense of sorrow and pity. She couldn't imagine how awful it must be to be held captive in a foreign land—no family, no friends, no freedom. She understood what it felt like to be stuck somewhere, but she knew it was nothing compared to what Joe was going through. She felt some solidarity nonetheless.

"Have you been in contact with them?"

"I have given the guards letters, but I don't know if they have sent them. There is not much mail," he said bitterly. Maggie shook her head and then abruptly walked inside, returning with a pen, paper, and envelope, and offering them to Joe.

"Write to your family. I'll make sure this letter gets sent."

"Are you sure?" he asked with raised eyebrows. Maggie lifted her chin and nodded. She returned to her chair and could feel the eyes of her family burning into her. She looked at them, willing them to say something. When they didn't, she sipped her lemonade and waited for Joe to finish. As dusk approached, so did the sound of the army truck. Joe jumped up, handed Maggie the finished letter, said goodbye to everyone, and started jogging around to the front of the house.

"You shouldn't have done that, Maggie," Richard said.

"Why not? The man has a right to correspond with his family. We receive letters from James and I get letters from Patty, too."

"It's not the same, and you know it. We could get in trouble for sending that letter. I think you should give it to Dad." Her father made to rise, but before he could do so, Maggie clutched the letter to her chest and ran inside to her bedroom. She shut the door and put a chair under the handle, then walked over to her window, pulled up the loose floorboard, and tucked the letter in next to her diary. She sat on her bed, her breath slowly returning to normal as she waited for a knock on her door. When the knock didn't come, Maggie unearthed the envelope, taking in Joe's large flowing script, and she tried to read the address. She carefully took out the page and turned it over. Joe had written on both sides. She wished she could read Italian. She knew it was a personal letter, but she wanted to know if Joe was really all right. She carefully folded the paper and put the envelope back in its hiding place. Richard's reaction to the letter and the look on Joe's face when he spoke of his home made her determined to post it.

***

Maggie drove to her shift at the hospital with Joe's letter safely tucked in the bottom of her handbag. It had been a week since she'd encouraged him to write it, and she'd spent that time worrying and waiting for her parents or Richard to ask about it. Rather than wait for a confrontation, she decided to find a way to send it. Reaching Colton's main street, she parked the Ford in front of the town hall and walked toward Patricia's house. If anyone asked what she was doing, she'd say she was checking in on Patricia's parents. It was a plausible story. She stopped and looked back towards the car, then crossed the street to the post office. Fumbling in her bag for the letter, she walked up the ramp and almost stumbled backwards when the door pushed out towards her. She grabbed the handrail to steady herself as Thomas came through the dark doorway and into the daylight.

"Maggie! I've been meaning to come and see you," he said with a broad grin. Ignoring the knot in the pit of her stomach, she greeted him warmly. This wasn't going according to plan. It was supposed to be a quick, clandestine errand. She had to get to the hospital, but she had to send this letter. Before she could change her mind, she blurted out her request while handing Thomas the envelope.

"A friend asked me to send this, but I'm running a little late for my shift. Would you mind posting it for me, please?" she said with a congenial smile plastered in place.

"Of course. Anything to help." She put her hand on his arm and thanked him profusely before ushering him back into the post office. Sitting in the car, she held her hands up and tried to stop them from shaking. She'd made a promise to Joe, and she'd had to find a way to send the letter without her family knowing, but had she made the right decision asking Thomas to send it for her? He was obviously keen on her, and she knew he would do what she'd asked. So why did she still have a knot in her stomach?

***

The heat of the afternoon sun was so relentless that it felt at least ten degrees cooler in the shade. Maggie sat perched in her favourite spot under the tree in the front yard. From her vantage point, she could see Richard on the tractor ploughing one of the far paddocks and her father walking through their small orchard, picking apples and tossing them in a hessian bag tied around his waist. Max was by his side, waiting for him to drop another apple on the ground. Her mother had left earlier that morning to spend the day with Joan.

"Hello there." A deep voice startled her. Maggie looked up into Joe's face as he came around the tree. She'd spoken with him a few days ago to let him know his letter was on its way to Italy. The grin on his face had produced a warm feeling that spread through her entire body. She stood up after making sure that Richard and George were still occupied. "I have something for you. To thank you for posting my letter," he said as he pulled a small silver packet out of his shirt pocket and dropped it into her outstretched hand.

"Thank you, but you didn't have to get me anything." She read the label and her eyebrows arched while her mouth formed a perfect oval. "Where on earth did you get chocolate from?"

"At camp. We get paid. No money, just tokens." He pulled out a small metal disk from the pocket of his pants. "We can buy things like cigarettes and chocolate." Maggie felt the warmth and weight of the token before handing it back.

"Well, it seems that you've got tokens, and we've got ration coupons, and neither of us can get what we really want." Maggie held his gaze and then sat back down and gestured for him to sit, too. He looked around before squatting down on one knee. She opened the wrapper and offered some to Joe, but he refused. She popped a small, slightly melted square in her mouth and let out a contented moan.

"How is your nursing going?" Joe asked. He'd been happy for her when she'd told him she'd decided to take Doctor Mosely up on his offer. The discussion she'd had with him had been a valuable part of her decision-making. Their chance meetings were becoming more regular, and she realised she looked forward to them. Maggie didn't feel the pressure to keep up appearances she felt when she was around other people. With Joe, she felt like she could be herself.

"It has its good and bad points." She balled the empty wrapper into her fist. "In truth, I question my decision all the time."

"It's not final. You can change it," he said. He was right. She could stop nursing if she wanted to. She didn't need to keep going just because everyone thought it was in her best interest. "I need to get back to work. We can talk another time, *si*." She watched his tall, muscular frame walking away and caught herself thinking about how it would feel to have his arms around her. Joe was sincere and worldly with a cheeky side, and he was the only person who listened to her without making a condescending remark. But he was also a prisoner of war, a foreigner, a man who had fought for the other side.

Sitting with her legs tucked under her while she sewed buttons on her dress, she was only half listening to the trio singing during Australia's Amateur Hour on the wireless. An advertisement for Rinso came on, and George got up to pour himself a drink.

"I saw Joe with you today. What were you talking about?" George asked, turning to face her. She bristled and pricked her finger.

"Nothing. I just asked how he was finding it here." She sucked her finger and kept her eyes on her dress. George sat in his chair and leaned forward.

"Well, I don't think it's appropriate for you two to be alone," he said, pointing at her with his glass in his hand.

"I don't see the issue. We were out in the front yard."

"Actually, your mother has seen you and Joe talking in the shed. And what about that letter? Did you send it without my permission?" Maggie looked over at Elizabeth, who stared at the needlework she was holding. She thought her parents had forgotten about the letter. Had Thomas mentioned it to Elizabeth when she last went to the store?

"The letter's gone. I spilled tea on it when I breakfasted in my room a few days after Joe gave it to me. It was ruined, so I threw it out," she said with a flick of her hand. "Speaking of tea, I might make myself another cup. Would anyone else like one?" she offered as she rose and walked to the doorway. Elizabeth murmured an agreement without raising her face.

"Maggie." She stopped and turned to face her father. "I'll thank you for obeying me when I say that you're not to speak to Joe alone from now on."

"What? Why not?"

"Because that's my decision, and it's final," George said, then sat back in his chair and took a sip of his whisky. She looked from her father to her mother, and neither of them looked back at her. She knew that there was no point arguing with him, and it was clear that her mother was on her father's side. She turned and stormed into the kitchen to make the tea. The water boiled and so did the frustration and anger boiling up inside of her. Why must he always treat me like a child? I'm a grown woman, for goodness' sake. And why is Mum acting like that? She returned to the sitting room and handed Elizabeth a cup, then resumed her sewing. The silence was awkward, but she was determined to sit it out. While she finished sewing on the last of the buttons, she thought about her father's comments. Why couldn't her parents see she was an adult, able to make her own decisions? She felt like she was just biding her time and that one day soon, she wouldn't live under her father's rule.

For the next few weeks, she went inside whenever Joe was close to the house. No doubt, he was wondering why she was avoiding him, but she'd known her father long enough to know that it was best to placate him, at least for the time being. She was sitting on one of the rocking chairs on the verandah with Max's inquisitive face pressed onto her lap. He raised his paw and started patting her leg, eager for a rub behind the ears. She couldn't resist his charms and gave in. Elizabeth came out of the house and sat next to her, chewing her bottom lip. Maggie continued to pat the dog while she waited for Elizabeth to break the silence.
"Your father and I are looking out for your best interests. We can't see that any good will come of it." Maggie didn't have to ask what she meant. Joe had just walked past the house and into the shed. "We don't know enough about Joe or his family. And once the war ends, he'll return to Italy, and where will that leave you?" Maggie bent down and put her face closer to Max. Elizabeth shifted in her seat. "You and the Williams' boy seemed to enjoy yourselves at

the New Year's Eve Ball." Maggie continued to snuggle Max, but when he heard Richard whistling, he leapt up and ran towards the paddock. Traitor. She kept her eyes on Max.

"You and Dad shouldn't concern yourselves with my business." Elizabeth opened her mouth but Maggie continued, "I've kept my distance from Joe as requested. I'm sure he's wondering why I've been so rude. And you're right, I enjoyed the Ball. And Thomas is nice. I've known him for a long time." Her words fell out before she knew what she was going to say. Elizabeth shook her head slightly and sighed.

"Maggie, dear, you've always been wayward, but I urge you to think about your future now. I understand you think you have a tough choice, but I see the right decision so clearly." She went back inside and left Maggie to contemplate her words. Her parents had forbidden any sort of relationship with Joe. Thomas was their obvious choice. He was a local lad, and his father had a good standing in the community. She thought of her parent's marriage. Their parents had been friends, and little George and Elizabeth had grown up together. They'd been all but betrothed in essence, if not practicality. Her mother had known that she would marry her father, and that was all there was to it. Maggie didn't have that option, and neither did she want it.

Chapter 6
Giuseppe
1944

Rather than deter him, the incident with Eugenio and the book spurred Giuseppe on. During the day, when he was working at Jarrah Downs, he spent a lot of time on his own. He met with Richard and George first thing in the morning when they doled out his jobs for the day. The manual work afforded him plenty of time to think. Marrinup was a large camp with a mostly transient population. It was where men came before being transferred to work on farms all over Western Australia. There were over 1200 Italian and German prisoners in the camp at any one time, and a lot of them couldn't speak a word of English. Only the farm workers had access to the Pidgin English book, but the guards were sporadic in their gifting of it. Something had to be done. Lying in bed after lights out, Giuseppe pulled the blanket higher and rolled over.

"You awake, *amico*?" he whispered as he leaned towards the bunk opposite.

"*Si.*"

"What about you, Eugenio? Giovanni? Domenico? Carlo?" They mumbled confirmations, and Giuseppe cleared his throat. "I think every man here has a right to learn English, and we can help them." He began to fill them in on his plan. Over the last few weeks, he'd been observing the interactions between the guards and prisoners, and distinguishing how much free time the prisoners had. Giuseppe determined they could use their meal and shower times, and the weekly trips to the oval, to secretly teach Basic English to the other men. He finished relaying his idea and waited in the silence that followed. Had he made a mistake telling them? Would they be willing to take the risk? Could he trust them? He held his breath and waited. Then, from the darkness, a voice whispered, "I'm in." Giuseppe puffed out his breath, and relief washed over him as Luigi agreed. Giovanni, Domenico, and Eugenio followed suit, but Carlo stayed quiet. "Carlo, what do you think?" he asked.

"I think...it is dangerous. What if we get caught?" Giuseppe heard the quiver in his voice. Carlo had been put in the cooler for two days after he'd got into a fight with another prisoner. He spoke little in the days following his detention. Giuseppe thought back to his night in the cell. Even during that one night, he'd experienced the humiliation and isolation that the detention cells were designed to encourage. He could only imagine what more time in there would do to a man.

"It's all right. You don't have to do it. But we will be careful," Giuseppe assured him.

"*Si*. We don't want trouble. But we have to help, don't we?" Luigi added.

"We'll take care, Carlo. We can do this," Giovanni said.

"Perhaps you think about it and tell us tomorrow?" Giuseppe suggested, and Carlo agreed. In the silence that followed, Giuseppe contemplated whether he was doing the right thing. He felt queasy and pressed a hand to his stomach. The thought of getting caught filled him with dread, knowing the dire consequences that would follow.

Giuseppe was standing with a tall chestnut mare in the front paddock, basking in the warm morning sun. He moved his hand back and forth over the horse's back and she let out a low whinny. He moved closer to whisper in her ear.

"You know what, Wanda? This plan of ours just might work." The horse snorted and turned her head away. A door slammed, and he looked towards the homestead and saw Maggie standing on the verandah. "What do you think is the matter with her?" Maggie had been shunning him for a while now. Whenever she saw him, she waved and then retreated inside or drove off without speaking with him. Giuseppe wondered whether he'd been wrong about her. He ran his hand down the horse's neck and hummed a song his mother used to sing to him when he was a child. A shiver ran through his body as if he could feel someone watching him. He looked back toward the homestead and found Maggie standing by the fence. He nodded to her but stayed where he was. He watched as she climbed the fence, jumped down onto the soft grass, and made her way over. She stood on the other side of the horse and stroked its shoulder. Giuseppe waited for her to make the first move.

"Joe, I need to apologise. I've been avoiding you, but I didn't want to." Giuseppe looked over at her. Her cheeks were slightly red, her mouth kept opening and closing, and she avoided his eyes. He glanced back toward the shed and homestead but couldn't see Richard or George.

"I understand. You do not feel the same way about me as I do about you. I will keep to myself from now on." He nodded in dismissal and grabbed the rope to lead the horse away.

"Please stop," Maggie said, moving closer and putting her hand on his. "It's not that. I do... I mean... I know I enjoy talking with you." Her eyes grew fierce with determination, and the fiery attitude that he had glimpsed the day they met came flooding back. "My parents can't stop me from doing what I want to do anymore." That explained why she had been avoiding him. George must have told her to stay away from him. He shook his head and sighed.

"Your parents only want what they think is best for you." She folded her arms across her chest.

"What do they think I need protecting from? You're a better man than some of the lads around here." Giuseppe shrugged. He had an inkling of what their issue was, but he wouldn't say it. Now that Maggie was speaking to him again, he wanted it to continue.

"Well, I am here to talk whenever you want to," he said, and she beamed at him.

"That settles it then," she said, before turning and heading towards the river. He watched her walk away and considered her parents' opposition. Were they frightened that they'd run away together? That was unlikely, given his circumstances. He gave the horse one last pat and then made his way to the fence. He looked towards the homestead again and shook his head. They were probably more worried about what people would think than whether Maggie was happy. It never ceased to amaze him how judgmental people could be, even when evidence contrary to their opinions was right in front of them.

***

The door of the recreation hall swung open, releasing a burst of noise as Giuseppe entered. He let his eyes adjust to the dim light, then walked over to a table near the far wall. Luigi was playing cards, and he dealt him into the next round. Across from him sat Mario and Pietro, two older men who worked on farms close by, and spoke a little English. Giuseppe looked around the room. There were six long tables with chairs on either side, all occupied by Italian prisoners who were playing cards or talking loudly, or both.

"*Come va il lavoro?*" Giuseppe asked.

"*Va bene*," Mario replied with a shrug.

"*Capisci il tuo capo?*" Giuseppe knew some men found it hard to understand their boss. Mario and Pietro nodded.

"*Vuoi imparare l'inglese?*" Luigi asked them.

"*Si, si*," came the reply. Luigi and Giuseppe exchanged looks, checked the room once more, and then launched into their first lesson.

They walked out of the rec room half an hour later with swelled chests and wide grins.

"This is it, Luigi." Giuseppe patted him on the back. "We are going to do it."

"*Si*. I'll tell the others." He walked over to the closest row of huts and went inside the first one. Giuseppe looked around the camp and felt like he could bear this place for a while longer.

***

Giuseppe ran across the oval to the group of men standing in the tree line. They'd made the most of the warm Sunday afternoon by spending it at the oval. Giuseppe sat next to Luigi and noticed that

Officers Thomson and Smith were sitting on the other side of the oval. It was the perfect opportunity. Carlo had eventually come around to the idea and their clandestine English lessons had been running successfully for a few weeks. They were mindful of where and when they practised, but with the number of men wanting to learn growing by the day, it was becoming increasingly difficult to keep it a secret.

"*Buongiorno*," Giuseppe called. "*Posso Aiutarla*?"

"Good Morning. Can I help you?" came the reply.

"Yes, please. Where is the toilet?" Luigi said, holding his crotch. The men laughed and answered, "*Si, per favore. Dov'e la toilette?*" They continued back and forth as they played the game. After almost an hour, Officer Thomson stood up, put his fingers to his mouth, whistled loudly and yelled, "10 minutes, lads". The score was 2-2. Antonio snatched the ball from Gunter and ran like a rocket towards the goal, dodging every man in his path. The Italians cheered and congratulated him before everyone started to walk back to camp.

Giuseppe felt a hand on his shoulder and flinched. He turned to see Antonio next to him.

"We win again," Antonio cheered and pumped his fist in the air. Giuseppe did the same before Antonio put an arm around his shoulders. "Thank you for the lessons. The boss talks to me now, so I don't spend all day in silence anymore." Giuseppe smiled and patted him on the back. Antonio had been one of the first to put his hand up when Giuseppe began to execute his plan.

"That's exactly what I wanted. I'm happy for you," Giuseppe said.

Antonio squeezed his shoulder and ran ahead to catch up with his roommates. Giuseppe felt a surge of happiness and a spring in his step.

The warm weather, pseudo-freedom, and camaraderie had put the men in an affable mood, and they were laughing and jostling with each other as they entered the compound gates. Major Browning strolled over to the group and attempted to step in front of Giuseppe, stopping him mid-stride. Browning stood with his chest pushed out and a smirk playing at the corners of his mouth. Giuseppe's heart raced and his stomach lurched as he looked around for Luigi. Browning nodded to Officers Grady and Harris, who were standing to the side of the crowd. They pushed through and grabbed Giuseppe under each arm, propelling him forward as Browning started walking towards the detention cells.

"Hey, what's going on? Let him go," Luigi yelled, making a grab for Grady's free arm.

"Get out of the way, Alberti!" Grady shouted, pushing Luigi back into the arms of Eugenio and Carlo. The group of Germans and Italians erupted into a deafening rumble and surged forward. Guards descended on them with their batons raised. The prisoners were forced back, but they continued to shout with their fists raised in the air.

"Get him out of here now!" Browning yelled at Harris and Grady. They hitched Giuseppe higher on their arms and dragged him away from the angry mob. Giuseppe looked back over his shoulder and caught sight of Luigi. The anger on his face mirrored that of the men around him. He began moving towards them again.

"Leave it, Luigi. It's all right," Giuseppe said, shaking his head. Luigi couldn't help him without risking a night in the cooler, too.

They reached the detention cells, and Harris and Grady forced him inside. The heavy door closed, but he could still hear the shouting crowd. The guards were trying to wrangle the men into their respective compounds, but they weren't cooperating. A gunshot rang out, and the camp fell silent. Browning's voice came through the speakers.

"Unless you want to be put in the cooler, you'll get to your huts now!" Giuseppe could hear the indistinct murmurs and heavy footsteps as the men obeyed the command.

Sitting with his back against the cold stone wall, his mind raced. Nobody had been caught, but Browning had somehow found out about the lessons. Surely, it wasn't wrong to teach English to the other prisoners. It was a way to help them and make their time here a little more bearable. Was it just Browning who had taken issue with it, or was the Australian government involved? Did they think the prisoners were going to create an insurgence and rise against them? He considered his options. He could tell them everything or he could say nothing.

When darkness fell, Giuseppe lay with his hands behind his head and pondered the other reasons for the prisoners' discontent. The conditions at Marrinup needed improvement. Many men didn't have the opportunity to send mail, let alone receive any word from their families. The food was only good when the gardens were growing well, but winters were long and summers even longer. The radio in the recreation hall had never worked well, and the picture shows they'd been promised rarely eventuated. There had been rumours that men were receiving increasingly harsher punishments for supposed misconduct. Escape attempts were becoming more frequent and when the escapees were caught, they were often sent to a camp somewhere in Perth. Giuseppe closed his eyes and let out a long breath. He'd just have to strengthen his resolve and take whatever punishment Browning doled out.

Giuseppe sat bolt upright, sweat dripping from his shaking body and his breath coming in short bursts. The images returned every time his eyelids closed. He saw men speared on the ends of bayonets or laying in trenches twitching and muttering incoherently. He shook his head and looked around, trying to ground himself in the present. He got up and walked to the door, where thin strips of light filtered in. It was impossible to tell what time it was, but from the lack of noise outside, he surmised that the reveille hadn't sounded yet. Footsteps crunched on the gravel, getting louder as they got closer. Giuseppe moved back and sat on the bed as the lock clicked and the door was hauled open. Browning stepped in, the dappled light behind him shadowing his face.

 "We know what you and your gang have been doing, Russo. We've got your man Alberti tucked up next door, and the others are spending some time in their huts under watch. What do you have to say about it?" He should have known they'd lock Luigi up too, but keeping everyone else in their huts was unnecessary. Still, Giuseppe didn't want to give in to Browning so soon. He raised his head and shrugged. Browning rushed towards him, stopping inches from his face. Giuseppe tried not to move. He wouldn't give Browning the satisfaction of seeing him flinch. Browning straightened and stood above him for a few more minutes. Giuseppe considered confessing. If he did, Browning might let the others go, or he could continue to punish them, anyway. He brought his knees up but stayed silent. "Suit yourself. Let's see if a little more time in here will loosen those lips," Browning said with a smirk that revealed his slightly yellowed teeth. Slamming the door, he barked at Officer Harris to lock it. Giuseppe put his head in his hands and rubbed his forehead. Perhaps they'd gotten too confident, or maybe there was a snitch among the men. Either way, it was his fault that everyone was in trouble. It was his idea. The shame felt heavy on his shoulders like a weight dragging them down along with his resolve.

"Hey, *amico*. Can you hear me?" Giuseppe moved towards the door, putting his ear to the gap between the heavy steel and the cold concrete. "Giuseppe? Can you hear me?" He put his mouth close to the gap.

"Luigi? Are you all right? What happened?"

"Si. The camp's been in lockdown since we got back from the oval. Harris and Grady dragged me out of bed around midnight, then gagged me, and brought me here. The others woke, but there was nothing they could do." Giuseppe put his hand to his forehead and wiped his brow.

"*Mi dispiace*. I'm sorry, Luigi. I didn't want anyone to get in trouble."

"It's all right. Don't tell the *bastardi* anything. We're not talking. They won't get to you through us, that's for sure," Luigi said. They heard voices coming from behind the cell block. Giuseppe knocked once and moved back to bed. He sat back and contemplated his situation. He didn't want Luigi to be locked up, but it was comforting to know that he was close by and that the men were on his side.

The next day was a repeat of the first, with Browning paying him another visit early in the morning. He stood above Giuseppe with a hand on his baton.

"You lot wouldn't know how to help yourselves. Alberti's not talking either, but since my money's on you being the ringleader, you can bloody well stay in here," Browning goaded, then marched out of the cell. Giuseppe moved closer to the door to hear the muffled conversation, but he couldn't make out the words. Instead, he heard a lock click and a door open, and then he heard Luigi call out, "*Rimani forte per te stesso.*"

"*Cercherò,*" Giuseppe replied, as a baton pounded on his door. He didn't know how long he would be in the cooler, but he knew he could do it as long as his resolve stayed strong and his dreams stayed away.

***

The shaft of light that filtered under the door moved around the cell, casting shifting shadows that became a measure of time during his weeks in isolation. The coolness of the cell was a blessing during the heat of the day, but at night, its hard concrete felt as if it was freezing Giuseppe to his core. Myriad thoughts clouded his mind, vying for attention. He thought of his family, wondering if he was still alive. He questioned whether Maggie had sent the letter. At other times, he trusted she had.

Mealtimes became a desperate source of interaction with the outside world. Giuseppe took to asking the guards questions about his fellow prisoners as they slipped trays of food through the flap in the steel door three times a day. As the days turned into weeks, the guards hovered during their deliveries, talking about which team had won the last wristball match or how the gardens were going. It was clear they were finding the situation difficult to stomach.

The shaft of light had reached its peak and Giuseppe was pacing his cell when Grady opened the flap and handed him his lunch tray. Grady stood and waited, telling him about how many tons the Germans had cut this month. Giuseppe mopped up the last of his soup with a piece of crusty bread and handed him back the tray.
"Do you think Browning will let me out soon?" Giuseppe asked. Grady looked at the tray in his hands and stayed silent for a few moments. Giuseppe watched as his brow knotted together, then unfurled.
"Look, Russo. We have to follow orders. We can't do much else." Giuseppe let out a long sigh.
"I understand," he said, then slunk over to the far wall. Grady left and Giuseppe paced the cell to keep his body moving. He heard footsteps approaching, then the door was unlocked and pulled

open, and Browning stood in the doorway.

 "Are you ready to talk yet?" Browning said, then walked over and stood in front of Giuseppe when he didn't receive a reply. Browning ran his hand along his chin. "I see two options here, Russo. Either you talk, or you don't work on the Sleeman farm." Giuseppe's head snapped up, and Browning snickered. Giuseppe cursed himself and bowed his head when he realised his mistake. Browning knew his weakness. Could he risk not seeing Maggie ever again? How much more could they punish him if he confessed?

"I only wanted to help them," he whispered. Browning signalled, and Harris brought in a chair. While Browning made himself comfortable, Giuseppe sighed and began his confession. Despite Browning's attempts to garner information, Giuseppe omitted the names of his fellow conspirators and ensured that Browning understood it was his idea. When he finished, he glanced away and ran his hands through his hair and down to the back of his neck.

"I'm glad you came to your senses," Browning said before he left the cell. Giuseppe assumed his confession and time already served would see him out of the cooler, but the cell door was closed again. Browning was making a point, and Giuseppe heard him loud and clear.

He woke the next morning to footsteps and muffled voices. It was early for breakfast, but he wouldn't complain. He looked up when Officer Grady pulled open the heavy door with a broad smile spread across his face.

"Today's your lucky day, Russo." He gestured towards the open doorway, and it took Giuseppe a moment before he realised he was being freed. He stood and stretched. From a small prison to a large one, he thought, as he waited for Grady to shut the door and lead him back into the Italian compound. Giuseppe lifted his head to the cloudy sky and let the light envelop him. When he opened his eyes, he saw Grady staring at him. His expression was almost unreadable, but perhaps there was a hint of sympathy or guilt. Giuseppe couldn't tell which.

Fear, anticipation, and excitement coursed through him. He looked at the ground and tried to make a beeline for his hut, eager to get his first conversation with his roommates out of the way. His stomach churned as he imagined the type of reception he would get from them. They had every right to hate him. The guards had placed Luigi in the cooler and kept the rest of the men under watch for days.

"Welcome back," Hans and Gunter called as he walked past the German compound. He waved but couldn't speak. His mind was elsewhere. He reached the hut but stopped near the doorway to smooth down his hair and straighten his weathered uniform. He entered the hut, his footsteps barely audible as he moved. The men were playing cards and didn't notice him come in. He watched for a moment before he saw Luigi's eyes bulge.

"Giuseppe, you're here!" Luigi ran over and embraced him. "They finally let you out. *Fantastico*!" Eugenio, Domenico, Giovanni, and Carlo looked up at the commotion before dropping their cards and rushing over. They huddled together, arms around each other's shoulders, all speaking at once. When the excitement had died down and they'd sat back down to their card game, Giuseppe coughed to get their attention. He had to tell them what had happened.

"Browning made threats. I had to confess," he said.

"We understand, *amico*," Giovanni said, patting him on the back.

"That's right. You did what you had to do," Eugenio said.

"I'd do it again in a heartbeat," Luigi said with a wink. Giuseppe looked at Carlo. He hadn't wanted to be part of the scheme in the first place, and it had all gone wrong despite their assurances that it wouldn't.

"*Mi dispiace*, Carlo," Giuseppe said with his hands to his chest. Carlo looked out the window, then back at Giuseppe before standing and putting his arms around him.

"All is forgiven," he said. Giuseppe let out a breath and thanked him. His chest felt open with immense relief. He'd never experienced anything like it in his life.

Chapter 7
Margaret
Mid-1944

The sound of thunder still echoed in the air—a remnant of the storm that had left a trail of destruction across the farm. Standing on the verandah, Maggie looked out at the branches strewn across the paddocks and the puddle-filled holes dotted along the driveway. She picked her way over to the shed. Grabbing a handful of feed on her way past the bench, she heard Lily's hooves scuffling the floor. She held out the feed and then ran her hands along Lily's shoulder and neck. The horse trembled when a rumble of thunder pierced the silence. Maggie wondered if Joe had made it safely through the storm. He hadn't been to the farm for weeks and nobody had told her why.

George walked into the shed and shook the rain off his jacket. He glanced up at Maggie, then picked up a pair of gloves.
"That was a terrible storm last night. We could do with some help to clean up," he said, handing them to her. She took them and followed him outside. "You start closer to the house, and I'll see what needs to be done here."
"Dad?" George turned to her. "Where's Joe?" He frowned, then straightened to full height.
"Well, he's not here, and this yard needs clearing up, so how about we just concentrate on that?" he turned and walked back to the shed before she could argue. While she gathered branches and piled them in the closest paddock, her mind conjured

possibilities for Joe's absence from Jarrah Downs. Perhaps someone convinced him to escape, or he was hurt working at the camp. He had told her about the prisoners building the camp where they were imprisoned. It seemed like an unusually cruel punishment to her. She stood near the pile of branches that would soon become a bonfire and looked at her mother and father standing on the verandah, deep in conversation. They knew why Joe wasn't on the farm and they weren't telling her anything. Maggie decided she was going to find out what had happened one way or another.

***

When another morning passed and Joe didn't walk down the driveway, Maggie saddled Lily and went to find Richard. She trotted along the boundary of Jarrah Downs until she discovered him fixing part of the wooden jetty that jutted out into the dam close to the back boundary. Maggie seldom ventured into the area, knowing it was where the larger cattle were kept. Her father had told her many times about how aggressive bulls could be. He understood the risks all too well, given that a bull was the reason for his limp. He'd just finished setting the wire on the fence he'd been mending when he walked back toward the house. He grabbed a rag from his toolbox and whipped it around to clear off the dust before wiping his brow.

The bull standing 20 yards away started charging towards him. George hadn't seen the animal until it was almost on top of him, and by then, it was too late. He ran to the fence and started clambering over just as the bull reached him and used its huge head to shove him as hard as it could, its horn piercing the back of his thigh. When the bull pulled back to gear up for a second shot, George fell over the fence into the next paddock. He lay there, unable to move, until Richard found him half an hour later. He'd dragged him onto the horse, then raced back to the house. The doctor on duty at Colton Hospital did the best he could, but George wasn't able to walk for weeks. When he eventually managed it, he had a permanent limp.

Maggie reached the edge of the dam, then dismounted Lily and let her graze. She gingerly stepped her way down the grass slope towards the jetty and sat next to Richard's toolbox with a thud.
 "Hey, Maggie. Hand me that spanner, will you?" Maggie picked through the bolts laying on the wood next to her and dropped one into Richard's outstretched hand. Sitting back on her haunches, she contemplated how she would address the matter of Joe's disappearance.
"You've been busy lately. It must be hard with Joe gone," she said.
"Yeah. My workload definitely increased again, but there's not much we can do about it." Richard tightened the bolts on the new planks of wood.
"He must be hurt badly if he can't come to work," Maggie ventured. Richard's hands stopped for a moment. He knew what was going on, but would he tell her and risk the wrath of their father? She bit her bottom lip and hoped he'd take the gamble. He dropped his tools on the jetty and sat up.
"He's not hurt. He's in solitary. The army bloke who usually drops

him off told Dad he broke the rules." Maggie frowned and tilted her head to the side. Richard was watching her closely.

"That doesn't sound like Joe."

"It doesn't, but that's what we were told," he said with a shrug.

"Did they say anything else?"

"No. I guess they'll let Dad know when he's set to come back to work." Maggie nodded. Joe wasn't a troublemaker. There had to be a reasonable explanation for whatever had happened. She felt eyes on her and looked up to find Richard staring. He ran his hand across his mouth and rested it on his chin.

"Well, if you don't need me, I'll go back to the house. Mum wants help weeding the veggie garden today." Maggie stood and whistled for Lily, then made her way back along the jetty, avoiding the tools and wood strewn in her path.

"Be careful, Maggie. You don't want to get hurt," Richard called after her. She didn't need to look back at him to understand that he wasn't talking about the jetty.

***

A powerful gust of wind slammed the front door shut. Maggie flinched and called out an apology to whoever might be in the house. Her shift at the hospital had left her feeling drained, and she was looking forward to a quiet night of reading. She walked to her room and dropped her handbag on the chair by the window.

"Dress nicely for dinner. We've got a visitor coming," Elizabeth called. Maggie rolled her eyes. It was probably another councillor or one of the CWA members and her husband. Over the years, Maggie had endured countless tedious dinners like this one. But after the day she'd had, she wasn't in the mood to play hostess.

She turned to close the door and spied her new dress hanging on the open wardrobe door. She and Elizabeth had made it the week before. She walked over and ran her hand along the fabric. It was a vivid emerald green silk that her mother had bought from an Indian man who'd been passing through the area. Since the war began, many men who were left behind had been displaced. They travelled the country looking for work or selling whatever wares they could get hold of. Elizabeth would offer them water, tea, or spare fruits and vegetables from the garden. Sometimes, George gave them a day's work and a makeshift bed in the shed, but he was always wary of them outstaying their welcome.

Maggie put on the dress and stood in front of the mirror. The dress looked beautiful. She twirled and watched it flare out. Her chest swelled and her smile widened. She floated downstairs and into the kitchen, thankful that her mother had been in a good mood the day the silk trader came through.
"Oh, darling, you look lovely," Elizabeth said as she held both Maggie's hands and twirled her around.
 "Thank you. So, who's coming for dinner?" Elizabeth turned back to the bench and picked up the knife to cut the carrots. "Mum?" Elizabeth didn't look up. A knot formed in Maggie's stomach.
"Can you please set the table for four?" She looked at her mother's back for a moment, then picked up the cutlery and went into the dining room. With the baby so close to arriving, it wasn't Richard or Joan. Perhaps Elizabeth was attempting to keep Mrs Fulton on side. Or perhaps it was Mr Sykes or Mr Jones. George had put in a motion recently that was stirring a bit of discussion

around town. He might have invited one of the councillors to try to win them over.

Right at 6 o'clock, Maggie heard an engine come to a stop. She peeked out the front window and saw a white truck with "Williams General Store" emblazoned in black on the door. Recognition dawned. Maggie checked herself in the hallway mirror. Her face showed no sign of the panic she felt. She had no reason to be nervous. It was just Thomas. She braced herself and then pulled the door open and greeted him. His eyes widened as they looked her up and down before he stammered a greeting. Maggie raised a hand to her mouth to hide her smile, then led the way down the hall to the sitting room. She could feel Thomas's eyes on her, causing the hairs on the back of her neck to stand up. She let out a quick sigh when she saw George reclining in his armchair, listening to the wireless. He stood and shook Thomas's hand, then asked him about the upcoming cattle sale. Maggie escaped into the kitchen to find Elizabeth. She faced her mother with her eyebrows raised and her hands on her hips.

"Why did you invite Thomas over?" Elizabeth averted her eyes. "Just for company, Maggie dear," she said before turning back to the oven. Maggie knew Elizabeth wouldn't be questioned further. She bristled at the thought of her parents meddling in her life again. How was she supposed to get through this dinner now? She grabbed the plates and stormed into the dining room.

George and Elizabeth sat at the ends, leaving Maggie and Thomas to sit opposite each other. With grace said and the meal divided between them, the sound of cutlery clinking against plates filled the air as everyone settled in to enjoy their food. Maggie's movements were mechanical, but she listened as George kept the conversation flowing by inquiring about Thomas's parents and the general talk around Colton. Working in the biggest shop in town meant Thomas was privy to a lot of gossip. George was keen to find out how his chances would be if he ran for mayor in the local government elections in October.

"I think you'll be a shoo-in, Mr Sleeman," Thomas said before taking another bite of roast chicken. George's pride manifested in his swelled chest.

"So, what have you been doing, Maggie?" Thomas's hand shook as he took a sip of water while he waited for her answer.

"My training's going well, and with Joan's baby due any day, I'm sure Mum and I will have plenty to do soon enough." She smiled to ease his nerves as much as her own. George picked up the conversation and Maggie picked up her cutlery and listened to the others converse until the meal concluded.

"Shall we retire to the sitting room, Thomas? We'll let the ladies clear up." George stood and waited for Thomas to do the same. Maggie watched them leave, then looked down at the table. She felt as if she had been observing the evening unfold from a distance, disconnected from her own body. A sense of déjà vu struck her, but she was glimpsing her future rather than the past.

"How do you think it's going?" Elizabeth asked, pulling her from her reverie. Maggie shrugged and took the plates into the kitchen. She couldn't shift the feeling that had set like concrete in the pit of her stomach.

Maggie followed Elizabeth into the sitting room, carrying a tray of tea and biscuits. Although she craved a moment of solitude to consider the thoughts and emotions that had stirred in her, she recognised the need to fulfil her role. She offered the refreshments and sat on the chair opposite Thomas. George claimed the conversation, and the evening continued as before. Maggie listened but rarely took part. Her thoughts were elsewhere. When the clock on the mantle struck nine, Thomas stood and bid everyone goodnight. Elizabeth indicated for Maggie to show Thomas to the door.

It was a cool evening, but the sky was clear, and the stars were out. Maggie shivered and rubbed her arms as they walked to the truck.

"I was hoping we'd get a chance to be alone," Thomas said. He looked at the ground, ran his hand through his hair and stepped towards her. "You look beautiful tonight. I mean, you always do, but more so tonight." He swallowed loudly. "You wouldn't mind if I visited you again sometime, would you?" He shoved his hands in his pockets, then removed them again and placed one hand on the back of the truck. Maggie's stomach filled with butterflies, and her mind was a jumbled mess. Did she want Thomas to visit again? What did that mean? Stuck somewhere between her head and her heart, she stood, contemplating her answer. Thomas's hand rose and tucked a loose curl behind her ear. Her cheek tingled with the light touch of his fingers. "Maggie?" She looked up into his face and saw the expectation in his eyes. She had to make a decision.

"Yes. You can visit again," she answered. He grinned, then leaned towards her. She felt her body rise and lean into him of its own accord. He kissed her softly on the lips, and when she didn't pull away, he kissed her again, this time for longer and with slightly more force. When they parted, she blushed at the heat rising within her.

"Goodnight, Maggie," he called, then jumped into the truck and drove down the driveway. She felt rooted to the spot as she watched the taillights move further and further into the distance. The heat had left her, and a sense of emptiness enveloped her. She wrapped her arms around her body. The air suddenly felt cold.

Standing by her bedroom window, she looked out at the sky dotted with stars, then shivered and hopped into bed, pulling the blankets up around her shoulders. She closed her eyes, but her mind raced. What was that feeling that had come over her at dinner? Why had she said yes to Thomas? Did she have feelings for him? She thought about her previous encounters with Joe. She thought they'd developed a deep friendship and she could see it becoming more. But he hadn't been at the farm in so long and she had no idea if he would return. Why had her parents felt the need to meddle in her private life and complicate things? The kiss with Thomas had stirred something in her, but she had a niggling feeling that wouldn't go away. She couldn't shake the sentiment that she'd looked into her future, and she didn't like what she saw.

***

"Margaret, what are you doing?" Matron Drysdale admonished. "You almost dropped that needle. Perhaps you should take a break." Maggie's cheeks reddened, and she bent her head and left the ward, heading for the staff kitchen. She knew her mind wasn't on the job, but she was embarrassed to have been called out like that in front of patients and other staff members. Perhaps a cup of tea would settle her. She stood near the table and checked the newspaper while she waited for the water to boil. It had become a weekly ritual for every member of her family since James had left to fight. Maggie scanned the long list of names. No James Sleeman. Next, she checked for Patricia's name. It wasn't on the list either. Maggie breathed a sigh of relief and then chided herself. These people had families who loved them, and they had fought and died thousands of miles away from them. Yet here she was in the comfort of her hometown, feeling sorry for herself over some silly romantic dramas. There was a time and place to mull over recent events, and this wasn't it. She finished her tea, straightened her uniform, and returned to the ward.

At the end of the shift, Matron Drysdale asked to see Maggie in her office. Maggie's stomach tightened, and she almost jogged to keep up as she followed the older woman through the corridors. Matron Drysdale sat behind her desk, but Maggie didn't take the other seat.

"Margaret, you came highly recommended by Doctor Mosely, and I respect his opinion. But I have to say I'm a little disappointed. You've been training here for quite some time, and you always do what's asked of you, but it seems that you are going through the motions." She leaned back and put her hands in her lap. "Some women are called to be nurses, but I don't think you are one of those women." Matron Drysdale waited for a response. Maggie brought her hand to her forehead, rubbing her fingers and thumb along her brow. Perhaps Matron was right. She certainly hadn't been called to be a nurse, and she'd had reservations about taking the job. She looked down at her uniform and then back at Matron Drysdale.

"I thought this was what I wanted, but if I'm honest, I much prefer the work I was doing in Doctor Mosely's office. I think I'm more suited to paperwork rather than people." Matron Drysdale brought her hands together on the desk in front of her.

"I concur. I'm sure Doctor Mosely would welcome your return." Maggie nodded and pulled the badge from her uniform, placing it on the desk.

"Yes. Thank you, Matron. I'm sorry for any trouble this has caused." Matron Drysdale waved a hand in the air.

"Not to worry. Now, I can focus my energies where they are needed." Maggie walked out of the office feeling lighter than she had in months. It wasn't that she didn't enjoy nursing; she just liked working in an office more, and it had taken a few words from someone who could clearly see it to help Maggie realise it.

***

The following Saturday morning, Maggie saddled Lily and took the long way over to Richard and Joan's. The air was so frosty her breath came out in small puffy clouds, but the sun warmed her to her bones. With Richard working at Jarrah Downs during the day and Joan almost at the end of her pregnancy, Maggie had taken to almost daily visits. Thinking about the prospect of soon becoming an aunty brought a smile to her face, and it was still there when she entered the small kitchen.

"You look chipper this morning. I wish I could say I felt the same." Joan grimaced, holding one hand on the bottom of her stomach and the other on the table. Maggie froze.

"Are you all right? What's happening?"

"Oh, nothing... there's just a baby who wants to be born," Joan said, but the look on her face told Maggie that the situation was serious.

"It's coming now?" she asked. Joan closed her eyes and nodded. Adrenalin jolted through Maggie, kicking her into action. She held Joan's arm and guided her into the bedroom before helping her onto the bed. There was no way she could help Joan on her own, and they didn't have a telephone. She knew she'd have to ride back home, but she didn't want to leave Joan in this state. Joan gripped Maggie's hand and closed her eyes, then let out a low groan as a contraction struck her. When it passed, Maggie let go of her hand and said, "I have to get Mum. I'll be as quick as I can."

"Oh, Maggie. Hurry. I don't think I can do this on my own," Joan said. Her face was white and her brow was sweating. Maggie gave her one last hug, then rushed out the door and sprinted over to Lily. Her pulse raced as they galloped through the paddocks to Jarrah Downs.

She jumped down and ran into the sitting room, panting and shouting all at once. Elizabeth dropped her knitting and sprang into action.

"Right. Tell your father and Richard and then ride back over there. I'll call the doctor and then take the car. Go! Now!" Maggie ran out to the shed where Richard and George were working under the truck.

"The baby's coming. There isn't much time. Hurry!" She watched as Richard's face changed from surprise to shock to excitement within seconds. She mounted Lily and started galloping back to Joan just as her father and Richard got into the truck.

Joan was sitting exactly as Maggie had left her. Sweat was dripping down her brow and into her eyes. Maggie grabbed a shirt from the chair by the window and mopped Joan's forehead as Elizabeth burst through the door.

"Maggie, I need hot water and clean towels," Elizabeth said as she moved to the other side of the bed and helped Joan to lie down. Maggie's hands shook as she filled Joan's biggest pot with water and set it to boil on the stove. She grabbed some towels from the cupboard before going back into the bedroom, where her mother was now checking to see how far along Joan was. Maggie averted her eyes and placed the towels on the bed, then stood back, unsure what she should do next.

"The baby's crowning, Joan. You'll have to push when the next contraction comes. You're doing well, love," Elizabeth said. It was all happening so fast. Maggie felt as if there was nothing else in the world besides the three of them in that small room. She knelt beside the bed and held Joan's hand. Joan's body stiffened, and she squeezed Maggie's hand and let out a low growl. "Push. That's it. Push, Joan. Nearly there," Elizabeth said. Maggie flinched at the pain in her hand.

"You're doing so well," she said, wiping Joan's brow with her free hand. She had no idea if Joan was doing well or if everything would be all right, but figured that her mother knew enough about childbirth to help.

The next contraction seized Joan's entire body, and she let out an animalistic growl. With one final push, everything changed. Joan fell back onto the bed just as Elizabeth pulled and lifted the baby simultaneously. Maggie stared in awe at the scene before her. Elizabeth wiped the blood and mucus off the crying baby before wrapping it in a towel and placing it into Joan's outstretched arms. Tears filled Joan's eyes as she put the baby on her chest and whispered in its ear, not caring about, or even noticing, anything else around her. Elizabeth watched for a moment before blinking back her own tears and beginning to clean up and tend to Joan. Maggie knelt beside the bed and put her little finger near the baby's open palm. It immediately curled its delicate fingers around hers and held on tight. Maggie had never felt such a powerful surge of love course through her body before. This infant was pureness personified.

The knock on the door burst the bubble of euphoria in the room. "Can I come in?" Richard asked.
"Just a minute, Rich," Elizabeth said. Maggie stood and helped her mother gather up the dirty linen and straighten the bed as best they could without disturbing Joan and the baby. Joan didn't even seem to notice that they were in the room. She was in a daze, staring at the beautiful infant in her arms.

"Well, is it a boy or a girl?" Richard asked as he gently sat down on the side of the bed. Joan looked at Elizabeth and Maggie, and they all burst out laughing. Richard looked at them with a raised eyebrow. "What's so funny?"

"I haven't even checked," Joan said, smiling and unwrapping the towel. "It's a girl!" Everyone erupted in cheers and congratulations before Maggie and Elizabeth left the new family to get acquainted. They walked into the kitchen and found George sitting at the table with steaming cups of tea, waiting for them. They slumped into chairs, exhausted but excited.

"Well, Lizzy, what have we got?" George asked.

"We have a granddaughter," Elizabeth replied with a grin. George's face lit up, and he embraced Elizabeth in a hug.

The men returned to the farm just before Doctor Mosely came by the house to check on mother and baby. Maggie took Joan a cup of tea but found her fast asleep. The baby, whom they'd named Grace, was awake, lying in her cot by the window. Maggie gently lifted her into her arms and began rocking from side to side. Her small grey eyes slowly closed and opened, and her delicate fingers clenched into tiny fists. Maggie rubbed a finger along her smooth cheek.

"You really are the most beautiful, most precious thing in the world," she whispered. She lowered her into her cot, then watched her chest rise and fall with each small breath. Could this precious baby be the catalyst for better times? Maggie hoped so.

Chapter 8
Giuseppe
Mid-1944

Giuseppe settled back into camp life quickly. After more than a year at Marrinup, he was so used to the routine that he often stirred just before the reveille, and his stomach grumbled on cue. This morning was no different. As he opened his eyes, he was greeted by the sounds of birds chirping and warbling, along with the sight of grey clouds drifting across the window. Stretching his arms out, his body tightened and then relaxed back onto the bed. Minutes later the reveille blasted and his roommates stirred. The loudspeakers buzzed, and a guard told everyone to get up. At that exact moment, Officer Harris shoved the hut door open and Giuseppe sat up.

"Tidy this room and put on your cleanest uniform. Now!" he yelled, then slammed the door. The hut was a flurry of activity as they all jumped out of bed and got changed.

"What's happening?" Eugenio asked.

"I'll see what I can find out," Luigi said, shoving his pillow on his bed and rushing out the door. Minutes later, he burst back in, panting. "There's someone official visiting the camp today. Nobody knows who or why, but Browning and his buddies look worried."

"Do you think we're going home?" Carlo asked. The men looked at each other for a moment, then continued getting ready.

Giuseppe pulled on a shirt. Was this it? Were they all going home? His fingers fumbled with the buttons. He shoved his shirt in his pants then stopped mid-tuck. What if someone higher up in the government had found out about the English lessons? What if they were coming for him? He turned to Luigi and saw his expression mirrored on Luigi's face.

"Don't worry, *amico*. We are with you," Luigi said, with an around Giuseppe's shoulders. A car horn blasted and the siren rang out. The men made their way to the centre of the compound and lined up in rows—Italians and Germans separated by guards. Giuseppe scanned the area, straining his ears to catch the murmurs of the crowd, but it appeared that no one had a clue about what was going on.

Major Browning, kitted out in a new suit and freshly cut hair, strode towards the assembly accompanied by a stranger. The man stood two inches taller than Browning. He wore dark-rimmed glasses and a pressed white uniform with a red cross emblazoned on the sleeve. Doctor Morel cleared his throat, stood a little straighter, and introduced himself.

"Good morning, gentlemen. I've come to ensure that the conditions of this camp are acceptable under the Geneva Convention. If any man wishes to speak to me in this regard, please make it known at an appropriate time." Murmuring erupted the silence. Giuseppe's mind went to the controversy over the Pidgin English books. Should he say something? What if Browning found out? He would never be allowed back to Jarrah Downs. But this might be his only chance to speak with someone neutral. The guards escorted the men back to their own compounds, and most went straight to the mess to digest breakfast and discuss the visitor. Giuseppe hung back with Luigi, who struck a match, lit a cigarette, and took a long drag before passing it to Giuseppe.

"What do you think, *amico*?" Luigi asked. Giuseppe sucked in slowly and then puffed out a cloud of smoke before answering. "I think this might be our chance. Morel isn't Australian. He's neutral. He needs to know." Giuseppe stopped when he saw the look on Luigi's face. The two men stood and finished the cigarette in silence, and then Luigi threw it to the ground and stomped his boot on it. Giuseppe watched him trudge back to their hut with his shoulders slumped forward and his head bowed. It suddenly occurred to Giuseppe that Luigi's jovial manner had been subdued since his time in the cooler, and it was all his fault. If he hadn't dragged Luigi into the lesson, his friend wouldn't be feeling like this.

With his mind made up, Giuseppe followed at a distance while Browning showed Morel through each section of the camp. As they neared the gate between the old and new Italian compounds, Browning leaned towards Morel and said something, then spun back towards the officers' quarters. Giuseppe bent his head and turned away as Browning hurried past. He glanced over his shoulder and saw Browning walk through the last set of gates. He looked back at Morel. He was alone, and Giuseppe couldn't see any guards close by. This was his chance. Giuseppe quickened his pace and fell into step beside him.

"Doctor Morel, may I speak with you in private?" Morel looked across at him and nodded. Giuseppe indicated to the closest hut, and they entered the empty room. He shut the door with trembling hands and took a deep breath before turning to face the doctor. Morel stood with his hands in his pocket, surveying the room. Introducing himself, Giuseppe wasted no time in recounting his experiences at Marrinup, especially the most recent happenings. The longer Giuseppe spoke, the grimmer Morel's expression got. When Giuseppe finished, Morel moved forward and put a hand on his shoulder, looking him in the eyes.

"Thank you, Mr. Russo. I appreciate your honesty and I'll investigate the matters you've brought to my attention." Giuseppe's stomach twisted at the thought of getting into more trouble for this.

"I... um... will they? Will I?" Giuseppe faltered, wringing his hands and swallowing hard. Morel's expression softened and he gently squeezed Giuseppe's shoulder.

"Rest assured. No harm will come to you, or your friends, as a result of what you've told me today." Giuseppe breathed a sigh of relief.

"Thank you, sir. Would you mind waiting a moment before leaving the hut?" Despite Morel's assurances, Giuseppe didn't want to take any chances. He left, eager to get away lest someone see them together. He felt relief and apprehension as he walked around the perimeter of the compound. His actions would either help everyone at Marrinup or get him into even more trouble. Either way, it was a risk he was willing to take.

After Morel's visit, Giuseppe had filled his roommates in on their conversation. The men started scouring the heavily censored newspapers for any word of Morel or the Red Cross investigation, but nothing had manifested. Browning and his allies continued to monitor Giuseppe's movements. The tension churned his stomach, and his nerves were so frayed that he'd brought his meals back up more often than he cared to count.

Sitting in the mess, he looked at his plate and wondered if he'd bring this meal up too.

"I think maybe Morel was a distraction. Nothing more," Domenico said as he pushed his empty plate to one side.

"We've got to have hope. You're always saying that, *vero*?" Luigi looked at Giuseppe and frowned when he didn't get a response. Giuseppe looked up and shrugged. He didn't feel like having this conversation again. His mood had lifted with Morel's arrival but had quickly waned when nothing had come of his confession. He stood and took his plate to the kitchenhand standing at the front of the mess. Outside in the cool night air, he looked up at the cloudy sky and thought about his roommates, especially Luigi. War wears down the spirits of good men, so all that's left is an empty shell.

***

The air was crisp, and the frost on the rocky ground glowed in the first light. Giuseppe stood at the hut entrance, listening to the kookaburras laughing and the magpies warbling. Hans had got hold of a book on Australian birds and had imparted what he'd learnt as the two men sat near the fence one afternoon. There was a territorial magpie near the watchtower at the far corner of the Italian section of the camp. Every so often, they'd hear a guard shout, "Bloody hell!" as the bird's black and white body streaked past the top of his head. It always elicited a laugh from the men and made Giuseppe smile as he thought of it.

The sun was cracking the horizon a little earlier each day. He'd been out of the cooler for weeks, but there'd been no mention of returning to the farm, and he was desperate to get out of the camp and see Maggie again. He began to walk the path around the perimeter of his section. Slowing at each watchtower, he noted they were all empty. He strode back towards his hut and heard the scuffle of boots and murmurs of Australian accents. The siren sounded for roll call, and a sea of men in maroon emerged from their huts and headed towards the centre of the compound. He greeted Luigi as he took his place next to him.

"Who's that?" Carlo asked. They jerked their heads and shielded the sun from their eyes, trying to get a better look at the figure leading the assembly of guards. The man was slightly taller than Giuseppe, with cropped grey hair, an aquiline nose, and a neat moustache. Browning was nowhere in sight. Giuseppe looked at Luigi, who shrugged a shoulder. He usually knew the gossip around camp, but he obviously had heard nothing about this. "Good morning. My name is Major Murray. In light of recent revelations during the inquiry conducted by Doctor Morel of the International Red Cross, I am now in charge of this camp. I would like to take this opportunity to remind you that while you are here, you are under the watch and protection of the Australian Army." Murray walked the length of the first row and then back to the middle. "You all know the rules of this camp, and you must all abide by them, or there will be consequences." Murray raised his hand and dismissed the assembly. Giuseppe looked across at Luigi, relief removing the lines between his eyes.

"What do you think?" he asked Luigi.

"Hard to tell, but I'll be happy with anyone other than Browning running this place." The surrounding men agreed. They made their way over to the mess, and Cambino caught up with them just before they stepped inside.

"You ready for work again, Giuseppe?"

"What? You mean the Sleeman farm?"

"*Si.* Murray says all workers need to return to their employment as of today." Cambino had already met with Murray, the guards, and the other camp leaders. "Things are going to change around here, *ragazzi*," Cambino said as he moved to the next group of men. Giuseppe felt his chest expand. He was finally going back to Jarrah Downs. He wondered what the Sleemans had been told about his absence. Had George or Richard said anything to Maggie? What would she think of him now? It had been almost two months since they'd last spoken, and so much had happened that Giuseppe felt he'd aged a year.

***

With his spine pressed against the canvas and his body jostling around, Giuseppe spent the drive to Jarrah Downs, pondering what to say to the Sleeman family. When the truck pulled up at the gate, he jumped down and looked around at the open farmland. He didn't realise how much he had missed it. He felt like he could breathe easier when he was on the farm. He watched the Sleeman truck come towards him. Whatever he was going to say to Richard and George, he needed to be ready to say it. "Jump in the back, Joe," Richard said, pointing to the back of the truck with his thumb. "We're heading over to the Watson's place to help with some fencing. Old Watto's been holed up in bed sick as a dog for a week." Giuseppe climbed up into the truck bed and sat on the battered toolbox, holding the side as they drove off. He looked back towards the house and saw a shadow pass Maggie's bedroom window. That conversation would have to wait.

The work kept them from returning to the farm until well after lunch. George, Richard, Joe, and Old Watto's son, Ted, had worked amiably. The usual banter flowed, but none of the men asked him why he'd been away from the farm, so he didn't volunteer any information. When they got back to Jarrah Downs, he saw Elizabeth and Maggie in the garden by the kitchen carrying cane baskets filled with fresh vegetables. They looked up as the truck pulled in near the shed. Giuseppe waved at them, and while Elizabeth gave a curt nod, Maggie beamed at him and waved back. He fought the instinct to move towards her. Instead, he pivoted and walked into the shed while Richard and George went over to the house.

Giuseppe hummed as he gently brushed Lily's coarse brown hair. The rhythm of the motion eased some of the tension he'd been feeling. He quieted when he heard someone come into the shed. He looked around the stall and spotted the swish of a dress. His heart skipped a beat as Maggie appeared and stood close to the bench. She picked up a hammer and ran her hands along it, then put it back down and looked over at him.

"You haven't been here for quite a while, Joe. Is everything all right?"

"Si. What did they tell you?" he asked with a quiver in his voice that he desperately hoped she wouldn't notice. She wrung her hands in front of her, then looked towards the door.

"Richard said you'd broken some rules and were put in solitary confinement. What happened?" Her voice was just as shaky as his, and she stood a little too far away for such an intimate conversation. He'd wondered what sort of reception he'd get, but he wasn't expecting Maggie to fear him. She turned back to the bench, picked up an old box of nails, and started sorting them into size. He walked over, put the brush down, and started sorting the nails, then told her everything. He told her how he'd come up with the idea and convinced the others to join in, and he told her about his time in the detention cell and how guilty he'd felt knowing that he was the reason his friends were in trouble. Maggie kept her gaze fixed on the nails as she absorbed his words.

"Being in that concrete darkness and knowing what I did to my friends was hard. But sometimes, I think it was worth it. The lessons gave the men something new to do," he concluded. She pushed the box of nails away and turned to him.

"Oh, Joe. You didn't just give them something to do. You gave them a chance to improve themselves and make their time here easier. I'm so proud of you for doing that." She put her arms around his neck, and he felt her body tremble, but he didn't want to let go of her waist. After a moment, she pulled back and looked at him, her fingers still laced around his neck. He couldn't read her expression. Her eyes narrowed slightly and a soft smile formed at the corners of her mouth. She leaned her face forward, closed her eyes, and gently let her lips touch his. It was the softest kiss he'd ever had. He kissed her, harder this time. Finally, they both pulled away. Their faces flushed, and their breath quickened. There was a cough from the doorway, and they let go of each other and stepped back. Richard moved to the bench between them and grabbed the hammer and box of nails.

"Come on, Joe. We've got work to do. Maggie, Mum needs you in the house." Giuseppe watched Maggie leave and then followed Richard outside. They went around the back of the shed where they'd laid out the materials to make a chicken coop. They often worked together in comfortable silence, but today was different. Giuseppe wanted to broach the subject of the kiss, but every time he tried, the words wouldn't form. Richard had always been kind to him, but Maggie was his little sister. Would he tell George what he'd seen? Giuseppe had only just got back on the farm. He didn't want to lose it again.

"Grab hold of that wire and pull it tight," Richard said. Giuseppe pulled the wire. Neither of them could move without the wire flying in their faces.

"Richard, did you...," Giuseppe faltered. Richard hammered a nail into the wooden framing.

"I won't say anything if that's what you're asking," he said. Giuseppe let out his breath. "But if you hurt Maggie, you'll have me to deal with." He gave the nail with a final blow, bringing his point home. That night, Giuseppe lay in bed listening to the incessant sound of crickets chirping and frogs croaking, and his thoughts turned to Maggie. She was book-smart but lacked knowledge about how the real world worked. She was feisty but shy, smart but naïve, and strong but weak. Giuseppe knew he was hooked.

***

Giuseppe was tightening the loose bolts on the front gate when a truck pulled up beside him. Old Watto's son, Ted, leaned out the window and asked him where George was. Giuseppe pointed to the paddock closest to the river where Richard and George were inspecting some cattle. He watched as Ted made his way over to the two men. Even without hearing the conversation, he could tell from the way Richard put his hand on Ted's shoulder that it was bad news. The men walked back through the grass, and Ted called out as he neared his truck.

"Hop in, Joe. We've got some commiserating to do." Giuseppe looked at George, who nodded his approval. Sitting beside Ted, his body relaxed into the seat, and he put his hand out the window, letting his arm push against the wind.

"So, do you like working on the Sleeman farm?" Ted asked, pitching his voice high and pronouncing each word slowly and precisely. Giuseppe agreed and suppressed a laugh as he assured Ted that he could understand English quite well.

"Right. Sorry, mate," Ted said with a laugh.

"But what is commiserating? I don't know that word," Giuseppe said.

"You know, my dad's been sick for a while. I guess it just got the better of him this time. He passed away yesterday."

"I am so sorry to hear that," Giuseppe said. He listened as Ted told him stories about Old Watto. He sensed it was something Ted needed to do.

The drive to the Dwellingup Hotel only took about twenty minutes, but it was the first taste of real freedom Giuseppe had had in a long time. When they pulled up at the hotel, he noticed five other cars and about half a dozen horses lined up outside. He looked down at his maroon uniform and bit his lip.

"You'll be right, mate," Ted said as they walked into the packed bar with Richard and George close behind. Giuseppe looked around the wood-panelled room that had a large fireplace on one side. In one corner, a young man played a battered piano, and some older men sang along, sloshing their beers on the wooden floor as they got carried away with the music. Richard walked up to the bar and ordered a round of beers, handing one to each of them.

"To Old Watto," shouted a tall, bearded man standing at the back of the crowd. Everyone in the hotel raised their glasses and cheered. Stories about Old Watto's antics came thick and fast. One man started a long-winded tale about the time he got caught stealing sleepers from the railway tracks and how he'd talked his way out of jail.

Although it was a sombre occasion, Giuseppe couldn't help but feel elated to be away from the confines of Marrinup and the constraints of Jarrah Downs. Sitting at a table on the side of the room, he started to relax. When he saw Luigi and Alessandro walk in a few steps behind their bosses, he waved them over. There was no shortage of beers, and everyone was in good spirits.

A loud whistle broke through the laughter, and someone shouted, "Coppers!" Giuseppe dropped his empty glass on the table and looked at Luigi and Alessandro. Both men were wide-eyed and tightlipped. They looked down at each other's uniforms. There was nowhere to hide. Two of the local constabulary entered the bar, calling out for any men from Marrinup to come forward. The room fell silent. Nobody moved.

"We know they're here. Move aside." Another minute passed before the crowd parted to make way for the police. The hairs on the back of Giuseppe's neck bristled and his fists clenched as the police approached.

"Right, you lot. Let's go." The larger of the two police officers moved toward their table and pointed his thumb back the way he'd come. The men looked at each other, then sighed and pushed back their chairs. Their taste of freedom and normalcy was over.

"Don't be too harsh, lads. It's our fault they're here," Richard said to the officers as they jostled the men to move faster. The policeman nodded but said nothing else. Giuseppe, Luigi, and Alessandro clambered into the back seat of the police car and the officer slammed the door shut. The driver turned around to look at them.

"We got a call from a guy by the name of Browning." The trio looked at each other. "He said you'd escaped, but we knew a lot of the farmers would be here tonight. Old Watto was a bit of a local celebrity around these parts. We'll have a word with the guards, but we can't promise anything." The officer turned around and shifted the car into gear. They remained silent during the drive back through the winding roads to camp. Giuseppe was terrified of another stint in the cooler and thought Luigi probably felt the same. Alessandro was a few years younger, and from the look on his face, he thought they were in for some real trouble, too. When the car pulled up near the guards' quarters, they stayed put while the taller policeman went in and emerged a few minutes later with Major Murray at his side. They opened the car doors and waved them out. Giuseppe inhaled deeply as he exited and stood with the others. Murray walked in front of them, looking at each man in turn. Giuseppe felt nauseous. Was he going back to the cooler? Or worse? He snuck a look at the two policemen who stood stony-faced with their arms folded.

"You're lucky chaps," Murray said, folding his arms. "I received a phone call from some very enthusiastic men who spoke highly of you. It seems you were at the hotel with your bosses' permission. We didn't endorse this expedition, but I understand there were special circumstances. Off you go." Murray dismissed them with a wave. Giuseppe felt lightheaded and held his stomach as Alessandro leaned over and vomited on the ground.

"That was close," Luigi said with his hand on his chest.

"*Si*. I thought we were in for a night in the cooler," Alessandro said, wiping his mouth. "It was a good afternoon, though. *Ciao*." He waved as he turned towards the back of the compound while Giuseppe and Luigi went straight ahead. Luigi sighed.

"That beer. And that freedom," Luigi said as he bunched his fingers to his lips, kissed them and let them go. Giuseppe laughed, gently elbowing him as they entered their hut.

***

Giuseppe was sitting in the mess with Luigi, Eugenio, Domenico, Giovanni, and Carlo. It was Friday night and the kitchenhands on duty had outdone themselves again by making gnocchi that rivalled any he'd enjoyed at home. The gooey texture melted in his mouth, and he closed his eyes and moaned. When he finished, he took his plate back to the kitchen and got some hot water to make everyone a coffee. Eugenio passed around some chocolates and Carlo offered his cigarette packet, while Luigi dealt the cards.

"Deal me in," said Cambino, parking himself on the bench next to Giuseppe. The game was quick, thanks to Luigi's questionable playing. After they'd all thrown their cards into a pile in the centre of the table, Cambino stood and bid them goodnight. Then he stopped and searched his shirt pocket. "I almost forgot. This came for you today." He handed Giuseppe an unsealed envelope and then went into the kitchen to check on the cleanup. Giuseppe inspected the envelope. On one side, the words "Reviewed by Censor" were stamped in red. On the other was his mother's handwriting. He felt his heart skip a beat when he saw her familiar scrawl. He hadn't heard from his family since he'd been in the staging camp in Egypt at the end of 1942. It felt like a lifetime had passed since then.

He had first been stationed in Southern Italy but had been transported to Egypt after the Allies captured him. While waiting in the desert heat for whatever was to come next, he'd written home, but he knew that delivering and receiving prisoners' mail wasn't

118

high on the Australian army's list of priorities. Then he remembered Maggie had given him the opportunity to write to his family. He'd often wondered whether Maggie had actually posted the letter, but now that he held this piece of home in his hands, he felt ashamed to have doubted her. He made his excuses to the group and went to his hut. Sitting on his bed and leaning against the wall, he opened the tattered envelope and carefully slid the missive out.

My Dearest Giuseppe,
I received your letter with much love in my heart. To know you are alive brings me great happiness, my son.
What a joy to hear you are in Western Australia! My cousin ____________________ lives in ________________. When you are free, you find him. He will look after you until you can come home to us. This Margaret sounds like a good woman. You must bring her home with you.
Life here has been hard. This war has brought many changes. I cannot write much so I just write this - we have suffered, but we are strong.
Take care of yourself, Giuseppe.
From your loving Mother.

A tear rolled down his cheek, but he didn't move to wipe it away. Not for the first time, he realised how much he was missing his home and family. He wished again for an end to the war. More and more frequently, men were trying to escape from the camp or their work farms. Despite all the escape attempts that had happened over the years, it hadn't occurred to Giuseppe to try it. He read his mother's letter a second time. He had family here somewhere. Perhaps he could escape and Maggie could go with him. He shook his head. He just had to bide his time. Now that Browning was out of the picture, conditions were much better at camp, and even though the work at Jarrah Downs was tough sometimes, the fact that Maggie was there made it bearable. Their last rendezvous played on his mind. Perhaps he'd been too forward in making the move to kiss her deeply. Then again, he'd felt her body relax into his embrace. But she'd left the shed without looking back. It felt as though there was a wall around her. He wondered whether it was a barrier that he would eventually get through.

Sitting with her back against the tree, Maggie could feel the sun's rays filtering through the leaves. When she realised she had read the same line for the fifth time, she snapped her book shut and threw it on the ground beside her. Pulling her knees up to her chest, she wrapped her arms around them and leaned her head on top. She couldn't stop the seemingly endless spiral of thoughts. She felt like she was being pulled in different directions by her head, her heart, and her parents. Kissing Thomas had felt like a dream, but afterwards, she'd felt guilty. The moments she spent with Joe left her with butterflies in her stomach. They both possessed qualities she found appealing, but their differences were striking. Her parents were steering her on a course that ended with a marriage to Thomas, and a life exactly like her mothers. It was a safe path, but would it make her happy? What direction was she headed with Joe? Perhaps the thrill of the unknown was what drew her to him.

She walked over to the paddock next to the shed, saddled Lily, and started for Richard and Joan's house. They'd had a fairytale courtship, and even now, when they looked at each other, Maggie could see the love they felt hanging between them like an invisible string. Joan would understand her dilemma. She let Lily loose in the paddock close to the house and walked into the kitchen. Joan was dressing Grace after a bath in the sink, and she placed her into Maggie's outstretched arms. Maggie felt her heart melt as her niece looked up at her with big blue eyes. She ran her hand across her soft cheek with its delicious peaches and cream complexion.

"You look just right with a baby in your arms," Joan said with a wink. Maggie scrunched her nose and laughed. Joan picked up a blanket, put it under her arm, and then grabbed a glass of lemonade in each hand. "It's such a beautiful day. Let's go outside. This little one needs some fresh air and sunshine, don't you, sweetie?" Grace felt warm in Maggie's arms, and as she lay her down and unwrapped her, the baby stretched her arms and legs out wide, then relaxed and looked around for her mother. Maggie took a sip of lemonade and considered how to tell Joan what had happened.

"Okay, Miss Maggie. What's the matter? Is everyone all right?" Maggie looked up and blinked a few times.

"Oh, yes, of course," she said before taking another sip. Joan put her arms behind her and leaned back.

"It's Joe, isn't it? Richard told me he walked in on you two in the shed." Maggie's cheeks warmed. Then a thought struck her. "Has he told Mum or Dad?"

"No, but you know they wouldn't approve. Are you worried about what other people will think if you get involved with him?" Maggie nodded. "Well, we can't help who we fall in love with," Joan concluded with a tip of her glass.

"But that's just the problem. I think I've fallen in love twice!" Joan arched her eyebrows and tilted her head. "I have feelings for Joe, but ever since I saw Thomas at his father's shop that day, I've felt a connection of sorts. Then, when Mum invited him for dinner, we kissed. It just happened. But I've shared a kiss with Joe, too. Oh, Joan, I don't know what to do." Maggie rattled on as Joan, listening patiently, tickled Grace's feet. She stopped and looked at Maggie.

"I can't tell you who to choose. But I'll say this - listen to your heart because it will always steer you in the right direction." The constant pondering had left Maggie feeling wound up, like a tightly twisted knot. She let her shoulders drop, feeling as though a weight had been lifted. She knew Joan could provide the guidance she needed.

The postman's car horn shrilled and they both looked up. Joan stood and bent to pick Grace up, positioning her so that the little girl could look at Maggie over her shoulder. Maggie blew a raspberry, and Grace smiled. They walked the 40 yards to the letterbox and Joan pulled out the envelope. Her eyebrows shot up, her mouth formed a perfect oval, and she let out a short, sharp, "Oh."

"What's wrong?" Maggie asked, taking Grace into her arms. Joan's hands trembled as she held the envelope up. Richard's name and address were front and centre, and at the top corner was the seal of the Australian Military Forces. They both knew what it meant. "We'll take it to Jarrah Downs. Rich should be back from town." She put her hand on Joan's arm. "It'll be all right." Joan gulped and nodded. James was already fighting in New Guinea, and now Richard would have to fight too. Joan was going to be on her own, looking after Grace and managing the farm.

What if something happened to Richard? How would they cope?

When they arrived, Maggie took Grace into the house, and Joan went to find Richard. Elizabeth took one look at her, then dropped her sewing, stood in front of her and grabbed her by the arms. "What's wrong? Is it Joan? Grace?" Maggie shook her head. "Richard received a letter from the Military." Elizabeth gasped, then ran out the front door, calling for George. Maggie followed, still holding Grace in her arms. The family congregated on the front verandah. Richard sank into a chair and bent forward, his head in his hands. Disbelief filled the air around them like a thick fog.

"I can't have two sons fighting in this godforsaken war. There must be something we can do, George?" Elizabeth's eyes implored him to act, but deep down, they all knew that he had no say in the matter. George shook his head and slumped into the other chair. Elizabeth wiped a tear from her cheek. Maggie felt as if the ground was shaking beneath her.

"Why now? Why did this have to happen now?" Richard said, running his hands over his forehead and through his hair. He stood and paced the length of the verandah. Joan moved closer to him, reaching out to hold his hand as tears formed at the corners of her eyes.

"There's nothing we can do. With luck, the war will end soon and you'll come back to us." Richard gathered her in his arms, bent his head close to her ear and whispered to her. Grace seemed to sense the tension and began to cry. Maggie jiggled and hummed to her but Grace wouldn't settle. She looked across at the horses grazing in the paddock near the shed. Perhaps they could help settle Grace's nerves and her own. She ambled over, gently patting Grace's back, then reached up to run her hand through Lily's mane. Her fingers trembled and she felt a hand cover her own. She turned her head to see Joe standing next to her. Her lips quivered and her breath came in short spurts as the tears fell. Joe took Grace, holding her over his left shoulder as Maggie melted into his right.

"I'm sorry to hear about Richard," he said, looking over at the family assembled on the verandah. They were engrossed in conversation, so he turned his head and kissed Maggie softly on the cheek.

"I wish this bloody war was over," Maggie mumbled between sobs.

"Me too," Joe said, stroking her hair. Both of them silently contemplated what the end of the war might bring.

***

Richard's departure left a void on the farm, and the resultant increase in workload meant Maggie was able to help. She saw it as an opportunity to convince her father she was capable of more than just domestic duties.

She woke with sore muscles and eased herself out of bed and into some old clothes. She reached the shed just as her father was backing the truck out.

"I'm going to town. Would you like to come?" Maggie slid into the passenger seat and enjoyed the quiet drive to Colton before George pulled up outside the general store. The bell behind the door jingled as George pushed it open and made his way over to

John Williams. Maggie moved towards the bulletin board. It was littered with notes about the war—casualty lists, ration orders, reminders from a woman in uniform that "There's a job for you in the A.W.A.S." Maggie had no intention of joining the Australian Women's Army Service or getting a "victory job". She was already doing her part by working with Doctor Mosely and helping her family to keep their farm going.

Wearing a cheeky grin, Thomas sauntered up and positioned himself next to her. Maggie smiled at him, then returned her gaze to the notice board.

"You'd be a pleasant sight in that uniform," Thomas said.

"As would you, I'd imagine." Thomas baulked then puffed out his chest.

"I'd enlist this week, but I'm not sure they'd take me." He turned to face her. "How about I take you out tomorrow night instead? They're playing You'll Never Get Rich at the hall." She returned his gaze, but there was something about his manner that irked her, and she took a small step back. She contemplated her options. Now that he'd asked to go out in public with her, the stakes had been raised. Maggie felt a shiver and rubbed her hands together before looking back at the noticeboard. Thomas was waiting for an answer. This was the moment she had to decide one way or the other. Remembering her conversation with Joan, she put a hand to her chest, then turned to Thomas with what she hoped was a congenial expression.

"That's a lovely offer, but I'm afraid I must decline. I... I don't believe a relationship between us would work. It has nothing to do with you." Maggie knew she was rambling, but the look on Thomas's face made her continue. "It's just that I wouldn't be a suitable wife. You deserve someone who would be happy to settle down here in Colton." He spun and walked away from her, banging the door as he entered the back room. Maggie hesitated, torn between wanting to follow him and fearing witnessing the pain etched on his face. Her stomach was in knots, but she'd made her decision.

Waiting in the truck outside, Maggie closed her eyes and inhaled deeply, letting go of the tightness in her chest. She opened her eyes and the tension returned as she saw George being accosted by town councillors, Jones, and Sykes. Their voices rose, but she couldn't make out what they were saying. She wound down the window as Sykes blocked George's path.

"Have you seen the news? The Japs have broken out of a POW camp in Cowra. They've killed the guards and are on the run," Jones said, holding up the newspaper. Maggie couldn't see the front page, but she watched George straighten his posture and move to the side of the footpath. She shifted closer to the window. She wasn't aware there were camps in other states, much less that they held Japanese prisoners of war. But why would that matter to the people of Colton, anyway? Sykes took a step closer to George.

"How do we know that lot up at Marrinup aren't planning the same thing? You've got an Eyetie on your farm. How do you know him and his mates aren't planning something? You haven't got your boys there to help you now." He pointed in George's face. "You need to keep a close eye on him, or we will!" Maggie grabbed the dashboard and gasped. She looked from the two men to her father. The vein in his neck throbbed, and he squared his shoulders.

"Gentleman, I appreciate your concern, but there's no need to involve yourselves with my business. I'm quite capable of identifying the moral character of those around me." He eyed the seething men for a moment, then stepped around them and hopped into the car. Apprehension filled the air, and Maggie stayed quiet until they were on the outskirts of town.

"Why were they so upset?" George looked across at her, then shifted his eyes back to the road.

"Let's just say that some people around here aren't as accepting as others." Maggie frowned and glanced out the window. He might have let Joe work on the farm, but he wasn't so accepting when it came to her and Joe.

"Do you think the men in Marrinup will do anything like that?"

"Definitely not. It's nothing for you to be concerned about." He slowed to go around a horse and cart and waved at the rider. "Did I see you and Thomas talking? Have you made plans?" Maggie stared straight ahead and angled her knees towards the door.

"I talked to him, but there aren't any plans. In fact, there won't be any plans. I told him I didn't want to see him." George's brow creased.

"I see." He pursed his lips. Maggie turned back to the window, and they drove the rest of the way back to Jarrah Downs in silence.

On her way to her bedroom, Maggie passed her father's study and heard the distinct murmur of her parent's voices. She stopped and put an ear closer to the door. What if her father really was worried about the men at Marrinup copying their New South Wales counterparts? Was he worried Joe was going to do something terrible? She quietened her breath and listened.

"It's madness, Lizzy. Those men in Cowra have created havoc by breaking out of that camp. They're no different from the men at Marrinup. They're all POWs and we've got one of them on our farm." She heard a glass being plonked on the table.

"But George, surely Joe is different. He's Italian, not Japanese, for a start, and he's been working here for such a long time. I also think there might be a good reason for him to toe the line, as it were," Elizabeth said. There was something in her mother's tone that caught Maggie's attention.

"Yes. I'm aware of what's been going on. I'm still considering the best way to handle that situation. Leave it to me. And as for whether we keep Joe on, I don't think we have a choice." The room had fallen silent. She tiptoed down the hallway and into her bedroom, then sat on her bed. Relief washed over her, closely followed by worry. Her parents knew about her and Joe. Had Richard or Joan said something to them? What had her father meant by "the best way to handle the situation?"

***

Dressed in their Sunday best, the Sleeman family sat in the first pew of the spacious Catholic Church, waiting for the sermon to begin. Maggie felt the emptiness of the spaces previously occupied by James and Richard. She looked over at Joan, with

Grace nestled quietly in her arms, and smiled as she returned her gaze. Joan held up Grace's hand and waved it. Maggie smiled and reached out to take Grace into her lap as Father Davis spoke. Playing with her niece somehow made time quicken, and before Maggie knew it, the service had ended.

The congregation filed out of the wooden doors and into the sunlight, gathering in clusters of family, friends, and acquaintances. George strolled over to a group of men standing at the side of the churchyard. Elizabeth, Joan, and Maggie, still holding Grace, walked towards the CWA ladies gathered under the gum tree.

"Lovely to see you, ladies. I trust you've been keeping up with your knitting. Our troops need their knitted kit," said Emma Fulton.

"Yes. We've managed quite a few, haven't we, girls?" Elizabeth said, nodding in Maggie and Joan's direction. The hairs on Maggie's arms stood up. There was something about the way Mrs Fulton's eyes were shining and her mouth curled at the edges that made Maggie's stomach clench.

"Indeed. It must be hard finding time to knit while also working at the surgery and helping with the farm, Margaret. I suspect that's why you turned down young Thomas Williams. Surely there wouldn't be another reason." Maggie watched as her smirk grew wider. "I'm sure Thomas, and any other local lad, would prefer the affections of a more virtuous young lady, anyway." Gasps erupted from the women standing with them.

"I beg your pardon?" said Elizabeth, barely able to stop her hands trembling. Emma Fulton sucked in her lips and glanced at the women standing on either side of her. Maggie felt her fists clamp and her heart race.

"It's not my place to pass on idle gossip, but there have been discussions about why your daughter might fail to take up the opportunity to court such a promising young man. There's speculation that it may have something to do with the help." Maggie couldn't contain herself any longer. She stood in front of the older woman and projected her voice for all to hear.

"You're right, Mrs. Fulton. It's not your place, so if you would just mind your own business, then everyone would be much better off." She folded her arms, willing the older woman to say something, but it was Elizabeth who spoke first.

"I suspect this display of yours has something to do with Thomas choosing my Maggie over your Sarah. However, I won't stand by while you drag my family's name through the mud. Idle gossip is the devil's work. Perhaps you're in need of the confessional on this fine morning. I'm sure Father Davis can oblige." Elizabeth pivoted and the three women walked towards the car park.

Maggie's hands clenched and unclenched. "Well, it looks like our CWA memberships might be in question now," Elizabeth said as she grasped Maggie's hand.

 "I can't believe you both gave that busybody a piece of your minds. Well done," Joan exclaimed. The women burst out laughing, the tension leaving each of them like a gust of wind. Maggie looked at her mother. She never thought Elizabeth would stand up to a bully like Emma Fulton. It suddenly occurred to her that her mother might not be the meek little housewife she thought her to be.

The smell of the soap tickled Maggie's nostrils as she washed the dishes from the family's Sunday roast. Elizabeth dried while Joan sat at the table feeding Grace. The morning's turn of events whirled in Maggie's mind. Why was her personal life gossip fodder for the women of Colton? And where had her mother found the courage to confront the queen bee in front of everyone? Elizabeth gently nudged Maggie as she picked up a plate.
"I hope you thought long and hard about turning Thomas down. I'm sure it was a blow to him." Maggie dropped a cup into the water and ran the dishcloth over it.
The decision had been tough, and she still agonised over whether she'd made the right choice, but she wasn't about to let her mother know that.
"He's nice enough, but I can't see myself settling down and living in Colton forever, and that's what would happen if I married Thomas." Joan placed Grace's empty bowl on the sink next to them and retreated to the sitting room. Elizabeth sighed.
"You've always been a bit...free-spirited. But I think there's another reason why you feel that someone from Colton isn't suitable." Maggie concentrated on scrubbing the already clean bowl. She could feel Elizabeth's gaze boring into her. "Maggie, dear, please consider your next move carefully. If it's what I think it will be, then I'll support you. But just know that there are people close to you who might not." Maggie creased her brows and looked up at her mother.
"I thought you weren't on my side." Elizabeth let out a soft groan

as she leaned on her tiptoes and placed the bowl in the cupboard above her.

"There are no sides here. I simply want you to be happy." Maggie wondered what had happened to make her mother have a change of heart.

Chapter 10
Giuseppe
Late 1944

Time seemed to stand still at Marrinup, with each passing day feeling indistinguishable from the one before. Giuseppe noticed the men around him slide into melancholia. Their faces drooped, their speech became monotone, and their moods swung from ambivalent to miserable. It appeared that the longer the war went on, the deeper they slid. They attempted to lift each other's spirits, but as the days dragged on, it became more challenging. One thing that did lift spirits was good news and it spread through camp like wildfire.

Giuseppe, Luigi, Giovanni, and Domenico perched on the bottom bunks playing cards while Eugenio and Carlo lay on the top trading sections of the newspaper. The heat of the Australian summer had yet to fully materialise, but it was too hot to be outside after Sunday lunch.

"Did anyone else notice the Germans have been going out near the gardens a lot? What do you think is happening?" Carlo asked.

"I asked Hans, but he didn't tell me much. Just that they are building something we can all use," Giuseppe said.

"Like what?" Eugenio asked. Giuseppe shrugged and threw down a pair of aces. Luigi groaned and threw his cards onto the bed.

"A better shower block? Or a bigger rec room?" Domenico said. There were a few nods and murmurs of agreement. Luigi stood up.

"I know what it is. They're building a dance hall, and we're going to have dances with the local girls," he said, swaying his hips and then falling back on his bed. The room erupted in laughter. Domenico threw his pillow at Luigi.

"Come on. Let's go find out," Giuseppe said, striding through the open doorway.

Shovels hit the ground with satisfying thuds. Giuseppe, Luigi, and Carlo stood with their sweat-soaked shirts sticking to them, watching the Germans clear the land and prepare it for concreting. They walked through the gates towards Hans, who was leaning against a tree smoking a cigarette.

"What's going on?" Luigi asked, pulling a slightly damp packet from his shirt and lighting one of his own.

"We beat the guards," Hans said, lifting his chin.

"Huh?" The other men looked at each other.

"We hit their target four weeks in a row," Hans said, pointing his thumb towards the guard huts. "2500 tonne. Now, we get to build a tennis court." Luigi looked at the others, a smile playing at the corners of his mouth.

"Shame we can't get some pretty broads out here to show us how to play. I've seen them in the papers in their little white skirts. It's enough to send a man into a spin." Luigi elbowed Carlo. The men burst out laughing. It was good to see Luigi behaving like his old self. Giuseppe bent down and picked up a shovel.

"Settle down, Luigi. We won't get to play with the ladies, but let's get this finished anyway," Giuseppe said. Over the next few hours, they flattened and smoothed the ground, then used wooden planks to form edges before pouring concrete into the makeshift mould. It would be a few days before it settled enough for them to have their first game.

As the sun began its slow descent, streaming in between the dark shadows of the tree line, the men, tired and dripping with sweat, headed back into their respective compounds. Hans, Gunter, Dieter, and Helmut waved and called *"Danke"* as they entered the German section. The Italians walked further on. They were strengthened by the knowledge that they'd achieved something and that there might be some fun to be had soon.

The sounds of laughter, music, and singing echoed through the recreation hall. Giuseppe, Luigi, and Carlo exchanged their tokens for Coca-Cola and chinked their glasses, celebrating the day's work. They stood near the window, hoping for a breeze and listening to Louis play the piano accordion. The rich, reedy, organ-like sounds reminded them of Italy. Cambino strolled over and lit up a cigarette.

"Did you hear about Aliberti and Ginchino?" he asked them. Everyone shook their heads. *"Scampare."*

"How hard are they looking for them?" Luigi asked. Giuseppe eyed his friend.

"Hard enough if what happened with Musitano is anything to go by," Cambino replied.

"What happened to him?" Carlo asked.

"He stole the boss's bicycle and rode it all the way to Perth. That's a good 6 or 7 hours away. The ride must have made him thirsty because the police found him in a pub." Everyone laughed. "The news was on the wireless all day. Somebody recognised the maroon uniform and told the authorities."

"So, he's in the cooler, then?" Carlo asked.

"No. They've sent him to the other side of Australia." The men gasped. Why had the government given him such a harsh punishment? Escape attempts usually only warranted time in the cooler. The sentence was surprising, but the escape attempt wasn't. It seemed that opinions, like morals, were wavering.

***

Standing in the paddock near the side of the homestead, Giuseppe hauled the roll of wire over his shoulder and watched as a white truck rattled down the driveway. He walked a few yards along the fence line before dropping the heavy load. A shiver ran through him, and he turned towards the house, only to be met with the penetrating gaze of a man standing by the truck. He was dressed in a dark grey suit and held a bouquet of bright pink roses in his hand. He smirked before turning and walking to the verandah. There was something about that look that made Giuseppe's stomach tighten. He grabbed the shovel and started digging. Why was the shopkeeper's son here, and why did he bring flowers? Was he here to see Maggie? Had she been seeing this man? He picked up a wooden post, shoved it hard into the ground, and bent to push the wire through the small hole in the side. He repeated the movements as he slowly made his way towards the house.

He was digging his fifth hole when he heard the front door hit the wall with a bang and turned to see what was going on. The young man stormed out of the house, his brow furrowed and mouth a thin line. He marched over to his truck and was about to get in when George came up behind the truck bed. The young man turned back. Giuseppe bent down next to a post to put the wire through.

"You need to watch out for these Eyeties, Mr Sleeman. Sneaky buggers, all of them. They'll stab you in the back as sure as look at you." The young man spoke loud enough for Giuseppe to hear.

"Not all of them, I hope," George said. "Look, Thomas, I'm sorry about what happened in there." Giuseppe risked a glance and noted the crushed roses dangling from the man's hand. Trying his best to appear not to be listening in, he picked up the shovel and moved along a few paces, then pushed it into the dirt with a hard thud.

"Yeah. Right. Well, I guess I'll see you around then, Mr Sleeman." Thomas nodded to George as he got in his truck, then threw the roses out the window, and barreled down the driveway. Giuseppe looked across at the older man. It wasn't so much the look on his face but the impassivity of his expression that made Giuseppe flinch. He thought he'd always been an excellent judge of character, but George Sleeman was a hard man to get the measure of. He stood up as George walked over to him and looked into the hole, checking its depth with a stick.

"Good job with the fencing, Joe. You'll have more to do when I'm in Perth next week, though. Think you can concentrate on the work?" he asked. Giuseppe looked him in the eyes. He might not have the measure of him, but he knew him well enough to realise that he was implying something.

"Yes. There is a lot of work. I'll do what I need to do," Giuseppe replied. George looked at him a moment longer, then grunted and walked back to the house.

Giuseppe had been back at Marrinup for an hour when he decided he needed to clear his head with a walk. As he passed close to the font gates, he heard raised voices and stopped. A truck rolled in, and the guards quickly closed the gates behind it. Officers Parson and Grady moved behind the truck and emerged again with a shackled man held up between their shoulders. They marched towards the cooler, and Giuseppe moved closer to the fence where Hans was taking in the scene.

"Who is it?" Giuseppe asked. Hans shrugged.

"An Italian, I think. Look, they're bringing in another one now." Hans nodded towards the truck. They watched as the guards forced the other man towards the detention cells. It was still light enough outside to see blood dripping down from a gash on his forehead. Giuseppe shuddered as he watched the two men being shoved into the cells and heard the doors slam shut. Memories of his time in the cooler came flooding back—the long days and even longer nights, the bitter cold that enveloped him, and the dreams that haunted him. He shivered and folded his arms. Aliberti and Ginchino had been gone for almost 3 weeks. Most of the prisoners thought they'd made a clean getaway, but it appeared that luck wasn't on their side.

"I wonder if it was worth it," Hans said, stubbing out his cigarette on a pole and dropping the remains on the ground. Giuseppe shrugged. Had those weeks away from Marrinup made Aliberti and Ginchino feel free, or had they felt like scared rabbits being hunted down by a pack of wild dogs?

"I'm sorry, Giuseppe," Hans said, pulling him from his reverie.

Giuseppe blinked a few times, then asked, "For what?"

"For this." Hans raised his hands and gestured to the camp. "My country is at fault. I feel ashamed for what the Fatherland has done to the world. To good people like you." Giuseppe looked up at the other man in the fading light. His blond hair had become lighter from many days spent in the sun and there were more lines on his forehead now. Giuseppe imagined that his own face had changed, too. He sighed heavily. Lost time was one of the true costs of war.

 "You did not do this, and you're not to blame. The real villains aren't in here with us. They are safe in their meeting rooms or private homes." He kicked at a rock and added, "I have seen and done some terrible things during this war, but you know what it has also brought me—friendship." He smiled, stuck his hand through the wire, and patted Hans on the shoulder.

"*Danke*," Hans said, looking at the ground.

"No. Thank you." He gave Hans's shoulder a slight pinch, then turned and walked back towards his hut with stooped shoulders. He put his hands in his pockets and drew down the corners of his mouth. Hans shouldn't be the one to feel guilty. He was a good person, a good friend. But could friendship really be a salve for all the horror they'd endured?

When he reached the doorway, Luigi was coming out, humming a tune as he slicked back his hair.

"You coming to the rec room? They've got some records, and we're..." Luigi stopped when he saw Giuseppe's demeanour. "What's wrong?"

"I just saw Aliberti and Ginchino put in the cooler."

"*Ah, Fanculo.* I thought those two would make it. Are you all right?" Luigi asked, his eyes full of concern.

"*Si.* I might stay in tonight. I'm not in the mood for company." Luigi nodded briefly, then walked away.

In the dimly lit hut, Giuseppe lay on his bunk with one arm resting on his stomach and the other covering his eyes. He stayed like that for a few moments before sitting up and reaching for the pen and paper on the shelf near his bed. He poured everything onto the page—the things he'd done in Italy, his capture and transportation to Australia, how awful he'd felt when he first arrived at Marrinup. Then he wrote about the Sleeman farm and Maggie. He wrote about the first time he met her when he couldn't tame the brumby, the time she'd sent a letter home for him despite her family's objections, their kiss in the shed, and how his day brightened whenever he caught a glimpse of her. Slowly, a smile spread across his face as his hand moved across the page. When he was done, he folded the paper and slid it under his mattress for safekeeping. That night, he slept better than he had in a long time.

***

At this time of year, the Jarrah trees that ran along the back fence line produced a perfect patch of shade during the middle of the day. Giuseppe sat with his back against a tree and unwrapped the bread roll Elizabeth had given him earlier that morning. He closed his eyes and gulped water from the canteen, and when he opened them, he saw Maggie approaching. He held up a hand and she waved back.

"Would you like some company?" she asked when she reached him. Giuseppe nodded and moved further around the tree, giving her plenty of space. Maggie sat on the grass and held out something wrapped in material.

"I baked a cake to celebrate you working at Jarrah Downs for a year." She smiled at him, then hesitated. "I suppose it's not really something to celebrate, is it? Sorry." Giuseppe put one hand on her arm, unwrapping the cake with the other. The scent of citrus wafted into his nostrils, and his mouth watered.

"It is a day for celebrating. It's been a year since I first met you," he said, offering her a piece. She smiled and took it. Giuseppe couldn't resist taking a massive bite, enjoying the burst of flavour as crumbs landed on his pants. He waited for her to say something, but she fiddled with the cake on her lap. He was on his last mouthful when she put the cake aside and moved onto her knees to face him.

"There's something I need to tell you." His stomach clenched, but he nodded for her to go on. "Thomas Williams, the shopkeeper's son, came to see me." She paused. He couldn't tear his eyes away from her face. "He made a formal offer of marriage in front of my parents." Giuseppe looked towards the homestead, then back at Maggie. What was he supposed to say to that? Had she been going round with him? Why else would he ask her to marry him? He took a sip of water. Whatever they had between them must not have been enough for her. But if she was happy with this other man, that was all that mattered.

"I'm sure this man will be a good husband to you. Congratulations," he said with half a smile. Her brow creased, and the corners of her mouth dropped.

"I turned Thomas down. I don't want to marry him. I'm in love with someone else." Giuseppe felt a wave of relief wash over him. When he'd seen Thomas at the house, the realisation that he wasn't the only man in Maggie's life had hit him like a kick in the stomach. But if she had been seeing Thomas, who else had she been going around with? Who had she fallen in love with? He picked up a twig and broke it into little pieces.

"Is he a good man?" he asked, throwing the remnants on the ground and picking up another twig.

"Yes. He's kind and thoughtful, and he accepts me as I am. I have definitely fallen for him and I'm fairly certain that he feels the same way about me. At least, I hope he does," she said, smoothing her skirt with both hands before looking up at him.

"I hope you will introduce me to him one day," Giuseppe said. He grabbed his water bottle and began picking up his rubbish. Maggie laughed, then moved closer to him, still on her knees.

"You already know him, Joe." She paused, then grabbed his hands in hers. She leaned forward, and he half rose to meet her. He let go of her hand to cup her face, then leaned in and kissed her lips, running his fingers through her soft golden hair. His heart pounded and he could feel hers quicken beneath him. They parted and sat back down, their breath coming in short bursts. Warmth spread through him as Maggie laid her head on his shoulder, running her fingers over his hands. He knew he wanted this with every fibre of his being, but there was so much uncertainty in the world. How could they even begin to build a relationship?

"Are you sure about this? We do not know how long the war will go on. Or what will happen when it finally ends," he said. She laced her fingers in his and looked up at him.

"I've never been surer. None of that matters. We'll figure it out."

"*Si*. We will." He brought her hand to his lips and kissed it softly. If she could be optimistic about their future, then so could he. They finished their lunch and sauntered back towards the house, holding hands, only letting go when they got closer. The unspoken rules of their clandestine relationship were already forming.

"You've finished lunch. Good. Jack's just dropped off a couple of brumbies. They're in the front paddock. We need to separate them and start breaking them in," George instructed when they rounded the corner of the house. Giuseppe nodded, walking towards the shed. Maggie followed a few steps behind.

"You're not thinking of helping, are you, Maggie? You're certainly not dressed for the occasion," George called out. Giuseppe turned back and saw her suck her cheeks in. She was about to say something, then changed her mind, spun around, and stalked to the house. Giuseppe and George made for the shed. With ropes dangling from their hands, they walked over to the paddock and stood by the gate, trying to figure out which brumby might be the easiest to work with. Of the three stallions and two mares, one smaller stallion stood away from the others. Nodding in its direction, George entered the paddock, then walked the fence line until he was as close to the brumby as he could get without scaring it. He motioned to Giuseppe to get into the paddock. The brumby stood still, watching Giuseppe's approach. With a lasso in one hand and the other arm held out wide, Giuseppe edged closer. The horse stiffened, snorted, and bolted towards him. "*Merda!*" Giuseppe sprinted towards the fence. George cursed and headed straight for the animal. Already spooked, it moved from side to side, keeping an eye on the older man's approach. George crept closer. He reached the little stallion and stepped back as he saw something move in his peripheral vision. He fell awkwardly on his left side and screamed out in pain. Giuseppe and Maggie, who had just climbed into the paddock, reached him at the same time. Giuseppe helped him stand, and they walked slowly to the gate with their arms interlocked around his shoulders.

"Keep the weight off his leg," Maggie instructed. "Why did you do that, Dad? Joe and I could have worked the brumbies." George squeezed his eyes and mouth shut. "Mum!" Maggie yelled out as she opened the gate and helped Giuseppe heave George towards the truck. Elizabeth was at their side, offering a reassuring hand as they carefully guided George into the back seat.

"What happened?"

"He fell on his bad leg. We've got to get him to the surgery."

"Right," Elizabeth said, fishing in George's pocket for the keys before getting into the driver's seat. "I'll let you know how we go," she said as she turned the key. The engine roared to life, and the truck raced out of the shed and down the driveway at breakneck speed.

"I can't believe he did that. He knows not to take risks like that. If he's injured his leg again, he won't be able to walk unaided." Maggie shook as the adrenalin left her body. Giuseppe wrapped his arms around her, his heart still pounding.

"It's okay. He will be all right," Giuseppe assured her, gently stroking her hair. They stayed locked in an embrace for a few minutes, savouring the warmth and comfort, before reluctantly letting go and heading inside. They sat in the kitchen while they waited for news. Maggie rose from the table and made them both a cup of tea. Giuseppe shifted in his seat. He'd never been in the house alone with Maggie. He wondered if this had occurred to her, but as soon as he saw her face, he knew she was only thinking about her father.

"Well, we can sit here and wait, or we can keep busy," he said. Maggie looked up. "We can break in that brumby together." Giuseppe pushed back his chair, picked up the empty cups and deposited them in the sink before turning and holding out his hand to Maggie.

They spent the next few hours working together. Giuseppe was grateful for the opportunity to keep Maggie's mind off her father. By the time the army truck arrived, the offending brumby had acquiesced enough to be led around the paddock. They were sitting on the gate watching it graze when Giuseppe heard the horn and jumped down, then turned and looked up at Maggie's face.

"I have to go. Will you be all right? I can tell them what has happened. They might let me stay a while."

"I'll be all right. I'm sure I'll hear some news soon enough. You'll be here tomorrow though, won't you?"

"Of course." He leaned forward and kissed her. The horn blasted again, longer this time. Giuseppe jogged down the driveway, turning back to see Maggie sitting on the fence with her face in shadow as the sun set behind her. The circumstances surrounding that moment might not have been the best, but the image of her on that fence was one that Giuseppe wanted to keep forever.

Chapter 11
Margaret
Early 1945

Maggie dipped her feet into the cool water, closed her eyes, and listened as the river rushed past and the birds chirped overhead. She wiped the sweat from her brow and washed her hands in the water. She'd never worked up a sweat like this before. Sitting behind the desk at the surgery certainly didn't elicit a drop of perspiration. She enjoyed the work, but more and more men were coming into the surgery for ongoing medical attention for wounds they'd sustained during combat. Doctor Mosely did the best he could for them, but they reminded Maggie that her brothers could return wounded. It had been a blessing that Doctor Mosely was so accommodating while Richard and James were gone and during her father's recent recovery.

Just as she felt her body relax into the grass, a short whistle eroded the peace.

"I thought I would find you here," Joe said as he cantered up on a grey horse. He dismounted and sat next to her, giving her a quick kiss on the cheek. It had been two weeks since the accident, and George had only just returned from the hospital. On strict orders to rest, he tried to oversee the running of the farm from his bedroom by giving Maggie instructions every few hours.

"I'm just taking a break before I go into town. Dad wants me to get some supplies and Mum doesn't want to leave him in case he tries to get out of bed on his own.”

“I can come with you.”

“Are you sure? Is that allowed?”

“I don’t care if it is allowed or not. You need my help,” Giuseppe said. He stood up and held out a hand to help her stand. Driving along the main street, they couldn't help but notice the energetic atmosphere. It seemed that the nice weather had lured people outside. Maggie pointed out the town hall and council chambers, the post office, the police station, the school she and her brothers had gone to, and the church that the Sleemans attended every Sunday. Maggie nodded to a woman and her daughter in the car coming towards them.

“There’s Emma Fulton and her daughter, Sarah. I’ve told you about them, haven’t I?” Joe nodded. “It looks like they’re heading out of town. Oh, and there’s my friend Patricia’s mum, Pearl.” She waved to the older woman walking along the side of the road. The woman returned her wave, then frowned when she noticed Joe next to her. Maggie pulled up outside the rural supply store and turned to Joe. “It must feel good to be out and about. Away from Marrinup and Jarrah Downs.”

“It does, but... I don’t know,” Joe said, looking down at his maroon uniform. One corner of Maggie’s mouth turned up. It hadn’t occurred to her that he would feel self-conscious in his uniform. “We should have borrowed one of James’s jackets. Never mind. We’ll be as quick as we can.”

List in hand, Maggie pushed open the door, with Joe following close behind. They made their way down the aisles, searching for the items George wanted. When they passed the livestock feed, Maggie nodded a greeting at Mr Harrison and Mr Jones, members of the town council and friends of her father's. They smiled and nodded at Maggie, then peered behind her to look at Joe. They turned to each other and whispered something. Maggie looked back at Joe. His lips were drawn together and he put his hands in his pockets.

"We should get what we need and go back to Jarrah Downs," Joe said, picking up a pitchfork and a shovel. Maggie watched the two men leave the store, eyeing Joe as they walked past, and felt a shiver run through her. Are they going to the police? Maybe Joe's not supposed to be in town after all. Will she get into trouble? Her mind whirled as they picked out the rest of the items, put them on George's tab, and walked to the truck with their arms full.

"What the hell is he doing here?" Maggie almost dropped the box of nails in her hand as she spun around to see Thomas standing inches away. Maggie took a step back and placed the box on the truck bed.

"I beg your pardon?" she asked.

"You heard me. He's not supposed to leave your farm. I could get him in a lot of trouble. Sergeant Connolly's in Dad's shop right now," Thomas said with a sneer. Maggie took a step forward.

"You wouldn't."

"I bloody well would." Thomas's eyes were slits and his fists clenched and unclenched. Maggie looked over at Joe standing on the other side of the truck. He nodded almost imperceptibly and hopped into the passenger seat. Maggie tried to get past Thomas, but he grabbed her arm. "That letter you wanted to send. The one I mailed for you. That was for him, wasn't it?" Maggie looked down. "I knew it. I bet your dad would be mad if he knew about it. Perhaps I'll make a visit to Jarrah Downs."

"What do you want, Thomas?" Maggie asked, wriggling out of his grip.

"You know what I want." He raised his eyebrows and pursed his lips. A wave of anger rose inside her. What right did he have to intimidate and bully her like this?

"Do you really think threatening me is helping your case?" she said, her voice quivering. "I've given you my answer, and I won't be changing it. If you want to tell my father about this, or any of it for that matter, then so be it." She pushed past him and opened the truck door before looking back. "He might be a foreigner, but he's more of a gentleman than you'll ever be." She slammed the door, started the engine, and put her foot down. Gripping the steering wheel until her knuckles turned white, she breathed deeply through her nose and blew the air out through her mouth. Once they'd reached the outskirts of town, she pulled over onto the side of the road.

"I can't believe the nerve of him. Who does he think he is making threats like that? What I do is none of his business." Maggie took her hands off the steering wheel and held them in front of her, opening and closing them to stop the shaking. She felt a hand on her arm and was startled.

"Whatever he decides to do, it doesn't matter. Everything will be all right." Joe's voice was calm. Maggie looked across at his smiling face. She knew he was just trying to make her feel better, but it was working. She rounded her shoulders and rolled her head from side to side, then shook it.

"It's just so frustrating. Why can't he take no for an answer?"

"I would not give up on you easily, either. I am just lucky you chose me," Joe said, winking. Maggie let out a chuckle, and Joe leaned across and planted a kiss on her cheek. She turned her head and their lips locked. Joe's hands entwined in her hair and then ventured down her neck and shoulders. They hesitated before moving to her waist. She reached down and guided his hand to her breast. He inhaled sharply, then kissed her more urgently. Neither of them noticed the truck approaching, but they quickly parted as its horn blasted. The passenger waved an arm out the window, whistling as he went past, causing them both to burst into fits of laughter.

The black Ford was the first thing they noticed when they pulled into the yard. They looked at each other, eyes wide, and foreheads lined with worry. Had Thomas beaten them here and told George that Joe was in town? Will Joe be taken away? Will he have to spend time in solitary again? Maggie's thoughts raced as she walked towards the house, leaving Joe to take the new tools and equipment into the shed. When she walked up the steps, she heard raised voices and dread filled every fibre of her being. Following the sounds, she entered her parents' bedroom. George was sitting up in bed while Elizabeth fluffed a pillow behind his back. Mr Harrison was seated on a chair near the side of the bed. Their voices hushed when she walked in, but the tension in the room was tangible. Mr Harrison cleared his throat and said his goodbyes, ignoring Maggie as he walked past. Elizabeth followed, glaring at Maggie.

"Sit down," George commanded. Maggie hesitated and then moved to the chair furthest from the bed. George sighed. "Mr Harrison tells me you and Joe were in town." Maggie stared at him, blank-faced. He took a sip of tea and fixed a measured gaze on her. "Do you realise that we, or to be precise, I could face significant repercussions if this was taken to the authorities? While Joe's working here, he's my responsibility. I trust you've heard the news about some prisoners from Marrinup escaping and making their way to Perth and beyond."

"Joe wouldn't do that," she said a little too loudly. George shuffled up on the bed and winced in pain.

"That may be so, but there are people in this town who think otherwise. It doesn't look good for a man of my standing to have his daughter flaunt the law so brazenly. This is not to happen again. Do you understand?" Maggie sat back and folded her arms.

"Yes, but if people in this town minded their own business, there wouldn't be an issue."

"People will always concern themselves with what's going on in other people's lives. It's human nature. The key to preserving our family's good reputation in this community is to ensure we abide by the law." George took another mouthful of tea and waved her off.

In the kitchen, she got a glass of water and sipped it, her eyes fixed on the shed. The screen door opened, and Elizabeth entered with an armful of vegetables for dinner. Maggie took the carrots and began peeling them.

"The people in this town are such busybodies," she said.

"That may be so, but Mr Harrison didn't come here to get you into trouble. You did that yourself by breaking the law, young lady." Maggie dropped a carrot on the bench, then picked up another.

"What was I supposed to do? We needed those things, and you wouldn't leave Dad alone and come with me. Joe should be allowed to go into town." Elizabeth opened her mouth to reprimand her further when there was a loud knock on the front door.

"I'll get it," Maggie said, darting from the room, grateful for the distraction. She wiped her hands on her skirt and opened the door to find a teenage boy in a uniform holding his hat and a piece of paper in his hands. The sombre look on his face made Maggie's body tense. Her mouth went dry, a shiver ran down her spine, and goosebumps rose on her arms.

"Good afternoon, Miss. Are your mother and father home?" he asked, looking past her down the hallway. Maggie stammered and then, in a rush of words, told the boy about her father's accident and subsequent immobility. She led him into the sitting room and called for her mother. Elizabeth entered and looked at the young boy and the envelope in his hands. Her hands flew to her chest.

"I think your father needs to hear this," Elizabeth said to Maggie, then turned to the young man. "Please give us a moment."

Once they had settled George in his chair, they held their breath and waited for the young man to speak. He swallowed hard, then looked from Maggie to Elizabeth before setting his gaze on George.

"Good afternoon, Mr Sleeman, Mrs Sleeman. I have a telegram for you." He passed the envelope to George, then stepped back. Maggie bit her thumbnail as she watched her father open it. His face crumbled as he read the words. He blinked a few times before thanking the young man and asking Maggie to show him to the door. As she left the room, Maggie looked back at her parents. Elizabeth sat on the floor, hunched over George's lap, her shoulders beginning to rise and fall rapidly. George looked down and patted her back, murmuring softly as his tears fell onto her hair.

Maggie's heart felt heavy in her chest. She felt like she was in a dream as she closed the front door, then leaned her head against it. She knew what the first few words on that telegram would be. She'd heard Mary read hers to Joan at a CWA meeting last year. We regret to inform you... but the question was which of her brothers had been killed? She'd never had a favourite as such, but she'd always had a soft spot for Richard. She thought about Joan and Grace and what this might mean for them. But what if it was James? He was the most patriotic of them all. Even as a young boy, he'd always stood up for what he believed was right. Before he left, he'd been resolute in his belief that he would go off to battle and come back triumphant.

Maggie returned to the sitting room to find her mother gone. George motioned for her to sit in the chair next to his. She looked at the sag in his cheeks and the hollowness in his eyes and wondered how he had aged so much in such a short time. "Maggie, dear, I have some terrible news." He paused and cleared his throat. "I'm afraid James has been killed in action." His voice trembled. The last three words hung heavy in the air. Maggie felt her body tighten and tears spring to her eyes. She ran from the room, out the front door, and over to the shed. Joe saw her coming and dropped the shovel as she barrelled into him. Her knees buckled under her and she cried uncontrollably. Joe held her up and stroked her back, waiting for her sobs to subside. In time, her body stopped shaking and her breathing returned to its normal rhythm. She looked up and took a deep breath. Joe's face was etched with worry.

"It's James. He's dead." Somehow, saying it out loud made the news more real, and she felt another wave of grief wash over her. It couldn't be real. Not James. He was going to come home and marry Kathleen Mitchell. They were going to set up a farm, and have children, and grow old together. He was going to have a wonderful life, but that had all been taken away. He wouldn't be coming home. "I need to go. I have to tell Joan," she said, letting go of Joe and walking towards the bench. Joe reached the bench before her and saddled Lily, then led her out into the yard while Maggie stood rooted to the spot. She felt an emptiness that she'd never felt before.

It was as if Lily knew Maggie needed to go fast, to feel the wind rushing past her, and to feel like her world hadn't shattered. Maggie reached down and touched the horse's neck, feeling the powerful muscles expand and contract. Lily galloped along the well-worn track faster and faster until Richard and Joan's small house came into view. Maggie slowed the horse down to a walk and dismounted once she'd reached the fence. Joan was sitting on the verandah, reading. She brought her finger to her lips as Maggie approached.

"Grace is sleeping," she said, and then noticing the look on Maggie's face, added, "What's wrong?" Maggie slunk down into the chair next to Joan and looked at her expectant face, holding in the tears that were ready to spill.

"Mum and Dad just received a telegram. James is dead."

"Oh, Maggie. I can't believe it. Is your mum all right? How is your dad taking the news?"

"It was awful. I've never seen them like that before. They were devastated. Broken." A sob escaped her, and Joan wrapped her in a hug. They sat like that for a while, crying quietly, before Joan stood and gently pulled Maggie's arm, urging her to stand. They tiptoed past Grace's bedroom and into the kitchen. Joan stood at the sink and began making them both a cup of tea. She glanced out the small window at Richard's car sitting in the shed, a mixture of grief and relief on her face. Maggie looked down at the table as the memory of her father stroking her mother's back played before her eyes. A faint cry from the bedroom pierced the silence. Maggie felt relieved by the break in the gloom.

"I'll get her," Maggie said, pushing back her chair. Grace lay on the white sheet, cooing and gnawing at her balled fists. Her pale pink cheeks were smooth to the touch, and she beamed a gummy smile as Maggie lifted her from the cot. She stood holding Grace over one shoulder, rocking side to side.

"Oh, sweet thing," she murmured, "it's such a travesty that you'll never know your Uncle James. He would have loved you. He would have let you do all the things your Mummy and Daddy wouldn't let you do." She smiled at the thought and then wept softly.

Once they were all back at Jarrah Downs, Maggie and Joan joined George in the sitting room, listening as Elizabeth's cries floated from the bedroom, punctuating the silent house. With their shock and grief exposed on their faces, their voices were barely a murmur. Even Grace's cooing did little to lift the sombre mood. Maggie's thoughts whirled around, and she swayed from disbelief to anger. This sort of thing happened to other families. It wasn't supposed to happen to James. He shouldn't have gone off to war. He should have stayed here. A soft knock on the door jolted the solemn group from their contemplation. Maggie answered and saw Joe standing on the step, holding a bunch of roses from Elizabeth's garden. The red, angry scratches running down the back of his hands reflected her feelings. She hugged him and started to weep again. She felt like she would spend the rest of her life crying for her brother.

They walked hand in hand to the sitting room, breaking apart just before they reached the doorway. Joe stood just inside the room and cleared his throat. George looked up, his face expressionless.

"Mr Sleeman, I am so sorry for your loss. It is not right that your son has been taken away from you like this. Please tell me if I can help in any way." Joe looked at the ground. Maggie felt the silence hang like plumes of smoke in the air.

"Thank you, Joe. We appreciate it," Joan said. She stood and took the roses from him, then picked up the vase from the mantle. Maggie looked at her father.

"Dad?"

"Yes. Thank you, Joe. Although, I'm not sure there's much you can do," George said. He shook his head and banged his hand on the arm of the chair. "This goddamned war has taken my son. The very war you've fought in and for the wrong side, no less." Joe looked at Maggie and then at the ground.

"I am sorry. I will leave you. I have a lot to do," Joe said, then walked out of the room. Maggie shot her father an angry look and followed Joe, catching him before he escaped out of the front door.

"Joe, wait! I'm sorry. Dad's hurt and angry, but he shouldn't have spoken to you like that." Joe shook his head.

"It's all right, Maggie. I understand. I saw many friends die on the battlefields. There are no winners in war," he said. Maggie grabbed his hand and led him down the steps and into the yard. They started to walk along the boundary of Jarrah Downs, at first in silence and then opening up about their grief. They found themselves at the river's edge, near the little old wooden shack that sat on the farthest side of the farm away from the homestead. Maggie picked up a rock and threw it into the water. It landed with a satisfying plop. She found a spot on the bank to sit, and as she settled in, she felt the gentle breeze rustling her hair. Joe sat down next to her. She leaned into his shoulder and inhaled deeply, letting her breath out in a long blow. She felt utterly drained and empty.

"What's going to happen now?" she asked.

"What do you mean?"

"I don't know. I just feel like the world should stop for a while, but it won't, will it?" she asked, looking into his eyes while her own were on the brink of tears. He put a hand against her cheek.

"No, *mi amore*. Tomorrow is a new day, and you will start it with one less loved one in the world. This is how life works. It takes a long time to feel like you understand it."

"Do you feel like you understand it?" Joe took a moment to answer.

"No. But I try to understand it a little better each day." They sat in silence, watching the water rush past. Maggie realised she had started and ended her day by the river, and it had been one of the longest days of her life.

Chapter 12
Giuseppe
Mid-1945

It had been three months since the Sleeman family had received word that James had been killed in action. The loss had left a lasting impact on each of them. George didn't allow Giuseppe to attend the funeral at the church in Colton for fear of community backlash. When the family and other mourners had returned to Jarrah Downs for the wake, he'd worked far enough away to avoid any confrontations. He'd observed the gathering crowd from his vantage point and noted that Major Murray and some of the other guards were in attendance. He could only watch on as Thomas stood close to the family and his stomach churned as he saw him hug Maggie.

While the Sleeman family grappled with their grief, the work at Jarrah Downs carried on. Giuseppe ploughed the land, mended fences, broke in and groomed the brumbies, fed the cattle, and did whatever else George directed him to do. Giuseppe approached the task of sweeping the stables with gusto, the dust swirling in the air as he worked. It was one job that he didn't mind doing, especially when it was raining outside. Maggie occupied his thoughts. He'd tried to comfort her as best he could, but she'd become distant. He understood that grief affected people in different ways. He'd thought she'd need him more during such a difficult time, but instead, she'd put her walls up again. He prayed she would return to him when she was ready.

A voice broke his thoughts, and Giuseppe turned to see Maggie entering the stables. He straightened and leaned on the broom handle, ignoring the urge to enclose her in his arms. She stood in front of him and hesitated before grabbing his hand and holding it with both of hers.

"I'm sorry for being withdrawn. These last few months have been hard, but I've had a lot of time to think. Losing James has made me consider what I want for my own life." Giuseppe tensed and swallowed hard. Had she changed her mind about being with him? Did she want the stability of marrying a local boy and staying in Colton instead? He bit his lip. She was waiting for him to say something, but he couldn't bring himself to do it. If she was going to end their relationship when it had barely begun, then he didn't want to bring on the pain any sooner. "I want us to get married," she blurted. Giuseppe's jaw dropped as he tried to process what she'd said and reconcile it with his own racing thoughts. Had he heard her correctly? Did she want to marry him? Could they even get married? "Joe?" Maggie let go of his hand and took a step back, her hands fidgeting in front of her. Giuseppe breached the distance between them.

"Oh. I thought you changed your mind," he said, scooping her up in a hug and twirling her around before setting her down and kissing her. Overwhelming joy surged through his entire body, and then he stood still. "But I should have been the one to ask you." He knelt on the ground and took her left hand, then lifted his head and said, "Margaret Sleeman, I have nothing to offer you but my love. Will you take me to be your husband?" Maggie laughed and pulled him up into an embrace.

The elation of the moment washed away the months of worry, leaving him feeling weightless and free. He cupped her face with both hands and kissed her, then wrapped one hand in her hair and the other around her waist. Then reality hit him like a blow to the head and he pulled back and looked at her. They couldn't get married. He didn't know what was going to happen when the war ended. He was probably going to be sent back to Italy. If that happened, they might never see each other again. "Maggie," he said. Her eyes grew wide, and she shook her head and brought a finger to his lips.

"Don't say it. I don't want to think about anything else. We will be together. I'll save every penny I earn for our new life. Whatever happens, we'll find a way." There was no mistaking the determination etched on her face.

***

"Giuseppe? Hey!" Giuseppe didn't see the pillow coming but felt it hit him in the stomach. "Thinking about your girl again, *si*?" Giuseppe laughed and threw the pillow back at Luigi, hitting him in the face. He'd told him the night before about the proposal. Luigi had thought it was hilarious that Maggie had been the one to ask. He knew Luigi would be happy for him, but he didn't expect his friend to shout out and hug him. The noise had woken the others, and within seconds, the entire hut knew. This sort of gossip spread quickly, so Giuseppe knew it wouldn't be long before everyone at Marrinup was aware of his engagement. He couldn't keep something like this to himself, and besides, the men needed some good news to cheer them up.

He stood and walked out the door, calling behind him, "Come on. Let's go see if Hans and the others want to play wristball." The guards were on board with the plan, and the men made their way to the oval.

"What's this I hear about you and the boss's daughter?" Mario said, elbowing Giuseppe in the ribs.

"I heard that she asked him," Helmut said with a laugh as he moved ahead of the group. Giuseppe was thankful that a game was imminent as the ribbing turned into taunts about who would be victorious. The overnight rain left parts of the oval waterlogged, but the men were unfazed, eagerly embracing the opportunity to get dirty.

The game was 2-2. After their last defeat, the Germans were playing to win. Giuseppe took an elbow to the chest and jogged to the side to join Hans under the shelter of the large gum. The German handed him a cigarette before lighting one of his own.

"Have you heard the news about my homeland?" Hans asked. Giuseppe shook his head. With Richard away and George not working much, he'd been so busy that he went to bed early most nights feeling completely exhausted. "Germany surrendered." Giuseppe coughed and bent double with the effort. Hans gave him a few quick blows to his back and continued, "It happened a few weeks ago, but we only found out when Heinrich got a letter from his brother." Giuseppe shook his head. He wasn't surprised to learn the news this way. Mail deliveries had been few and far between during their years at Marrinup, and the censored newspapers offered minimal insights into world events.

"What will happen now?" he asked.

"Well, they haven't released us yet, so I don't know." Hans shrugged and took a drag of his cigarette.

"Maybe they will wait until their war with Japan has ended too? Do you think they will let us go free after that? Will they send us home or just open the gates?" Giuseppe asked, his voice coming out higher with the last two questions. Hans put a hand on his shoulder, shook his head, and said, "I wish I knew." A cheer erupted from the oval, and the two men looked across to see the German team shouting and jostling each other. Hans ran over to join his comrades, and Giuseppe joined the group of dejected Italians. After the initial commiserations, Giuseppe told them the news. Surprise and confusion seemed to be the consensus. They took their time walking back to camp, quietly pondering what they'd heard. Why hadn't the Australians let them go yet? There was no war with Germany now. Surely, they were no longer a threat. Not that they ever really were.

"I think there will be more escapes now." Luigi punctured the silence. A couple of men nodded.

"They will not just let us go free. They will make us go back to Italy. I'm sure of it," said Giovanni as he kicked an old can along the path.

"What do you think we should do?" Eugenio asked the collective group, but nobody had an answer. There wasn't much any of them could do. They walked the rest of the way in silence.

***

Making his rounds of the farm, Giuseppe pulled his raincoat shut and strolled along the fence line, looking up at the bulbous grey clouds. It felt like the rain hadn't stopped for days. The grass was longer and the everlasting daisies were starting to pop up in the paddocks. Giuseppe bent over and plucked some flowers for Maggie. Straightening up, he heard a long, low groan. He looked around and moved in the sound's direction. He came across a cow lying on her side in the long grass, her round stomach protruding like an over-inflated balloon. The cow groaned again and swished its tail. Giuseppe moved towards its rear, preparing himself for what he was about to witness. He could see the calf's legs, but it appeared to be stuck. He stooped down but looked up when George called out and made his way over.

"Bloody hell. We've got to pull that calf out quick," George said, kneeling next to Giuseppe with a loud grunt. The two men gently moved the cow's legs and manoeuvred the calf into a better position. With their arms covered in mucus, they each reached a hand inside and pulled. The cow groaned again and the calf came out in a rush of liquid, landing on the ground in front of them. They both fell back onto their heels and watched as the exhausted cow swung her body around to lick the calf clean. She eased herself up and continued licking as the calf bleated its existence to the world. A soft smile played on Giuseppe's lips as he sat and watched mother and baby bond. Despite growing up on a farm, he'd never had the opportunity to see an animal being born, let alone help it into the world. George was silent, but Giuseppe felt him glance over a few times before he grunted and stood up. Giuseppe followed his lead, monitoring the calf as it tried to stand for the first time. George looked around, then back at Giuseppe.

"I guess now is as good a time as any," he said, clearing his throat. "Joe, there's something that needs to be said, and I would like this conversation to be kept between us." Giuseppe's whole body tightened. Did George know about his relationship with Maggie? Was he going to tell him to leave her alone? What if he sent him back to Marrinup for good? He straightened and nodded. "I know you and Maggie have become close." George paused and ran a hand across his chin, clearly not comfortable with the conversation he felt he had to have. "You must know that we don't think it's right for her. We don't know how long this war will last. The news mentioned that when it does end, all POWs will be sent back to their own countries. What will happen then? Will you break Maggie's heart?" Giuseppe bowed his head. What could he say to that? He didn't know how long he'd be in Marrinup or what was going to happen when the war ended? He had no intention of hurting Maggie, that much was certain. Raising his head, he fixed his gaze directly on George.

"I do not want to hurt Maggie... I love her."

"If you loved her, you'd do the right thing. What will it take?" Giuseppe shook his head.

"I do not understand," he said. George folded his arms, and his lips formed a thin line.

"What will it take for you to leave her alone?" Giuseppe had no intention of leaving her alone. Maggie had finally made her feelings known, and they were happy amidst the difficult circumstances. He couldn't just pretend nothing had happened between them. George mistook his silence for consideration.

"Look, I'm willing to give you £10,000 if you'll stay away from

Maggie. That's a lot of money, Joe. Think about what you could do with it. You could buy a farm back home and set yourself up. You could travel anywhere in the world. You could do anything you dreamed of." Giuseppe's brow furrowed and he shook his head slightly. George looked towards the house before turning to him again. "I'll let you think about it, but I want an answer by the end of the week," he said, then spun on his heels and stalked towards the house, leaving Giuseppe alone in the middle of the paddock.

Giuseppe moved under the nearest tree as the rain turned to spears of ice. Leaning against the trunk, he lit a cigarette and watched the newborn calf toddle awkwardly behind its mother and thought of his family's farm. He never imagined he would have that kind of money, and here it was, practically thrown at him. He could do so much with it. He could buy livestock or build another house on the farm. He could help his brother and sister. But at what cost? Over the last two years, he'd grown to love Maggie more than he'd loved anyone before. He thought about her as soon as he opened his eyes, and she was in his thoughts as he fell asleep. Sure, there had been a few rocky moments, but they were beginning to find their footing in this relationship. They had only just made plans to get married. He couldn't break her heart. He dragged the last of his cigarette before throwing it to the ground and stubbing it out with his boot. He had four days to ponder his decision.

***

Giuseppe walked the familiar track around the compound,

nodding and stopping to chat with fellow prisoners. Sunday afternoons were usually spent relaxing, but there seemed to be a buzz in the air. Luigi would know what was going on. Giuseppe strode over to the recreation hall, where Luigi and Carlo were playing cards.

"Deal me in," he said, sitting opposite Luigi and nodding at Carlo. He examined his hand and put the cards back down. The sound of Cambino's booming voice reverberated through the hall as he bounded in, issuing orders to the men in his wake. Mario and Giovanni, carrying a large machine, moved to the back of the room and set it down gently on the floor. Antonio started moving the tables to one side. Giuseppe looked at Luigi and Carlo questioningly. With a collective shrug, they all rose in unison.

"What's going on?" Luigi asked Cambino.

"We're setting up the projector. You're in for a treat tonight, lads."

"Projector? You mean they're going to let us watch a picture show?"

"*Si*, that's the plan."

"*Grandioso*!" Luigi exclaimed. As Giuseppe and the others rearranged the tables, the sound of scraping chairs and shuffling feet filled the room, while Cambino focused on adjusting the projector. Giuseppe went back and forth, moving the chairs into place with precision while Luigi whistled in tune with the music. Giuseppe knew his silence hadn't gone unnoticed, and Luigi would quiz him about it later, but right now, all he wanted to do was lose himself in a repetitive task.

He'd managed to avoid being alone with George for the rest of the week. But he knew his respite from the confrontation wouldn't last. He'd gone over their conversation so many times that he wasn't sure if he'd imagined some of it. He still couldn't believe that George would offer him money to stay away from Maggie. But it wasn't just the offer he had to think about. He had to decide whether to tell Maggie what had happened. He had a few choices. If he rejected the offer, he'd keep seeing Maggie. He could tell her about it, but it would fracture her relationship with her father. He could stay silent, but then he'd be starting their marriage, keeping something from her. Then, there was the question of what George would do if he decided not to take up the offer. Would he dismiss him from the farm? He might never see Maggie again. And if he took up the offer, it would be the same conclusion. He didn't know what to do.

The dinner bell snapped him from his reverie, and he joined the throng, headed for the mess. The chatter was louder than usual, and he could almost smell the anticipation in the air. The last major thing to happen at camp was the change in command, and that seemed so long ago.

Dinner comprised a stew made from vegetables procured from the garden near the mess, followed by dumplings and cream. Luigi slurped the last of his dessert, then slapped his spoon and bowl down on the table.

"Out with it," he said, glaring at Giuseppe. Giuseppe looked up and back down into his almost empty bowl. He could ignore Luigi, but he knew better. Luigi wouldn't stop asking until Giuseppe told him what was on his mind, but he didn't want to discuss it in front of the other men. He stood, picked up his bowl and spoon, and said, "Let's go for a walk."

The floodlights lit up the compound, and the two men strolled around the perimeter. Luigi made small talk about the upcoming picture show, but Giuseppe could tell he was eager to find out what was troubling him. He inhaled deeply, then embarked on a lengthy dialogue about what had been happening at the farm. He didn't look at Luigi until he'd finished recounting his conversation with George. Luigi's mouth opened and closed a few times before he shook his head.

"Is this true? He offered so much money? What are you going to do?" Giuseppe shrugged and kicked a rock. Luigi was silent as they rounded the corner and passed the watchtower. He didn't speak until they'd almost completed an entire circuit, then he stopped and turned to Giuseppe. "You love this girl, *si*?" Giuseppe nodded. "You want her to be happy, *si*?" He nodded again. "And she wants to be with you, *si*?" Another nod. "There's your answer, *amico*." Giuseppe put his hands in his pockets and looked up at the cloudy sky. Was it really that simple, though? Luigi raised his hands. "Look, you know I like *i soldi*, but *amore*? Love trumps money." Luigi's hands squeezed Giuseppe's upper arms. "This is what you do. You turn this man down. Then you and Maggie will marry and have children and be happy, end of story." Giuseppe smiled without it reaching his eyes.

"If only it was that easy," he said.

"It can be. You will see." Luigi was so sure he had the right answer, but Giuseppe was doubtful. George had told him what would happen if he left Maggie alone, but he hadn't mentioned what might happen if he didn't. "Come. Take the night off from your worries. Let's go see the show." Giuseppe rolled his shoulders back and shook his arms out. Luigi was right. He'd worried enough about it this week. He was well overdue for some fun and entertainment. They all were.

Sitting on the hard bench as the truck rattled down the road, Giuseppe felt his nerves rattling, too. He smoothed his hair and ran his hands down his thighs. He repeated the process on and off for the next 15 minutes until the truck pulled up at the gate leading to Jarrah Downs. He jumped down to the ground and watched the truck drive off. Not once during the last two years had he wished to be back on that truck, but today, he felt otherwise. He turned and ambled up the driveway. He wouldn't be able to avoid George today. They'd have their regular Monday morning meeting in the shed.

The house was still dark as he approached, but there was light coming from the entrance to the shed. He inhaled deeply and headed towards the open door, the voice in his head turning over his conversations with George and Luigi. His rational mind knew that taking the money would set him up for the future. He was going to be sent home, so why not take the money and buy a farm near his family home in Rimissa? He could grow produce and raise cattle. He'd have a place to live and an income to live off. But his irrational mind, or more so his heart, knew that he couldn't live with himself if he did that to Maggie. It would be an entirely selfish decision. His heart would break to leave her that way. He walked through the door, still feeling like he wasn't entirely sure if he had made up his mind.

"Bit cold this morning, isn't it?" George's voice dissipated his thoughts, and he blinked a few times to bring himself back to reality. He greeted George, grabbed a grooming brush from the bench, and then strode towards the horse stalls. He stiffened when George followed. Giuseppe laid his hands on Lily's neck and immediately felt his body relax. If only he could mount the horse and gallop away at this very moment. George slapped a rope over the low wall of the stall.

"Right. The cattle in the back paddock are off for the chop this week. Mr Pickering will be dropping off some brumbies on Wednesday, so they'll need to be broken in. I want them ready to sell ASAP. I've bought some pigs. They'll be delivered on Thursday. And the gate near the dam is coming off its hinges again. Can you get onto that this morning?"

"Yes. I can do that," Giuseppe said and continued to brush Lily. George stood watching him for a moment before walking away. He stopped in the doorway, then turned on his heel and headed back towards Giuseppe. George stood in front of him with his hands on his hips. Giuseppe tried to swallow the lump that had formed in his throat, but it wouldn't budge. This was the conversation that would determine which way his future went.

"Have you given any thought to my proposal?" He put the brush down, then squared his shoulders and rose to his full height. He locked eyes with George, his gaze unwavering.

"*Si*. Yes. Mr Sleeman, your offer is generous, and it would change my life." George's face broke into a subtle smile of satisfaction.

Giuseppe took a deep breath before continuing. "But I am afraid I cannot accept it." The colour drained from George's face and the red hue of anger took its place. His breathing became laboured, and he started shaking his head.

"Surely, you cannot be serious? I've offered you the chance of a lifetime." He pointed at Giuseppe's chest as the words tumbled from his mouth. "You are to stay away from Maggie. I forbid you to speak to her again. You are done, young man. This will be your last day at Jarrah Downs." George stalked out of the shed, leaving Giuseppe rooted to the spot. A familiar feeling of foreboding came over him. What had he done? This wasn't how he wanted things to go. He stayed in the shed until he'd composed himself enough to face George should he run into him again. It was clear that George wouldn't tell Maggie the truth, and Giuseppe didn't want her to believe he'd left her on purpose. He hovered near the shed and the paddocks close to the house, keeping watch for any sign of her. Later in the morning, Elizabeth brought out some scones and tea, gently setting them on the bench.

"It's a shame Maggie's gone to work for the day. She loves to see Lily freshly groomed," Elizabeth said. She stood with her hands folded in front of her and gave him a curt nod before leaving. It was an odd comment and even stranger that Elizabeth had brought the food and drink out to the shed rather than leaving it on the verandah as she usually did. He resigned himself to the fact that he wouldn't get the chance to say goodbye. That afternoon, he climbed into the truck and looked back at Jarrah Downs one last time, his heart heavy.

Chapter 13
Margaret
Mid-1945

"I let him go, Lizzy. I told him the truth. He's not right for our Maggie. She'll marry the boy of Williams or another local lad, and that's that." Maggie stood frozen, listening at the door of her father's study. She clenched her fist and sucked her lips over her teeth to dampen her rising anger. Once again, her father was meddling in her personal life. Joe's dismissal explained his most recent absence from the farm. But it was entirely unfair to fire him when he did nothing wrong. Hearing footsteps approaching, she darted to the sitting room and picked up the book lying on the arm of the chair.

"Maggie dear, what are you doing up?" Elizabeth asked as she entered the room.

"I couldn't sleep," she replied, holding the book up by way of explanation. Elizabeth eyed her for a second. "Well, it's getting late. You should probably go to bed." She'd had little time to digest the news and her anger hadn't fully dissipated. She stood in front of Elizabeth.

"I wish you would stop treating me like a child," Maggie huffed.

"Where's Joe? Why hasn't he been here?" Elizabeth looked towards the study and then back at Maggie.

"I think you need to discuss that with your father."

"So, Dad's behind it, then?"

"Your father has made a decision. You need to speak with him."

Maggie harrumphed and marched to the study. Without bothering to knock, she barged into the room and positioned herself in front of George's desk, hands firmly planted on her hips.

"Why hasn't Joe been here?" she demanded. George raised his eyebrows but didn't respond. "Where's Joe?" she asked. George sat back and put his hands together on the desk.

"I decided we don't need his help anymore, and that's the end of it."

"I think there's more to it, isn't there?" Maggie asked. George stood and walked around to Maggie, then rested his hands on her shoulders.

"Now is not the time. What's done is done. We all need to move on with our lives." Maggie shrugged off his hands. How could she move on with her life? What if he'd been moved to another camp? What if she never saw Joe again?

"But Joe needed this work. What if they've sent him away? He could be anywhere by now. Why would you do this to him? You have no idea what you've done."

"Maggie..." George tried to hold her hand, but she pulled away and stormed out of the room, slamming the door as she went.

***

The scent of plum blossoms filled the air. Joan and Grace were sitting under the trees, enjoying the sunny spring weather. Grace toddled towards Maggie as she approached. Maggie picked her up and squeezed her gently before depositing her back on the grass. She plonked down on the rug next to Joan and noticed the creased letter sitting in her lap.

"Is that from Richard? How is he?" she asked. Joan nodded, a small smile briefly gracing her lips before she handed over the letter. Maggie raised her hands. "Oh, I don't need to read it. I'm sure it's personal." Joan shrugged.

"It's pretty standard, actually. You know Richard." Maggie laughed. Richard had always been the same—traditional, reserved, and taciturn. She took the letter and read it.

Dearest Joan,

My troop is stationed in Borneo. Our camp is surrounded by jungle and its accommodations are basic at best. The weather is shocking. It rains a fair bit, but it's still hot and humid. We're sweating profusely, but we can't take our shirts off or we're swamped by the biggest mosquitos I've ever seen. The food is awful too.

We're up here fighting the Japanese. We heard the Americans have dropped a couple of atomic bombs on Hiroshima and Nagasaki. Those bombs are the worst kind. They've completely decimated the cities. Hundreds of thousands of people were killed, and many more have had to leave their homes. Nobody is winning this war. Not us, not them.

How are you? How's the family? Missing you all.

Your loving husband,

Richard

Maggie handed the letter back to Joan.

"You're right. Typical Richard. He's always been a man of few words and his letters aren't much better. I'm sure he misses you both very much."

"Yes. Well, same here." Joan turned away and then turned back to face Maggie. "I'm sorry. I get a bit upset that he's missing out on seeing Grace's new tricks. Did you see how well she's walking? Clever little cookie!" Joan said as she picked Grace up and cuddled her.

"I've found out what happened to Joe." Joan's eyebrows shot up, and she put Grace back down on the rug.

"Out with it then." She folded her arms and waited. Joan had been supportive when Maggie had told her she wanted to be with Joe. She'd even managed to get George and Elizabeth away from the farm on a few occasions to give them time to themselves. She'd been worried when Joe hadn't been coming to work.

"Dad's kicked him off the farm for good. I don't even know if he's still at Marrinup. They could have sent him away already. He could be anywhere." Maggie blinked to quell the tears that had formed, then leaned forward and tickled Grace under the chin to distract herself.

"Hmm. Well, I don't like our chances of getting your father to change his mind, but first things first. We need to find out if Joe's still at Marrinup. I've got a plan." Intrigued, Maggie stopped tickling Grace and looked up. "You remember Richard's friend Norm Halliday? He popped over the other day to check in on us. His dad's a guard at Marrinup." Maggie's mouth dropped open.

"I'll ask him if his dad could get a message to Joe."

"Yes! That would be swell. Once I know he's there, I can figure out what to do next."

"Leave it with me." Maggie couldn't erase the wide grin from her face.

The following week felt long, and Maggie's thoughts revolved around Joe's whereabouts, Joan's plan, and what the future might hold. At work, Doctor Mosely commented on her lack of concentration when she transcribed his notes into the wrong patient's file and called another patient by the wrong name. She'd also found it hard to think about anything else while she was at home, too. Sitting on the verandah, listening to Max's snores coming from the chair next to her, she heard a motor and saw Richard's car rattling up the driveway, dust billowing behind it. Joan almost skipped up the stairs in her hurry to reach Maggie. "Go and tell your mum you're coming to my place for the night. No questions. Just hurry." Maggie found her mother in the vegetable garden and relayed the news, knowing she'd have no issue with the plan. Maggie slid into the passenger seat and turned to Joan. "What's happening? Where are we going? Where's Grace?" As Maggie bombarded her with questions, Joan did her best to provide rapid-fire responses.

"It's a surprise. I can't tell you. And Mrs Winthrop said she'd look after Grace for a bit. Now, hop over the back and put on that dress," Joan commanded with a smirk. Maggie climbed into the back seat and saw the dress lying flat across the leather. She looked at Joan's face in the rearview mirror, a mixture of disbelief and excitement rushing through her. "I made a couple of adjustments," Joan said. Maggie picked up the dress, running her hand along its length and letting it fall onto her lap. The sleeves had been shortened and lace had been sewn to the bodice, but it was still the same beautiful, timeless dress that Joan had worn when she married Richard. Did this mean what Maggie thought it meant? Was she about to be married? Where? How? Thoughts swirled in her mind, creating a buzz of excitement. She looked back at Joan.

"It's perfect. Thank you." Joan beamed.

"It was nothing. Now, put it on. We're almost there." Maggie rearranged her limbs to get out of her yard dress and into the gown. Finding matching heels on the floor, she put them on as Joan pulled the car to a stop. She'd been so caught up in getting changed that she'd neglected to pay attention to where they were going. Maggie looked out the window and instantly recognised where they were. Her family had picnicked at Marrinup Falls over the years. It was a lovely spot where the seasonal Marrinup Brook flowed gently over the large grey boulders. Getting out of the car, Maggie ran her hands over her dress to smooth out any wrinkles, then turned her gaze towards the group standing under the trees.

She recognised Joe, but she had no idea who the other two men were. One man dressed in a military uniform was slightly shorter than Joe, with dark hair and hazel eyes. Giuseppe had mentioned his friend Luigi on many occasions. Maggie guessed it must be him. The older man had similar features and wore a black cassock. The ankle-length garment buttoned at the front and had a stiff, white collar. Maggie couldn't help but notice how impeccably dressed Joe was, with his crisp suit and polished shoes. It felt like such a long time since she had seen him.

"Here. These are for you," Joan said, holding out a bunch of red and white roses. Maggie took them and hugged her. Joan squeezed her and said, "Now, go and get married." Walking towards the group, her mind raced. Was this really happening? Was she about to marry Joe? She felt like she was in a dream. When she reached the group, Joe engulfed her in a tight embrace.

"You look absolutely beautiful, *mi amore*," he whispered in her ear before the sound of a cough from the priest made them break apart. Joe gestured towards the man standing on his left. "This is my best friend, Luigi. Luigi, this is the love of my life, Maggie." Maggie blushed and Luigi hugged her, then kissed her on both cheeks. Father Romano, who had also come from Marrinup, did the same.

"Are we ready to begin the ceremony?" Father Romano said. Maggie handed the roses to Joan, and then her hand flew to her stomach to quell the butterflies. Giuseppe held her other hand in his and gazed into her eyes. The next few minutes seemed to pass by in a blur. When Father Romano asked, "Are you prepared, as you follow the path of marriage, to love and honour each other for as long as you both shall live?" tears sprang to her eyes. She looked at Joe and visions of their future flashed in her mind—a happy home filled with love, laughter, and children, their grandchildren visiting them, and the two of them sitting on their verandah in matching rocking chairs reminiscing about the wonderful life they'd had. Her heart felt like it was ready to explode.

She stood taller and replied with a firm "I am." When Joe responded the same way, gazing at her, a tear rolled down her cheek and she wiped it away with the back of her hand. They didn't exchange rings, but they knew they didn't need a ring to get married.

"You may now kiss the bride," Father Romano said. Joe leaned forward and put one hand around the back of her neck and the other around her waist. She stood on her tiptoes to reach him. They shared their first kiss as husband and wife, and she felt like the rest of the world slipped away. Joan and Luigi clapped and cheered as they parted.

"*Congratulazioni amico! Evviva gli sposi*!" Maggie gave Luigi a quizzical look. "*Mi scusi*. It means "Long live the bride and groom"." Luigi smiled and hugged Joe and Maggie to him before encouraging Joan to join in as well.

After sharing their congratulations, Luigi and Father Romano got into an army truck and left Joan, Maggie, and Joe at the Falls. Settling next to Joe in the backseat of Richard's car, Maggie closed her eyes and tried to remember all the details of what had just happened. It seemed to have passed by in a haze. One minute, she was sitting on the verandah with Max, and the next, she was in the back seat of Richard's car, a married woman with her husband sitting beside her. Maggie didn't know what was ahead of her, but she knew it was a time of change and that she was ready for it.

***

Outside the Dwellingup Hotel, Joan parked the car and they all eagerly piled out, their bright smiles still fresh on their faces. Before they entered the pub, Joan pulled Maggie aside.

"The accommodation isn't grand, but it's all I could arrange at short notice. Molly, the publican's wife, was a friend of my mother's. She'll be discreet."

"Oh, Joan, it's perfect. I can't thank you enough for what you've done for us." Joan shooed Maggie's comment away as if she did this sort of thing all the time. Then she looked across at Joe, who was leaning against a pole waiting for them.

"Will you be all right tonight? I mean, is there anything you'd like to ask me?" Joan ran her hand across her mouth and lifted her eyebrows. Maggie paused for a moment, until realisation dawned, and her cheeks flushed with embarrassment.

"No. Thank you. I think I'll be fine. I've read a lot of books, you know," she said with a wink. The two women chuckled, and Joe walked over to them.

"Thank you, Joan. Maggie is lucky to have you in her life," Joe said.

 "I'm lucky to have her and now you," Joan said as she hugged Maggie and stood on her tiptoes to kiss Joe's cheek before heading to her car. Maggie waved profusely as Joan pulled out of the gravel car park.

Alone at last, Maggie and Joe looked at each other and burst into laughter.

"Did that all just happen?" Maggie asked.

"Yes, and I am the happiest man alive because of it." He hugged her, then grabbed her hand and led her into the pub. Molly showed them to a large wood-panelled bedroom with an attached bathroom at the rear of the building. The aroma of flowers filled the room. A heart made of rose petals had been laid on the bed, the nightstands held candles, and two bottles of beer were sitting on the small table by the window. Joe opened both bottles, handing one to Maggie.

"To us and the wonderful future we are going to have," Joe announced. They clinked their bottles together before taking long swigs. Maggie had had little time to process the afternoon's events, but now, as she stood in the room with Joe, she felt nervous. Her hand shook as she took another swig of beer. She looked around the room, at the painting on the wall, at the candles by the bed, at the rug on the floor, anywhere but at Joe. She knew she wanted what was about to happen, but she was nervous. Joe took the bottle from her hand and placed it on the table. He held her hand and brought it to his lips, kissing it, then turning it slightly so that he could kiss her wrist. Then he kissed her forearm and elbow before slowly making his way to her shoulder and neck. She swallowed and a soft moan escaped as he gently nibbled her ear. He started to softly tug at her dress, and she gently brushed his hand away. She took a step back, undressed and watched him do the same. Goosebumps rose on her skin, and she trembled with fear and excitement. He pulled her close before walking her backwards and laying her on the bed.

***

Sunlight streamed through the curtain, basking the room in a soft glow. Maggie rolled over and placed one arm across Joe's bare chest, then bent a leg across his. Her breathing was slow and steady, and she felt relaxed and content. She noticed the rhythm of Joe's breathing change and felt him twitch next to her before he opened his eyes, a grin spreading across his face. He kissed her, and she felt warmth spread through her entire body. They lay curled up in each other's arms. They'd not spoken much since before her father had sent him away and were preoccupied the previous night. Maggie knew they had to talk about their future, but was she ready to face what Joe might say? He laced his fingers in hers.

"I have to go home, but I will come back for you, and we will build a new life together. We will have our own farm with lots of cattle and brumbies and an enormous vegetable garden."

"That sounds wonderful. I've been saving my pay from the surgery."

"I've been saving my tokens."

"We're going to have a good life, aren't we?" She looked up at him.

"*Si.* The best." He leaned down and planted a kiss on her lips, then kissed her more urgently. Afterwards, they showered and dressed. Maggie was grateful that Joan had the forethought to organise some plain clothes lest she wear her wedding dress again. They sat by the window enjoying a breakfast of tea with toast and strawberry jam. They couldn't stay in the room all day, but when there was a knock on the door, Maggie's heart sank.

"It's time to go, Russo," a voice said. Joe looked at the door, then back at Maggie, and shrugged in resignation.

"It's Halliday. I have to go back to camp." Maggie sighed. "It's just for now, not forever," Joe said as he pulled her to her feet.

"But when will I see you again?" she straightened the collar on his uniform.

"I'm not sure, but we'll find a way. We found a way to get married, didn't we?" he said. They walked to the door and held each other until another knock broke the silence. Joe gently shut the door behind him, and Maggie turned back to the room. She was a married woman. The thought brought a smile to her face as she remembered the events that had taken her from the verandah at Jarrah Downs to that small room in the Dwellingup pub. Her euphoria was short-lived as she sat on the chair looking at the suit Joe had left behind. They might be married, but Joe was back in a prisoner-of-war camp, and she was about to resume her everyday life, which had increasingly been feeling like its own kind of prison.

***

It was nearing dusk as Elizabeth, Joan, and Maggie pulled into Colton's main street. The lights were on in the blue CWA building, casting a warm glow through the windows, signalling that it was almost time for the meeting. They walked into the bustling hall with their arms laden with cakes and slices. They unburdened themselves at one of the trestle tables housed along one wall, then turned around as the chatter in the hall dulled. The eyes of every woman in the hall were on them. Elizabeth's eyebrows knitted together, and she eyed Joan and Maggie questioningly. The younger women looked at one another and shrugged. Maggie gulped and hoped it had gone unnoticed. Elizabeth, ignoring the stares, turned and rearranged the food they'd brought in. The unmistakable nasal pitch of Emma Fulton's voice filled the room.

"I don't think we'll be needing your help this evening, ladies." Elizabeth braced herself as she turned back around.

"I beg your pardon?"

"I said we won't be needing your help this evening. In fact, I think our membership might be at capacity. We may have to defer certain memberships for the time being. You understand, of course, don't you?" Emma Fulton pushed through the three women, picked up the slice that Maggie had set down, and handed it back to Elizabeth.

"Actually, Emma, I don't. Can you please explain?" Elizabeth said, taking the slice and placing it back on the table. Maggie looked across at Joan, who shook her head almost imperceptibly.

"Well, the other ladies and I have come across a bit of news that puts us all in a rather awkward position. I'm sure you're aware of it, and I can't fathom why you'd think it wouldn't be an issue."

"I honestly do not know what you're referring to." A sneer spread across Emma Fulton's pinched features as she glanced at Maggie. She sucked her lips in, then put a hand on her chest and sighed.

"I hate to be the one to enlighten you about the goings on in your own family, Elizabeth, but it seems that young Margaret here is a blushing bride. Albeit to a quite undesirable husband." Elizabeth's mouth opened and closed, and then she turned to Maggie. She started to shake her head slightly but stopped when Maggie looked at the floor. Maggie's stomach tightened and her mouth went dry. She looked up into her mother's face and saw shock, shame, and disappointment in even measure. Elizabeth turned to look at Joan.

The younger woman matched her gaze. It felt to Maggie as if the world had stopped and they were all moving in slow motion. Emma leaned in so that only those closest to her could hear her words. "You are not welcome here anymore. Please leave before you make even more of a spectacle of yourself than you already have." Tears sprang to Maggie's eyes as a satisfied smile spread across Emma's face. Elizabeth seized Maggie's hand and marched out the door with Joan trailing behind. Elizabeth's grip tightened as she almost dragged Maggie up the street towards their car.

"I don't even need to ask. I can see the truth of her words in your eyes," Elizabeth exclaimed. She let go of Maggie's hand and stood back, gasping and shaking her head. "I just can't believe this. What were you thinking?" She pointed at Joan. "And you. I have no doubt that you played a role in this. How could you? What will George say? What will he do?" Elizabeth was almost on the brink of tears. Maggie tried to touch her mother's arm, but she pulled away from her. A shiver ran through her. She knew she had to explain.

"I didn't do this out of spite. I did it for love. I love Joe. Please don't be upset with me, and don't blame Joan." Maggie looked up at the stars and then back down at her mother. "If this war, and losing James, has taught me anything, it's that we need to live; we need to take a chance and do the things we want to do because we are not guaranteed time." Elizabeth blinked back tears and allowed Maggie to hold her arm and gently manoeuvre her so that she leaned against the car. Maggie wanted to explain but knew there were no words that her mother would hear right now that would make this all right.

"When did it happen?" Elizabeth asked. Maggie looked over at Joan.

"You have to tell her the truth," Joan said. Maggie squared her shoulders.

"A month ago." Elizabeth's face drained of colour.

"A month! You've been married for a month, and I didn't know? How did I not know what was happening with my own daughter right under my nose?"

"I'm sorry, Mum." Tears rolled down Maggie's cheeks and she couldn't bring herself to look at Elizabeth or Joan. She did the right thing by marrying Joe, but at that moment, she felt like the worst person in the world for betraying her mother's trust. She realised that Elizabeth had to come to terms with her only daughter getting married without her knowledge and also without her presence. Maggie felt a hand wipe away her tears and arms wrap around her. She began to sob and Elizabeth did the same. Joan put her arms around both of them, and they stood like that for a few moments before Elizabeth took a deep breath, pushed Maggie to arm's length and looked her up and down.

"Well, I am disappointed, to say the least. But I also understand why you did what you did." She looked at Joan. "And Joan, I was a little harsh earlier. Please forgive me."

"There's nothing to forgive." Joan nodded. Elizabeth turned back towards the hall.

"As for the CWA, well, I never enjoyed being ruled by Her Majesty Emma Fulton, anyway." Laughter filled the air as the three women chuckled and hugged each other, savouring the moment before they got into the car. "The only problem now is what we tell your father. He's only just agreed to have Joe back on the farm."

Chapter 14
Giuseppe
Late 1945

Giuseppe lay on his bed, staring at the wooden slats across the top bunk. It wasn't the slats that held his interest, but what he'd placed there. A picture of Maggie that she'd given Officer Halliday to pass on to him a few days after their wedding. It had been just over a month, but he could remember every moment as if it were yesterday. She'd looked stunning in her dress and had almost brought him to tears when she'd said her vows. He'd been so nervous at the wedding, but even more so when they reached the hotel. Leaving her and heading back to camp, not knowing when he'd see her next, had been one of the hardest things he'd had to do. His sadness had been short-lived because when he'd entered his hut, confetti and congratulations rained down on him. His roommates had dragged him to the recreation hall. Music blasted from the gramophone, and they enjoyed a few bottles of Gunter's homemade schnapps. They celebrated, albeit without the bride. The guards didn't bother them, and Giuseppe reasoned that Halliday had filled them in. The festivities lasted most of the day. Men came in and out of the hall; some only stayed for one drink while others spent the day talking, playing cards, and consuming the food that the kitchenhands dropped off. For a few brief hours, the men forgot where they were.

Tiptoeing to the shelves, Giuseppe picked up some paper and a pencil before retreating to his bed. He'd been so distracted lately that he hadn't thought to write to his mother and tell her the news. He lit a cigarette and began writing at length about Maggie and their clandestine wedding. As he neared the end of his letter, Cambino burst into the hut.

"Get up! Get to the rec hall. There's some big news," he called out, then was gone before they'd comprehended what he'd said. With wide-eyed looks, they jumped out of bed, threw on their clothes, and sprinted to the hall. Prisoners and guards in all states of dress were piled in; some hadn't even bothered to get out of their pyjamas. The radio was at full volume, but the murmur of excited voices made it difficult to hear. Giuseppe looked at Luigi, who shrugged and pushed his way forward. Giuseppe followed close behind. As they moved towards the front of the room, a man's voice boomed from the crackling speakers.

"Fellow citizens, the war is over. The Japanese Government has accepted the terms of surrender imposed by the Allied Nations, and hostilities will now cease. The reply by the Japanese Government to the note sent by Britain, the United States, the USSR and China has been received and accepted by the Allied Nations.

At this moment, let us offer thanks to God. Let us remember those who gave their lives that we may enjoy this glorious moment and may look forward to a peace which they have won for us."

As the Australian Prime Minister, Ben Chifley, declared the end of the war with Japan, the hall filled with a palpable sense of relief and anticipation. When the speech ended, some men cheered while others looked confused. The war might have ended, but they were still stuck at Marrinup, and they didn't know when they'd be freed. Luigi gestured towards the exit, and Giuseppe and the others followed. As they made their way back to their hut, the weight of the news hung heavy in the air.

"With no war, they must let us go," Eugenio reasoned.

"Maybe, but they will not just let us walk out the gates." Giovanni bounced a tennis ball as he spoke. "They will ship us all back to Italy. What will we be returning to? The aftermath of a dictator who joined a war that reduced our homes, and our country, to rubble."

"I won't go back," Luigi muttered. Giuseppe knew Luigi didn't have a family, or a home, to go back to, but what was the alternative? To escape? If he was caught, he could be charged and sent back to Italy as a criminal rather than a returned soldier. On the other hand, if he didn't get caught, he could stay here in Australia. Some of the men had grown fond of the country over the last few years. It's warm weather, the laid-back larrikin attitude of most of the people, and the sense that it was a place where they could make a go of things. They'd seen it out on the farms. Giovanni and Carlo had been working on neighbouring farms about half an hour's drive from Marrinup. The owners were good men who didn't mind having a drink with them when the work was done. They'd told them about the opportunities around here to buy farms or build businesses. Australia really was the lucky country.

"Are you going to try and escape?" Carlo asked. Luigi shrugged and shook his head.

"I don't know. I guess so. What choice is there?"

"You could go back to Italy and try to come back legally. There are a lot of Italian families living here who came out years ago. Although, now the men are in internment camps." Domenico had been quiet up to this point. Confusion filled the air as the others exchanged puzzled glances. This was the first they'd heard of internment camps. "My boss told me about it. The Australian government rounded up all the Italians and Germans. They called them enemy aliens. Some had been living here for years, but that didn't matter. There are camps all over the place—Bunbury, Harvey, Kalgoorlie." Giuseppe wondered why Maggie or Richard hadn't told him about this. Were his relatives in these internment camps? Were they going to be let out now that the war was over?

"What happened to their farms and businesses?" Luigi asked.

"Some were sold. Some men have their family and friends looking after them."

"So, they'll let those men go now?" Giuseppe asked.

"I guess so." Domenico shrugged, as he went into the hut. Giuseppe nodded to the others and continued on. He needed to think.

He walked the familiar track around the edge of the camp, but he wasn't alone. Others were wandering around the camp too, his thoughts mirrored on their faces. He passed the guard tower and waved a greeting to Officer Halliday, who returned it with a nod. Giuseppe was overwhelmed by a range of emotions, but betrayal was the one that lingered. He thought he'd become friends with Richard. They'd talked a lot while they worked. He really missed him now that he was away fighting, but why hadn't he told him about these other camps? Had it just slipped his mind? The long days hadn't been the same without Richard there, helping him wrangle the brumbies and mend the never-ending lengths of the fence. George had been a firm but fair boss, but when Giuseppe knocked back his offer, he'd told the guards that Joe wasn't needed at the farm. Then he'd called by the camp a month later to ask Major Murray if Joe could return. He'd often wondered what had made George change his mind.

***

As the morning turned into afternoon, the cool and crisp air transformed into an oppressive heat. Giuseppe to sweat profusely as he lay beneath the tractor. Turning the wrench on the jammed bolt, he felt it shift quickly. His hand slipped, and his knuckles hit the metal hard.

"*Fanculo.*"

"Hurt yourself, mate?" Giuseppe hit his head as he scrambled out from under the tractor. One hand on his head, the other raised in the air. He stood and looked at the figure before him. He knew the man well enough, but something about him had changed, something other than the fact he was missing an arm. Giuseppe broke into a smile and hugged the man, patting him on the back. "You are home. This is good news. Everyone will be so glad to see you." Richard's smile was fleeting and didn't reach his eyes.

"Truth be told, I'm not sure I'm ready to see them yet." Giuseppe looked around. The yard was empty, so he gestured to the truck. He watched Richard haul himself in, then grabbed some water and the slice Maggie had brought him earlier. He drove to the farthest corner of the farm, near the little shack, before shutting off the engine. They walked to the river bank and sat under a large

Jarrah tree. He pulled off his boots and socks, then stood in the shallows, letting the water bring his body temperature down. He bent and splashed water over his face, then walked back and sat beside Richard. The sun filtered through the branches, the water flowed past, and the air was fresh except for the slightest hint of cow dung. They ate in silence. Richard would talk if he wanted to. Pushing him into it wouldn't help. Giuseppe laid back on the grass with his arms bent under his head and closed his eyes.

"They came out of the jungle before we knew what was happening. There were so many of them. I'd just lifted my rifle when I was hit. I looked down at my arm, and I knew they wouldn't be able to save it." Giuseppe opened his eyes and squinted at Richard, who was staring at the water. He didn't dare say anything. He waited for Richard to continue in his own time.

"It happened a month or so ago. The infirmary was... I still hear their cries in my sleep. I can see the horror on Johnno's face as the bullet hit his skull." Richard's shoulders trembled as he silently cried. Giuseppe sat up and watched the water. Slowly, Richard composed himself. "What's Joan going to think of me? I won't even be able to hold Grace. And the farm. How will I look after this place and my own?" Richard fell silent, and Giuseppe seized the opportunity to speak.

"I know you are worried. But I have seen you and Joan. She will not care about this." He waved at Richard's side. "And Grace will just be glad to have her Pappa home. As for the farm, I will be here as long as I can." Richard gave him a half smile.

"Thanks, mate."

"Would you like to hear my news?" Giuseppe said with a smirk.

"Maggie and I got married." Richard's face lit up.

"That's great. Does Dad know?"

"Not yet," Giuseppe said, grinning. Richard threw his head back and laughed.

"Gee, I hope I'm around when he finds out. You'll need someone to stop him from killing you."

"What? You think he will not welcome his new son-in-law into the family with open arms?" The two men burst into laughter again.

By the time Giuseppe pulled the truck back into the shed, it was almost time to walk up the driveway and wait for his lift back to camp.

"Come to the house with me." It was more a question than an order, but Giuseppe obliged. As they neared the verandah, Elizabeth came out the door carrying a tray laden with lemonade and scones. The next minute felt like it happened in slow motion. Elizabeth saw Richard and her mouth dropped open. The tray fell from her hands. She started yelling his name and running towards him. She noticed his missing arm and missed a step, almost falling over. She recovered, reached him and hugged him tight. "Oh, my boy. Richard. I'm so glad you're home," Elizabeth cried into his shoulder. George, Maggie, and Joan, with Grace on her hip, came outside to see what the commotion was. It seemed as if everyone had the same reaction. Their faces lit up at the sight of Richard, then startled when they registered his missing limb before they composed themselves and smiled again. George hugged him quickly before stepping back. Maggie faltered before gently squeezing him in a hug and then moving away to allow

Joan and Grace through.

"Hello, sweetheart," Richard said to Joan. "I hope you don't mind being married to a cripple." He said it with a smile, but it was clear that he was worried about her reaction. At first, Giuseppe thought Joan was going to cry, but she gathered herself together, lifted Grace higher on her hip, and folded into Richard's embrace. The little family stayed like that, murmuring to each other until Grace started to cry. Maggie's eyes were filled with sadness as she looked at Giuseppe, and he instinctively moved closer to her. He wanted to hug her and tell her that everything was all right, that Richard was still himself, that nothing would change, but he couldn't. Not because George and Elizabeth were standing a few feet away, but because he knew Richard was a changed man in more ways than one.

As they sat down for dinner that night, he relayed the news to Luigi and the others.

"He'll learn to live with the dreams. We all have them, *si*?" Luigi said as he looked around the table. The others agreed.

"First, they lost James, and now Richard comes back like this." Giuseppe shook his head.

"It's not unusual. Think of how many of our people back home are living with that sort of news as well. For all we know, some of these men's families might think they're dead," Luigi said as he lifted a hand, gesturing around the room. He was right. From what Giuseppe could gather from his mother's letters, their town had lost many young men. His best friend Antonio among them. His mother relayed the heartbreak of the Calabrese family at losing their only son. Giuseppe had vowed to visit them when he returned home. Whispers had begun to circulate the camp of another impending escape attempt. Each time it happened, the men left behind wondered if they were brave enough to do the same.

Maggie was waiting for him when he returned to Jarrah Downs the following Monday. The soft morning sunshine cast a beautiful glow across her face as she sat on the gate.

"Have a great day," Officer Halliday said with a wink as he drove off. Giuseppe turned to Maggie. Her slightly furrowed brow was the only sign that something was wrong, but she hid it behind a smile as he approached.

"*Buongiorno, Bellissima*." He put his arms around her and gently lifted her down, kissing her as he set her on the ground. They started down the driveway hand in hand. Giuseppe waited as Maggie mentioned how lovely the sunshine was and how she was glad it was going to be a pleasant day.

"What it is?" he asked. She looked at him, her eyes filled with a mixture of curiosity and hesitation.

"There's something wrong with Richard," she said. He gently pressed her hand, and she continued. "Joan says he tosses and turns all night and ends up going and sitting in the kitchen. That's on the nights when he doesn't wake up screaming. He cries when he watches Grace play. He gets angry when he can't do something with only one arm, and he's quieter than usual. He's just not himself."

"Of course not. He has been to war and lost an arm because of it.

He has seen awful things, horrible things. Things that I cannot even say to you." He shuddered before he continued. "It is hard to turn your mind off to it. Believe me, I know." Maggie stopped and turned to him.

"Can you help him?" She looked up at him expectantly, and he wished he could help, but he knew there wasn't much he could do.

"I will do what I can, but I cannot promise anything. I think every man deals with this on his own." Maggie pondered his answer, then grabbed his hand and started walking again.

"So, what does *Bellissima* mean?" she asked.

"Beautiful. And so you are." Giuseppe winked and felt his stomach flip as a smile spread across her face. "Do you think you can meet me by the river today?"

"Yes. I've got the day off, and Mum and Dad are going to Perth to see one of Dad's friends." They kissed and parted as the house came into view.

Concentration eluded Giuseppe. He overfilled the horse trough, cut a length of wood a yard too short despite measuring it twice, and almost took a swig of oil instead of water. His mind was on Maggie and what he hoped would happen later in the day. The cows he was trying to move must have sensed he wasn't really up for the task. He sighed and followed a cow that had strayed off from the herd.

"You need to be quicker than that." George was standing near the gate, watching the scene play before him. He opened the gate and Giuseppe's body tightened. Does he know about Maggie and me? Is he coming to tell me to get off the farm again? Giuseppe folded his arms across his chest. "You've been doing this for years, Joe. I'd have thought you'd have it down pat, but I guess your mind is elsewhere." Giuseppe tried not to smile. If he only knew, he thought. He turned to face the older man and noticed that he seemed to have aged. Perhaps the shock of losing one son and having another return handicapped had taken a toll. He looked tired, not angry, so Giuseppe relaxed his arms at his sides. "With the war over, you must be thinking about home. I spoke with Major Murray. He said the camp will continue on while the government sorts a few things out. I imagine they'll close the internment camps first. Those men didn't fight against ours." He shot a look at Giuseppe. "Then they'll work with Italy and Germany to get you lot back to where you came from. It shouldn't take more than a few months, I'd imagine." He waited for a response. Giuseppe took a moment to gather his thoughts. Now, he had some accurate information about what was going to happen to him and his fellow prisoners. And he knew he had a few more months left with Maggie. It seemed that George was no longer concerned about him now that he knew he was going to be sent back to Italy sooner rather than later. Giuseppe weighed his words. He didn't want to give anything away or offer false hope.

"Yes. I am happy this war is finally over, and I can start my life again." Satisfied, George nodded and walked back towards the gate. He turned back and called out, "Well, we're off. Richard is staying here tonight to keep an eye on things. See you tomorrow." Giuseppe waved and turned back to the cows, pondering his situation. A few months left of being forced to live in a prison camp with 1300 other men and working on a farm that wasn't his, but also, a few months left of being able to see Maggie almost every day.

He checked the clock in the shed. It was time to head to the river. He grabbed a small roll of wire and put it over his shoulder. Then, he walked out of the shed and took the long way past the house and around the dam before arriving at the little clearing. Maggie was lying on her back on a blanket, reading. His eyes travelled up her exposed legs. Dropping the wire, he lay down next to her and draped his arm across her middle.

"I spoke with your dad earlier." Maggie rolled onto her side, and they faced each other. "I have a few more months before I am sent back to Italy." Her lip quivered. He reached up and cupped the side of her face, then kissed her softly. They made love in the dappled shade, with the river quietly flowing beside them. As they lay in the contented afterglow, he tried to brush aside the feeling of impending disaster that had settled in his stomach.

The rotting streamers from the heady days post-war still lingered on the poles and fences of Colton months after the celebrations ended. The fear and uncertainty that everyone had felt during the war was quickly replaced with a renewed sense of hope. Maggie had felt it and seen it in people's faces as they began to relax back into their regular routines. On her way into the surgery, Maggie pulled on a piece of purple streamer that had lodged itself onto the gates. She unlocked the door and threw the streamer remnants in the bin before settling at her desk by the window. She checked the diary. She was in for a busy day, but at least that would make the time go quicker. Deciphering Doctor Mosely's notes and rewriting them neatly into a new patient's file, she was startled when she heard a noise in his office. She looked around the room but nothing seemed out of place, so she crept towards his office. She rounded the doorframe and found the doctor sitting at his desk, rifling through a stack of papers.

"Doctor Mosely, I thought you weren't here yet," she said. He jolted, then looked at her with wide eyes.
"Maggie. You're here. Good. There's something we need to discuss before the first patient arrives." Maggie began fidgeting with the hem of her blouse. She was certain she'd locked up the day before and that the new patient files were all in order. Surely, he would not ask her to rethink her nursing training? Doctor

Mosely stood behind his desk, twirling a pen and switching from one foot to the other.

"You're a fantastic employee. You're good with the patients and know how to keep things in order and, more importantly, confidential. But I'll have to let you go." Maggie blinked a few times, unsure she'd heard correctly.

"Pardon me?"

"Your recent nuptials have been brought to my attention. You know married women aren't allowed to work." She stood completely stunned and speechless. She opened and closed her mouth, but couldn't seem to form the right words. The shock on her face made the doctor keep talking. "Look, I think it's a terrible rule. Women can work just as well married as they can without a husband. But this directive has come straight from the medical board, and I can't go against their decision." Maggie finally found her voice.

"But I need this job, Doctor Mosely. Isn't there anything you can do?" He ran a hand through his thinning hair.

"I'm afraid my hands are tied, Maggie. I wish I could help, but I can't. If I go against the medical board, I could lose my license." Maggie stood motionless. The only sound came from the tapping of the pen and the rushing in her head. This wasn't happening. How would she be able to save for her new life with Joe if she didn't have a job? How did the medical board find out? Someone must have told them. No doubt Mrs high and mighty herself, Emma Fulton.

"How did they find out?" she asked.

"I honestly don't know, and I don't think they'd tell me if I asked.

My guess is someone from Colton doesn't like what you and Joe have done." Maggie raised an eyebrow. "Don't look at me like that. I have absolutely nothing against it. And I think you're an amazing worker. I certainly don't want to let you go. I'll be run off my feet again." There was a knock on the door. They looked at each other before the doctor shrugged. Indignation ran through her before dissipating with the doctor's aftershave as he left the room. This was unfair. She could work just as well now as she did a few months ago. But there was nothing she could do about the situation. The system was broken. She returned to the reception area and put her few personal items into her handbag. She threw her favourite notebook into her bag and took one last look at her desk before turning on her heel and marching out of the door, ignoring the astonished look on the faces of the waiting patients.

Maggie marched towards the car. She wasn't in the mood to speak to anyone. She kicked at a rock on the path and watched it hit a fence.

"Hey, stranger." She'd recognise that voice anywhere. She swivelled and saw Patricia coming towards her arm-in-arm with a beau. His hat was pulled low over his eyes. He wasn't wearing a uniform, but Maggie assumed it was one of the soldiers Patricia had talked about in her letters.

"Patty, you're back! It's so good to see you." She strode towards them but hesitated as they came out of the shadow of the trees.

"Thomas?" The smirk on his face made her skin crawl.

"Hello, Maggie. How are you? How's Richard?" he asked, casually. Maggie answered, her voice laced with forced politeness. She looked at Patricia and asked how long she'd been back in Colton.

"Only a few days, but I have so much to tell you," Patricia said, then turned and told Thomas she'd meet him in the store. After planting a quick peck on her cheek, he shot Maggie a smug look before striding across the street.

"Isn't he a dreamboat? He's been so wonderful since I got back. And while I was away, actually. He sent me quite a few letters. It was a lovely surprise when he knocked on our door and asked if I'd like to go to his house for dinner. We've practically been inseparable since then. Sorry, I didn't tell you I was coming home. I wanted it to be a surprise, and by the look on your face, I'd say it was." Maggie could see the glint in Patricia's eyes and the glow that radiated from her, and she knew exactly how she felt. She'd written to Patricia plenty of times over the last few years but hadn't told her about what had happened with Thomas, and by the looks of it, Thomas had kept quiet, too.

Maggie's letters were full of news of Colton, and she'd mentioned Joe a few times but hadn't told her about their relationship. It had felt wrong to write about her happiness while her friend was dealing with death and destruction every day. Patricia had written about some of the awful things that had happened to her and other nurses overseas. Maggie didn't want to ruin her bliss.

"It certainly was. That's lovely to hear, though. I'm glad you're happy," Maggie said with a smile. Patricia beamed back.

"I am happy. So happy, in fact, that I'm getting married." Maggie froze for a moment. If Patty was marrying Thomas, surely she should tell her what had happened? But did it matter now that she was already married? Maggie hugged her.

"That's wonderful news. Best wishes in the world, Patty. You deserve it." Maggie's eyes followed Patricia as she made her way across the street and into the busy entrance of Williams General Store. She held a hand to her knotted stomach. She had decided not to tell her, but would Thomas keep it quiet too? She didn't want to see her friend get hurt, but she had the distinct feeling that Thomas didn't care who he hurt.

As she made her way back to Jarrah Downs, the drive only deepened her melancholy. Joe was mending the water pump near the trough but stopped when he noticed her approach. She sat on the ground next to him and told him about what had transpired that morning.

"I can't believe Doctor Mosely let me go. How will we save for our future now? And I don't like keeping secrets from Patricia, but I also don't want to hurt her. What do you think I should do?"

"Well, we cannot do much about your job if that is the law. And I do not know what you should do about Patricia." She looked across at him. She had expected more of a response, and he was usually more attentive when they talked.

"What's wrong?" she asked. He shifted so that he sat across from her.

"I have something to tell you. I should have told you a while ago." The knot in her stomach returned. How many revelations would she have to deal with in one day? "Your father came to me a few months ago with an offer." Maggie bristled as Joe paused and looked towards the house as if George might hear what he was about to disclose. "He told me if I left you alone, he would give me £10,000." Maggie's jaw dropped, and she sat back on her heels. Joe moved forward. "That was before we married." He picked up her hand. "Your father does not know me at all. I would never have chosen money over you." Maggie leapt to her feet, anger rising in her, and her breath coming faster and faster.

"I can't believe he would do such a thing. Did he think I'd forget about you and marry Thomas? This is ridiculous. Who does he think he is?" She clenched her fists and turned towards the house. Joe stood quickly.

"Wait. What are you going to do?"

"I'm going to have it out with him once and for all. I'm not a pawn in his game. I make my own decisions." Joe turned her away from the house. His hands enclosed her upper arms, and he gently squeezed them before pulling her to him.

"I can see how this upsets you, but if you say anything, he will know that I told you. It might cause trouble for me. He might send me away again." Maggie looked up into his eyes and could feel her breath becoming slower and steadier. He was right. Her father would know that Joe had told her, but something had to be done. She couldn't let him get away with this.

"I need to do this, Joe." He looked across the paddock for a few seconds before his gaze returned to hers. Then he nodded.

"All right. But please wait until I am not here." Maggie agreed and relaxed back onto the ground. "So, you are not angry with me?" he asked as he sat next to her.

"Why would I be angry with you? It was my father who was wrong.

I mean, you should have told me when it first happened, but you've told me now." Joe smiled, then went back to mending the water pump, leaving Maggie to consider how to broach the subject with her father.

Maggie sat in her favourite chair in the sitting room, looking out at the sky painted with hues of orange and pink. Joe was safely back at Marrinup, and when she heard the car pull up, she knew her father was home from the council meeting. She watched the clock and waited ten minutes before marching into the study. George looked up at her and smiled.

"Maggie dear, how are you?" His smile faded when he noticed the look on her face. Maggie stood on the opposite side of the desk, narrowed her eyes, took a deep breath and launched into the speech she'd rehearsed a million times in her head that afternoon.

"I know about your offer to Joe. How dare you gamble with my life, my feelings, and my future! You had no right to do that. I'll never marry Thomas or any other boy from around here, and you know why? Because I'm already married...to Joe." Inwardly, she enjoyed the shock on her father's face. Outwardly, she held her head higher, waiting for his response. He flustered, and his cheeks flushed pink.

"You can't be. Who would? How? I think you're mistaken."

"I am not mistaken. Joe's my husband. We were married by a Catholic priest. And furthermore, I no longer want to live under the same roof as a man who would treat me like cattle he can buy and sell to the highest bidder. I'm moving into the shack tonight."

She turned and rushed to her bedroom, ignoring the yells behind her. She snatched her suitcase from beneath the bed and frantically tossed clothes in. She dragged it from her room, stopping in front of the linen press to gather candles, matches, and blankets. In the kitchen, she bent down and rummaged through the cupboards for food and cooking implements her mother wouldn't miss. The back door opened, and she jumped and banged her head on the cupboard.

"What's going on?" Elizabeth asked, her brow creased with worry. Maggie's words rushed out in a stream. Elizabeth pulled her close, rubbing her back. As if struck by a blow, Maggie reeled back to look at her mother.

"Did you know? Were you in on it?" Elizabeth's eyes widened.

"I assure you, I was not. I wholeheartedly agree that your father shouldn't have done that. He went behind my back as much as yours. But, is staying in the Shack the answer to all of this?"

"It is for now." Maggie picked up her suitcase and started for the door.

"Wait," Elizabeth called after her. "You'll need more than that." Elizabeth pulled out a bag and started filling it with more food and cooking utensils. George walked into the kitchen just as Elizabeth handed the bag to Maggie.

"For goodness sake, Lizzy, don't enable her." Elizabeth raised her eyebrows as she looked at George.

"I beg your pardon. I'll help my daughter in whatever way I want to. Thank you very much." George's mouth gaped as Elizabeth stalked out of the kitchen and helped Maggie carry the bags over to the stables.

"Thanks, Mum," Maggie said, hugging her tightly.
"You know I would do anything for you, for any of you children. Even defy your father if need be." Maggie let go and looked at her mother as if seeing her for the first time, then she mounted Lily and waved as she galloped towards the shack.

Lily stood patiently as Maggie secured her to the hitching rail. Maggie would have to sort out better accommodations for her tomorrow. She hauled her suitcase and bag up to the old weatherboard one-roomed building and pushed on the jammed door. It opened in a rush, and she stumbled into the stuffy room. The fading light struggled to penetrate the dirt-covered windows, casting a dim glow. There was no electricity, so she lit a candle and set it on the wobbly wooden table to her right. The interior was bathed in light, exposing the cobwebs and the layer of dust that coated everything. The shack had minimal furniture and fittings. Aside from the table, it contained a sink built into a low cupboard with no doors, two wooden chairs, and a bedframe covered with a mattress that sagged almost to the floor. Maggie sighed and resigned herself to the task ahead.

Grabbing an old blouse from her suitcase, she turned to the sink and used both hands to turn the tap. As rust-coloured water spluttered out, she sent a silent prayer up and waited for it to clear before wetting the material. She spent the next hour wiping everything in sight, sweeping out cobwebs and mountains of dust, setting up the kitchen, and making the bed. After she finished, every muscle in her body ached and her head pulsed with pain.

She moved the candle to a stump that acted as a bedside table before blowing it out and giving in to exhaustion.

A kookaburra's laugh pierced her dreams. Maggie stretched and opened her eyes. Sunlight streamed through the now clean windows, bathing the room in a warm, inviting light. Maggie took in the space. Now that it was clean and she'd set up her things, the shack felt cosy. She dressed and went outside to greet Lily and give her breakfast. The sun was coming up over the trees and the air was cool. She closed her eyes and breathed deeply. It was a new day, the start of her new life, and she felt a sense of calm run through her body.

Maggie spent the morning working in and around the shack, making it as comfortable as possible. She had expected her mother or father to come looking for her and felt a mixture of relief and disappointment that they hadn't. Did they think this was a whimsy and she'd be back under their roof tonight? Were they giving her time to calm down? Maggie didn't need time to calm down. She had done nothing wrong. It was her father who needed to think about what he'd done. He had interfered in her life one too many times. He wanted what was best for her; that was obvious, but he didn't know what was best for her. She was the mistress of her own destiny, and that destiny included Joe.

Whistling as she collected small branches down by the river, she didn't hear the horse approach.

"Things went well then," Giuseppe said with a grin. She burst out laughing.

"I wouldn't exactly say that. But I think this is for the best. I need my own space and we need somewhere we can be together, at least until we know what's going to happen to you. Have you heard any more news?" Joe shook his head and raised a shoulder. He turned to survey the little cottage, and Maggie watched his face. The war had officially ended months ago, but nothing had changed for the men at Marrinup. She'd never say it, but in a way, Maggie didn't mind because it meant that Joe wasn't going anywhere. She knew it was selfish to think that way.

"So, this is ours then?" he asked. Maggie took his hand and led him over to the shack. "Wait." He turned her around and, in one swift movement, bent and scooped her up into his arms before walking through the door. They laughed as he gently placed her upright and looked around the room and back at Maggie.

"It's not much, I know."

"It is *perfetto*," Joe said. He grinned and pulled her into his arms, then turned his head and nodded towards the bed with a wink. Maggie let him lead her towards it. Afterwards, they lay with their hands entwined in the air in front of them, making plans for their future. Maggie rolled over and leaned one hand on her head, the other playing with his fingers that lay across his chest.

"You know, this shack is pleasant, but it's missing something," she said.

"What?" His brows furrowed and a look of confusion crossed his face. She waited a beat before answering.

"A crib." For a second, the puzzled look remained before realisation spread across his face.

"We are having a baby." It was more of a question than a statement, but Maggie nodded and fell into his outstretched arms. "Well, I'm fairly certain we are." Maggie hadn't menstruated for two months. She'd wanted to talk to Joan about it first, but telling Joe now had felt right.

"You will be an amazing mother. And I am going to be the best father I can be." Maggie knew he meant every word. She lay next to him and listened as he talked about all the things he would do with the child growing inside her. She smiled and basked in the glow of sharing the good news for a while longer before getting up to make them both some lunch.

Down by the river, Joe dragged over a fallen log for them both to sit on while they ate.

"You have not told your parents, have you?" Joe asked. Maggie shook her head. It had been playing on her mind for weeks, but with everything that had happened lately, she figured everyone had enough to worry about. "I have not seen George today. I can only imagine what will happen when I do." Maggie stared at the water. Surely, her father wouldn't punish Joe for this?

"I would avoid him for a few days if I were you. He knows I know about the offer. And he knows we're married. He'll need to get used to that before I tell him we're having a baby."

"You will have to tell your parents eventually." Joe leaned over and kissed her goodbye, then headed towards the dam, leaving her to her thoughts. She accepted she would have to tell her parents about the pregnancy, but the thought of doing that terrified her far more than telling them she was married. She blamed her reluctance on all that had happened—the war, losing James, and Richard's injury, but in reality, she was frightened of what they would think. She also had to admit that as much as she wanted this baby, she was scared. Becoming a mother was always part of her plans, but it seemed like a far-off dream, not something that was going to happen so soon.

Giuseppe dug his hands into the warm soil and lifted out a handful of dirt and potatoes. He rubbed the potatoes clean and dropped them into the bucket beside him. He looked over at Luigi, who sat back on his haunches and took a swig of water from his canteen. He hadn't told Luigi the latest development. Although it was something to celebrate, he felt that keeping it to himself was the best approach. Luigi's mood had been unpredictable lately, and he didn't want to give him a reason to spiral downward. Luigi's boss had accused him of stealing, and he'd had to stay at camp while the investigation was pending. While Giuseppe's relationship with Maggie flourished, a pang of guilt washed over him when he thought about Luigi's hardships. He gently tipped his bucket of potatoes on the ground in front of Luigi. He knew a taste of home always made the men feel better.

"Gnocchi tonight?" he asked. Luigi smiled and counted the potatoes before placing them back into the bucket. The two men walked the short distance to the kitchen at the back of the mess. They didn't mind taking their turn at cooking duty, and Sundays were easier because they had more time to prepare a decent meal. They washed up and started peeling the pile of potatoes on the bench. Giuseppe nicked his thumb with the knife and ran it under the tap before covering it with a towel. A shadow fell over the open door, and Cambino surveyed their haul.

"Three less for dinner tonight," he said as he sat on a stool and took a long swig of water.

"What do you mean?" Giuseppe asked.

"Nobody can find Gallo, Costa, and Moretti. They must have made a run for it last night. The police are onto it, but I don't think they'll find them or even look too hard, for that matter," Cambino said with a one-shouldered shrug. "Parson and Grady were very talkative last night after a couple of glasses of Gunter's schnapps. It sounds like we're not going anywhere just yet, but there'll be some changes around here." Giuseppe threw the towel in the wash bag and picked up the knife again.

"I noticed they didn't have the parade on Friday, and the gate between the Germans and us has been left open for two days now," Luigi said. Giuseppe agreed that the lack of parade had been a welcome start to the morning, but the news about the latest escape was no surprise. For the past few years, men had been finding ways to escape from Marrinup. Some had made it as far as Perth, but they'd been caught every time. But with the war officially over, how would the Australians feel about their escape attempts? Would they allow them to walk away with no repercussions? Giuseppe filled a large pot with water, set it to boil, and then turned back to the others. His life revolved around Maggie and the baby now. Could he escape, and would Maggie come with him?

"Don't even think about it, *amico*. It won't work," Luigi warned.

"Why not?" Giuseppe asked. Cambino stood and headed for the door.

"If I don't hear it, I can't speak about it," he said with a wave before he disappeared. Luigi put down the potato and knife and looked squarely at Giuseppe.

"You have nowhere to go. You cannot take Maggie away from her family. You need to go home and try to come back legally." Giuseppe sighed heavily.

"What about you? What are you going to do?"

"That's different. There's nothing here for me. I'll go back to Italy." He didn't want to admit Luigi was right. He had to start his new life with Maggie the right way.

***

With his morning's work completed, Giuseppe walked along the river towards the shack. He heard singing as he approached and stopped to listen for a moment with his face towards the sun and his eyes closed. As the weeks went by, he'd been spending more and more of his day at the shack. Richard ignored his absences as long as the work was done, but neither George nor Elizabeth had spoken to him about Maggie's move. Perhaps they were just biding their time until he was sent home. He brushed the notion aside before opening the door. Maggie and Joan were sitting at the table, their fingers busy weaving paper chains, as Grace perched on the soft rug, playing with colourful ribbons. Christmas was just a few days away, and the two women had been busy decorating the shack. Since it was the first Christmas after the war officially ended, it seemed to Giuseppe that everyone wanted to make it a memorable one.

"This place looks *Bellissima*," he exclaimed. The two women obviously hadn't heard him come in because they both dropped their chains and let out a brief shriek.

"Don't sneak up on us like that," Maggie admonished. Giuseppe surrendered with his hands in the air before giving Maggie a peck on the cheek. "Could you please tie this chain up to that rafter?" Maggie asked, handing him a long, colourful paper chain. He reached up and hitched it to the rafter before taking the next one offered by Joan.

"I was just telling Maggie how much better Richard has been. I think I need to thank you for that. He told me the two of you talk sometimes," Joan said, holding up the string and scissors.

"It's nothing," Giuseppe responded. Although, in truth, he felt that his talks with Richard were mutually beneficial. Since the day he returned and they sat by the river, they'd often had lunch together, away from the homestead and shed when the weather permitted.

In an effort to lighten their load, both men opened up and shared the burden of their dreams and memories. He looked at Maggie and saw a scowl pass across her face before she composed herself. Was she mad at him? Did she expect him to tell her these things? The conversations with Richard were not for women to hear.

"Well, thank you anyway," Joan said before adding, "Do you think the guards will let you spend Christmas Day here? Elizabeth and George are hosting lunch, and it's only fitting that you join us now that you two are married." Giuseppe balked at the idea. He wanted to spend more time with Maggie, and her parents were aware of their nuptials, but they didn't know about the baby. They hadn't even spoken to him directly about Maggie moving into the shack. As for the guards, they had become more lenient, but was

it enough to let him be away from camp for longer periods?
"I am not sure what the guards will say. I do not think I would be
welcome here, anyway." Joan frowned and bent to pick Grace up.
Maggie came to stand in front of him with her hands on her hips.
"Well, you're my husband, and if they don't like it, that's just too
bad. I'm going over there this afternoon to tell them you're
coming. You just square it away with Major Murray." Giuseppe
knew from the set of her jaw that her mind was made up and that
he'd be joining the Sleeman's for lunch on Christmas Day.

Later that evening, he walked to the guard's quarters and
knocked on the door of the largest hut. Major Murray answered,
dressed in civilian clothes. From the moment he arrived, Murray
had shown unwavering respect for all the prisoners in his care. He
didn't act like a dictator and abuse his position of authority as his
predecessor had. Giuseppe knew what he was about to ask for
was a huge favour that Murray had every right to refuse. He ran
his hands through his hair as he greeted the older man.
"You look like a man on a mission. You'd better come in." He
moved aside and held the door open. The hut was furnished with
a large bed, a sturdy desk, and leather chair, a small settee, and
a dresser with a radio on top. The walls displayed charcoal
drawings of the camp and vignettes of the surrounding bushland
and its inhabitants. Giuseppe's eyes honed in on a picture of two
kookaburras perched together on a branch. He squinted at the
signature in the bottom right corner.
"Did you draw all of these?" Murray nodded. "*Bellissima.*
Beautiful." Giuseppe swallowed the lump in his throat and turned

back to face him.

"Thank you, Mr Russo. But I think you're here for something other than to view my amateur art." Giuseppe's face flushed with colour as he shifted his weight from one foot to the other, his stomach churning with nerves and his palms moist with sweat.

"Major, I was wondering what your thoughts were on some of us spending Christmas Day at work. On the farms, I mean," he said. He watched and waited as Murray considered his reply.

"It would be against the rules, but at this point, I believe the rules need to change." Murray moved to the dresser and poured two small glasses of rum. He handed one to Giuseppe before taking a sip of his own. "Look, Mr Russo. Can I call you Giuseppe? The war is over, but I'm still under orders to keep Marrinup going, and I intend to follow those orders." He stopped to take a sip. "However, should a respected prisoner happen to not come back from work on a day of celebration, the guards might be inclined to look the other way."

Giuseppe let out a slow breath before thanking him. "Before you go, I think there's something else we need to discuss." Giuseppe stopped. He placed his glass down on the dresser, then shoved his hands in his pockets so Murray couldn't see them shake. "I heard about your recent wedding. I offer my congratulations, but I feel I must also offer a word of caution. Men are escaping from camps all over Australia more frequently than ever. I understand it must be frustrating for you. Nevertheless, I urge you to follow the process. Do things the correct way, and you'll be able to return to Australia without the government breathing down your neck."

Giuseppe nodded. Murray was right. He couldn't even think about escaping. There was too much at stake. He thanked Murray again and bid him goodnight before leaving him to enjoy his rum.

***

On the morning of Christmas Eve, Giuseppe rose later than usual and packed some clothes and a parcel into a sack.

"I hope old Sleeman doesn't kill you when he finds out what you've done." Luigi laughed. Giuseppe rolled his eyes and shook his head. Trust Luigi to set his nerves on edge before he'd even left camp. "Easy. It was a joke," Luigi said with his hands in the air. "I'll walk you to the gate." There were only a few people out and about as the two men made their way through the camp. The prisoners were granted a few days off work, so many took the opportunity to sleep in.

"At least I don't have to explain this to anyone," Giuseppe said as they reached Officer Grady at the gates. He was the only prisoner heading to work, so Grady let him sit up front. *"Buon Natale, amico,"* he called through the open window. Luigi reciprocated and waved back.

The day was already heating up, and Giuseppe felt his body warming with the heat coming through the windscreen as they made the short drive.

"I'll see you back here in two days, then," Grady said as he pulled away. Giuseppe looked at him, his eyebrows furrowing as he raised his hands, questioning what he meant. "Murray's orders." Giuseppe stood frozen for a moment as the words registered. Then he thanked him and watched the truck drive away.

221

Richard, Joan, and Maggie were standing under the large willow tree. He dropped the sack at his feet, then put his arm around Maggie's waist.

"What are you all doing out here?" he asked. "Has something happened? Am I not allowed to be here?" Maggie put a hand to her chest and scoffed before breaking into a laugh.

"I hope you're ready for your first real Australian Christmas," she said. He tilted his head and she added, "You're coming to lunch tomorrow." His eyebrows shot up.

"We had a hell of a row with Mum and Dad, but in the end, they gave in. Well, the three of us didn't give them much choice." Richard chimed in.

"*Fantastico*! Thank you. You don't know how much this means to me." He hugged Maggie tight, then shook Richard's hand and hugged Joan.

"Right, well. Enough of the pleasantries. Let's crack on before Dad comes out and gives us what for." Richard and Giuseppe headed to the shed while Maggie and Joan went into the house.

They only had a few jobs to finish, and they completed them by lunchtime. Giuseppe emerged from beneath the tractor to find Richard packing away the tools.

"I'm off. See you tomorrow. It's going to be an interesting day," he said. Giuseppe looked towards the homestead and decided to take the long way to the shack. George and Elizabeth might have agreed to have him join them for Christmas lunch, but had they agreed to let him stay at the shack with Maggie? They wouldn't have been able to tell her no, anyway. She was certainly asserting her independence now. Had she told them about the baby yet? He got the impression that Richard and Joan knew. Maggie told Joan everything, but telling her parents was a different matter. George would not react well to the news.

The sun was still high in the sky. Maggie was perched on the log by the river bank. His spirits lifted with the thought of the coming celebration and a few days away from the confines of the camp. "*Buon Natale*! Merry Christmas!" he called out as he approached. He sat next to her and said, "You always seem to surprise me." "What do you mean?" she asked. Richard had told him about the confrontation with their parents and how Maggie had stood up to her father. Right from the start, Giuseppe had perceived her fighting spirit, but for reasons he didn't understand, she had suppressed it. It was only in the last year that she had started taking a stand for herself and he was proud of her for it. "I have something for you." He pulled out a parcel wrapped in a clean pillowcase and handed it to her. She took it and felt the weight, then began to carefully unwrap it. "You didn't have to bring me anything," she said. As she unfolded the last piece of cloth, he watched her face intently. Her face lit up as she held two wooden carvings in her palm and ran her fingers over them. He'd been working for weeks on the figurines of Mary and baby Jesus in a manger. "I am glad you like them. We have a nativity scene on our mantle at home. I thought we should have a set of our own to place here in the shack. I hope we can use it for many Christmases to come." "They're lovely." She held the baby Jesus up and ran her thumb across it. Giuseppe pulled a carving of a sheep from his pocket and laughed, thinking of the amount of swearing he'd heard every time Luigi nicked himself with the knife.

"Luigi made this for you," he said. Maggie took it and placed it on the log beside her, next to the other figures.

"You're both very clever. Wait here. Let me get your present." She jogged to the shack and returned with a large parcel wrapped in brown paper, held together with string. Giuseppe sat on the log and unwrapped his gift. A tan-coloured shirt, long black trousers, and a black button-up jacket fell into his lap. He picked them up and held them to him, measuring their size.

"*Fantastico*. Did you make them yourself?" he asked.

"Yes. With a little help from Joan and Mum. Now you'll have something new to wear to lunch." Giuseppe pulled her into a hug. He had been wondering whether to wear his maroon uniform or his army regalia. Neither had seemed appropriate. They rose and walked towards the shack.

"Do you think things will be all right tomorrow?" he asked. Despite everyone's assurances everything would be fine, he worried there might be a confrontation. She stopped and looked up at him with a smile.

"I think it will be the best Christmas we've all had in years," she said before standing on tiptoes and planting a kiss on his lips.

***

Maggie pulled open the homestead door and stepped in, but Giuseppe stayed on the verandah. He looked at his feet and wiped his hands on his new trousers. Maggie turned back to him, fixed his collar, and looked at him squarely in the eyes.

"Are you ready?" He shrugged a shoulder and raised his hands. "Relax. It will be fine." The radio was on in the background and the smell of roasting meat and vegetables wafted through to them as they walked to the dining room. Richard and George sat at the table, and Joan was standing next to the window holding Grace. "Come in, you two. Take a seat." Richard said, pointing to the space opposite him. Joan smiled at them. Maggie looked at George, but he offered more of a grunt than a greeting. They took their seats and a moment later, Elizabeth called out from the kitchen. Joan and Maggie left to help, and an awkward silence fell on the room. Giuseppe looked around, keeping his eyes everywhere but in George's direction. His stomach churned, and he wrung his hands in his lap. Richard gave him a reassuring smile, but it did little to quell his nerves. Relief washed over Giuseppe when Joan and Maggie returned and deposited dishes onto the table. Maggie sat next to him and he squeezed her hand beneath the table.

Spread before them was more food than Giuseppe had seen in years. A large chicken took pride of place in the middle, and around the sides was roasted pumpkin, potato, and carrot. Covered dishes held steamed beans and peas while a plate was piled high with fresh buns still warm from the oven. Giuseppe's stomach growled loudly, and Elizabeth let out a laugh.
"I think that's our cue to begin," she said. Giuseppe looked at her, and she nodded slightly. After saying grace, George carved the meat, and they filled their plates, chattering about how good the food looked. The conversation flowed easier as their bellies got

fuller.

"How do you celebrate Christmas back home?" Elizabeth asked. Giuseppe swallowed his mouthful and lay his knife and fork on the edge of the plate.

"We attend mass and have a feast at home with all of our family and friends."

"Quite similar to us then," she said, smiling. Giuseppe nodded. There was something about the way Elizabeth looked at George after she said it that made Giuseppe wonder if there was more to her questioning.

After lunch and dessert had been cleared, they moved to the verandah to relax with a drink. The sun was high, but the heat was bearable thanks to a slight breeze. Richard handed Giuseppe a beer. Before taking it, he looked at George and was given a slight nod. He could feel Maggie's eyes on him. He said thanks and took a long sip. George stood up and walked over to where he and Maggie were sitting on the steps.

"Take a walk with me, Joe," he said and gestured to the path. Giuseppe shot a glance at Maggie and the others. Richard shrugged, and the three women looked surprised but encouraging. He didn't really have a choice, and besides, he wanted to hear what the man had to say. The two men fell into step. Giuseppe kept his hands in his pockets and his breath slow and steady, even while his mind was racing. Was George going to offer him money again? Surely not. The man must know by now that he loves Maggie and would do anything to be with her. George stopped and snapped off a tomato.

"Well, Joe, I believe I underestimated you. I thought you'd take the money and run. You really love Maggie, don't you?" Giuseppe agreed but didn't offer more. "I've thought long and hard about this, and I think the time has come for me to accept what's happened." He turned to face Giuseppe. "I don't believe your relationship will be an easy one, and if you break my daughter's heart, I'll never forgive you."

"I do not intend to do that."

"Good. Pretty soon you'll be returned to Italy, and then you'll have to apply to come back to Australia. Elizabeth and I will continue to look after Maggie in your absence, and I'll assist, if I can, to get you back here." Giuseppe shook his head in disbelief. It felt as though one minute George hated him, and now here he was offering to help him. It was unfathomable.

"I... uh... thank you, sir," Giuseppe muttered. George grunted and gestured for them both to return to the house. Giuseppe sat back down on the step next to Maggie. She arched her eyebrows, and he mouthed the word "later." He had to process what had happened before he could speak to her about it.

This is perfect, Maggie thought as she reclined on a towel, watching Joe flick a fishing line into the river. The festive season had been the most wonderful time of Maggie's life. The tension finally subsided as her parents reluctantly embraced her relationship with Joe, putting an end to months of pressure. Everything had fallen into place. As the new year progressed, the rules at Marrinup relaxed even further, and Joe was able to spend more time at Jarrah Downs. He sat next to her with a thud and reached across to stroke her stomach. She'd had to let out her dresses as her flat belly morphed into a little pooch. She often cupped it with both hands, thinking about what the future would bring. Joe bent his head to her stomach and murmured in Italian, then looked up when they heard the familiar gallop of a horse approaching.

"We need some help, Joe," Richard said, jumping down. "We have to get the cattle loaded and need an extra pair of hands. I certainly haven't got enough," he said with a quick smile. Joe walked to the small enclosure next to the shack where Lily and another chestnut mare were grazing.

"I'm coming, too," Maggie said. They saddled up, then raced across the flat, and past the dam towards the back paddock. Maggie reached the gate first and pumped her fist in the air in victory. She dismounted and walked towards the cattle yard, where George was attempting to entice a large cow inside the metal barrier and up onto the ramp. Richard and Joe stood on the other side of the railing.

"In you get, lads. We need these bloody cows loaded," George said. He stood holding the railing, trying to control his breathing. The two men jumped into the enclosure and began clapping and yelling to move the cows on. Maggie looked across at George. His face was red and sweat dripped down his brow. His whole body seemed to expand and contract with each difficult breath. She moved to his side.

"Let me take over for a bit, Dad. We'll get this sorted," she said as she began to climb the railing. There was a commotion at the back of the herd, and the cows surged forward, knocking the barrier; the pins jumped out of the locks, and the railing toppled, taking Maggie with it. The three men raced over and pulled the barrier off her. Maggie struggled to open her eyes, but a wave of dizziness washed over her. She was seized by intense, crippling pain. Her hands flew to her stomach and she let out a scream. She felt Joe put his arms beneath her and pick her up. The men were yelling at each other, but she was in too much pain to comprehend what was being said. She felt dampness between her legs.

"The baby," she cried.

"You will be all right. We are going to take you to the hospital," Joe said, gently lifting her up into the front seat of the truck. He climbed in next to her while George started the engine. The drive into Colton seemed to take forever, and Maggie felt as if she was drifting. This couldn't be happening. She couldn't lose the baby.

She prayed Joe was right and everything would be all right. The dizziness subsided, but the pain in her abdomen did not. Propped between her father and Joe, she couldn't move without inducing more pain. Joe wiped his hand across his face several times, then gently squeezed her hand when he saw her watching. She glanced in her father's direction and noticed his fingers gripping the steering wheel, the knuckles turning white. She closed her eyes. Why had she done that? Why had she climbed up on that railing? What if she lost the baby? George pulled the truck into the hospital car park, narrowly missing a car, then coming to an abrupt stop at the entrance. Joe climbed down and reached for her. She wrapped her arms around his neck and let him lift her out. A nurse met them at the entrance, yelling for a stretcher. Maggie cried out in pain as Joe laid her on it. The emergency room was a jumble of doctors, nurses, and voices calling out. She noticed the lights above her flickering on and off. As she was wheeled away, Joe released her hand, his touch lingering for a moment.

Her mouth felt dry, and she licked her lips as her eyelids fluttered open. In the sunlit hospital room, her mother and Joe stood on opposite sides of the bed, while her father watched from the window. She mumbled, and Elizabeth squeezed her hand. "You're awake. How are you feeling?" Elizabeth said as she held a cup to Maggie's mouth. Maggie tried to sit up, but the pain in the lower half of her body made her flinch and lie back down. "Sore. What about the baby?" She looked at Elizabeth, who looked across at Joe. He blinked slowly and swallowed before answering. Her hands flew to her stomach. She knew what he was going to say.

"We have lost the baby," Joe said. Tears welled in her eyes before one rolled down her cheek. He wiped it away with his fingertip.

"We are so grateful that you are all right. We'll give you two some privacy," Elizabeth said. She squeezed her hand again before gesturing to George. After they'd left the room, Joe settled himself on the bed and gently wrapped his arms around her, providing comfort as she wept.

"I wanted this baby so much. I wanted us to be a family. Now that's not going to happen," she said between sobs.

"Shh... I know," he soothed, "I wanted this too. We will be a family when the time is right." Joe stroked her head. She felt empty as if a void had opened inside her. This wasn't supposed to happen. This baby was going to make them a family. Joe was going to be allowed to stay in Australia. Everything was supposed to turn out right. Maggie turned her face into his shoulder and cried herself into an exhausted sleep.

***

"Maggie dear, you've got a visitor," Elizabeth called out from the verandah. Maggie picked up the basket of vegetables she'd collected. As she rounded the side of the house, she saw Patricia standing on the front steps, talking with her mother.

"Patty, I haven't seen you in an age. How are you?" she said as she reached them, and the two women embraced.

"It seems like we've all been a bit busy lately. I was just stopping by to give you this," she said, handing Maggie an envelope.

231

Maggie slipped out the handwritten card. She and her parents had been invited to attend the wedding of Miss Patricia Hollows and Mr Thomas Williams.

"How exciting! Do you need help to organise anything?" she asked, passing the card to her mother. Patricia looked at Elizabeth and then at Maggie.

"Actually, Maggie, do you think we could talk in private? Sorry, Mrs Sleeman." Maggie hesitated for a second. What was this about? Did she just want to talk about the wedding? Or had Thomas told her what happened while she was away?

"Of course. Excuse us, Mum. We'll go for a walk." Maggie motioned towards the front yard, and they silently made their way down the steps. She knew she wouldn't have to wait long for Patricia to start the conversation.

"Mum convinced me to go to a CWA meeting a few days ago. I hadn't felt like going since I came back. I'd barely been in the hall for five minutes when Kathleen marched up to me and almost dragged me outside." Patricia stopped walking and turned to her. Maggie bristled. "Any idea what gossip she was so eager to pass on?" Patricia glared. After her last run-in with Emma Fulton, the whole of Colton, and probably the whole district, knew about her and Joe. But did Patricia know about Thomas's attempts to court her, and more importantly, did she know about their kiss? She decided to start with the topic that she knew wouldn't have been kept a secret.

"I take it you know about Joe," she said.

"Well, I know now. I can't believe you didn't say anything. You mentioned him in a couple of letters, but I had no idea you'd fallen for him. Why didn't you tell me?"

"I'm sorry. I guess I didn't know how you'd react. With you being so close to the fighting and all." Maggie glanced back at the house and then looked at Patricia. She'd expected annoyance but saw a look of acceptance on her face. She'd known Patricia her whole life. She didn't want to keep secrets from her anymore. "Well, since we're disclosing things, there's something else I need to tell you. Let's go to the shack and have some tea." They hopped in Patty's parents' car and drove to the small building. "Oh, it's lovely. You've done a great job of making it feel like a little home," Patricia exclaimed as she ducked her head and went inside. Over tea and cake, Maggie told her everything about her relationship with Joe, and about the baby she'd miscarried. With Patricia holding her hand, Maggie felt secure in their friendship, and she placed her other hand on top.

"Patty, I have to tell you something and it might be a bit upsetting." Patricia let go of Maggie's hand, folded her arms, and sat back in her seat. "Thomas and I... we courted. Sort of. We kissed," Maggie stammered out her confession, while a look of satisfaction spread across Patricia's face.

"Finally! Maggie, I already know."

"You do?"

"Of course. Do you really think Emma Fulton and her clique wouldn't want to pass on that news as soon as they found out Thomas and I were together?"

"And you're not mad at me?"

"Well, I'm a bit annoyed that you left that bit out. But you know what? Thomas and I are happy. I confronted him, and he told me everything." Patricia took hold of Maggie's hand again. "It's in the past, and I don't want it to come between us. I want you to be at my wedding, and if Joe is still here, he's more than welcome to come, too." Maggie felt relief wash over her.

"How did I get to have a friend like you?" she asked. Patricia shrugged.

"Just lucky, I guess." They spent the afternoon making plans for the wedding. As Maggie waved Patricia off, she was relieved that at least one part of her life was falling into place.

***

Joan dealt the cards with a flourish of her hands. Maggie appraised them and snuck a glance at Joe. The tension between her father and Joe had dissipated in the wake of grief for the little life lost. Perhaps it was the catalyst that George had needed to realise that Maggie was no longer a child but a married woman. Whatever it was, as she glanced at Joan, Richard, and Joe, Maggie felt a warm glow of appreciation that the people she loved most in the world were now getting along.

They'd lost the last round, but Maggie was determined to win this one. Joe took a sip of his beer and peeked over the top of the bottle at their opponents before winking at her. She pulled her lips over her teeth to stifle a smile and inwardly cursed herself for her terrible poker face. Joan held Richard's cards up for him and looked around the room.

"Maggie, you've turned this shack into a perfect little home for you both. Well done," Joan said. In the months since the accident,

Maggie had turned her hand to sewing to keep her mind from dwelling on lost possibilities. The shack had new curtains, tablecloths, bedspreads, and tea towels, while Joe was sporting new shirts and trousers. Richard played his hand, then got up and grabbed himself another beer. He placed it on the bench, then reached across to hand a bottle to Joe before taking his seat.

"Thanks," Maggie said, beaming. "It's kept me busy. I just hope we can stay here for a while longer yet." Richard sat bolt upright and turned to Joe.

"I forgot to tell you. Dad heard from Murray this afternoon. He said they're closing down the camp next week and all the prisoners would be deported. I'm sorry, mate." Maggie gasped.

"For goodness' sake, Richard, you could have told us earlier," she said.

"Would it have mattered? The outcome is the same," Joe replied, his mouth turned down at the corners. Maggie felt her chest tighten. This was it. Joe was really leaving. And nobody could tell her when, or if, he would come back. Her breathing quickened, and she tried to swallow her feelings. She threw her cards on the table and ran out the door.

The moon was full, and the stars were hiding between long, puffy clouds. Standing on the river bank, she folded her arms and looked at the blackness of the water. She perched on the log and rested her head in her hands. Her body trembled with every sob that escaped her. She stiffened when she felt a hand on her shoulder. She hadn't heard Joe come after her. He pulled her up into his arms, his embrace a gentle attempt to ease her pain.

"I am so sorry. I will do whatever I can to get back to you. Please do not cry." He rubbed his hands up and down her back.

"It's not fair. You should be able to stay here," she moaned into the crook of his neck. "We could tell them we're married. Dad could say that you have work and a home here. Surely, that will help your case."

"That might help me to return, but I must go." He held her at arm's length and studied every feature of her face before settling on her eyes. "We have one more week together. I think we should keep living as if nothing is going to change." Maggie saw in his eyes the sadness his words tried to hide. Could she do as he asked? Could she pretend she wasn't about to lose him? As he leaned in, he kissed her with a fervour that sent shivers down her spine. When they parted, she knew she had to do it for him as much as for herself.

***

In the days that followed, Maggie caught herself mulling over the future and had snapped Joe out of his thoughts on more than one occasion. They had tried to continue their routine, pretending that nothing was changing. Maggie spent her days helping where she could with farm duties or visiting Joan and Patricia. Joe continued on as he had for the last few years, stuck between Jarrah Downs and Marrinup. He'd only returned to camp three nights that week, and their last night together had come around all too quickly.

As the morning light filtered through the window, they savoured their last precious moments of privacy before getting ready and riding to the homestead. George had agreed to drive Joe back to

Marrinup and had the car waiting for them when they arrived. Maggie stood back and watched as Joe said goodbye to Elizabeth, Richard, Joan, and Grace. He hugged them each in turn, and Maggie could see that all of them fought to keep their feelings in check. They might have held some hope of Joe's return, but it was clear they also thought they might be saying goodbye for the last time. Her chest tightened and she had to turn away. She felt a hand grab hers and she let Joe lead her to the car. When they reached it, Joe turned to embrace her, and she shook her head.

"I'm coming with you," she said. George puffed his chest and was about to protest when she turned to him. "I have every right to see him off properly." She stared at each of them, daring them to tell her she couldn't go. When nobody said a word, she squeezed past Joe and scooted across the back seat.

The drive to Marrinup was filled with a heavy silence, broken only by the occasional sound of a heavy sigh. Her palms were sweaty and she let go of Joe's hand and folded her arms. She couldn't bring herself to voice her thoughts or look at Joe, so she stared out the window instead. She felt as if she was in a dream. How could such a familiar landscape seem so foreign? They drove down the gravel road towards the looming wooden gates. George spoke with the guard on duty, who peered at them through the back window, and then signalled for the gates to be opened.

Once inside, Maggie gulped as she took in the rows of small huts, the larger halls, the gardens, the guard towers, and the long barbed wire fences surrounding it all. The camp was precisely as Joe had described it. The beauty of the Australian bush, and the creatures that inhabited it, was no match for the brutality of this makeshift prison. How had it felt to be confined here for so many years? How many men had looked into the bush and thought of escaping? She looked across at Joe and wondered if he'd ever contemplated escaping. He squeezed her hand, and she moved over to hug him. There was so much she wanted to say and so many questions she wanted to ask, but now there was no more time.

"It's all right," he murmured in her ear. She didn't want to let go. Joe pulled away and hopped out of the car, walking to her side to open her door. He held a hand out, and she braced herself before taking it.

An older man in uniform was waiting for them in front of a large building.

"Major Murray," Joe whispered to her as she stood beside him. Joe had mentioned how much this man had changed Marrinup for the better since he'd taken over. He was also the man who might have the power to help Joe stay, or at least assist in his return. After polite introductions, Murray motioned towards the office, and they followed his lead. Inside, he stood behind a desk and pushed some paperwork towards the front.

"Would you mind signing this, Mr Sleeman?" Murray said.

"What's this about then?" George asked as he scanned the page.

"It's just to confirm that you've returned Mr Russo, and acknowledge that the contract between yourself and Western Command has come to an end." Murray held out a pen to

George, and Maggie's chest tightened. She had to do something and she had to do it now. Murray needed to know how much she wanted Joe to stay; how much they all wanted him to stay. Maggie let go of Joe's hand and stood in front of Murray, looking up into his face. Murray furrowed his brow and looked from Joe to George, then down at Maggie.

"Major Murray, surely something can be done about this. We all want Joe to stay here in Australia with us. What can we do?" Maggie pleaded, but Murray looked past her. She felt her pulse quicken with anger and frustration. Did this man know he was destroying her life? Did he even care? She looked back at her father and Joe, but they shook their heads.

"Mrs Russo. I'm sorry, but this is the way it has to be," Murray said, keeping his eyes focused on the wall behind her. She placed a hand on his arm.

"Please!" she begged. She'd thought she could stop it from happening if she came. She'd thought there might be a last-minute reprieve. It was only then that she noticed the redness around Murray's eyes. The realisation that Joe was definitely going to be transported back to Italy hit her. She let go of Murray's arm, wiped her tears away with the back of her hand, and then moved to stand near Joe. He wrapped his arms around her.

"Shall we give them a few minutes?" Murray said to George, who nodded. When the two men had left the room, Maggie's sobs grew harder, and she dropped to the floor. Joe sat holding her and rocking her gently.

"I love you. *Mi amore.* I have to go, but I will come back, whatever it takes." His voice shook, and Maggie looked up into his face.

She noticed the tears he held back, the set of his jaw, and the tightness of his lips. She realised at that moment that she'd loved him from the start. Why had she wasted so much time? They could have had more time together. Why had she listened to everyone else? Why had her parents clung to their stubbornness? "I love you so much. I made so many mistakes, but it was always you, Giuseppe." A sound escaped his throat when she pronounced his name. He stood and pulled her to her feet just as Murray and George walked back in.

"It's time to go, Maggie," George said. She closed her eyes, hugged Joe once more, then turned and walked out the door. Her stomach was in knots, and her body shivered as she sat in the passenger seat waiting for her father. She chanced one last look towards the building and saw Joe lift his hand to his heart, then his lips. She did the same and vowed that this would not be the last time she saw him.

Chapter 18
Giuseppe
Mid-1946

A loud thud startled him awake and he rolled over to check the cabin floor. The stark light from the porthole illuminated the figure spread-eagled on the steel below.

"*Fanculo*," Luigi said as he stood and rubbed his hip. Giuseppe burst out laughing and Luigi stood on the bottom bunk to punch him in the arm. The two men grappled playfully before the cabin door opened and Cambino walked in.

"We're stopping in Port Said in about an hour. Who's ready to be back in Egypt?" Everyone in the cabin shrugged and mumbled.

"How long has it been?" Eugenio asked. Giuseppe tried to count the years and months, but he'd lost track.

"About three and a half years, *amico*, but just think it's one stop closer to home," Domenico replied. Eugenio huffed and turned towards the wall. Giuseppe rolled onto his back and stared at the ceiling. The ship's constant movement lulled him, and his thoughts turned to home. What would he find there? How many people had his town lost? Was there even a town left? He leaned down over the side of the bunk to find Luigi lost in thought. He'd received a letter from his aunty just before they'd left Marrinup, and Giuseppe knew it hadn't been good news.

"When we get to Italy, you know you can come with me to the farm. You'll be welcome there."

"*Grazie*," Luigi said. Giuseppe saw the twinkle return to Luigi's eye before he added, "You've got a sister, *si*." Giuseppe screwed his eyes and bunched his lips, ready to object, but Luigi laughed and moved to the doorway. "Come on, let's go up on deck."

They had departed Fremantle on the Chitral the morning after he'd said goodbye to the Sleemans. Extra cabins and bunks were hastily installed on the troop ship they were travelling on. Giuseppe had read in the newspaper that after the Australian government had sent all the prisoners of war home, it was going to try to increase Australia's population via immigration. "Populate or perish" the headline had read. Giuseppe felt it was another blow. Australia wanted more citizens to address labour shortages and boost the economy, but it was sending him and his comrades home when so many of them wanted to stay.

Standing at the railing, Giuseppe watched Egypt's land mass grow more prominent on the horizon. He swallowed the lump that formed in his throat as his thoughts returned to the staging camp and the events that had put them there. A cigarette floated into his line of sight.

"You look tense, amici," Luigi lit it and handed it to Giuseppe, who took a long, slow drag. He closed his eyes, rolled his head back, and blew smoke into the sky.

"Just thinking too much," Giuseppe said.

"Less thinking, more drinking, I say. I'm looking forward to a nice cold drink. Wine, if they have it, beer, if they don't." Giuseppe agreed. A drink would ease the tension that had settled into his body.

When they got to shore, Giuseppe took off his boots so he could feel the sand between his toes. He stood on the beach looking back at the troop ship that dominated the horizon before walking the short distance into town. Port Said was bustling with crowds of people, animals of all descriptions, and stalls set up in every available space. Giuseppe hadn't seen this many strange faces in a long time and it unnerved him. The noise in the bustling market was deafening, a stark difference from the relative quiet he had grown accustomed to onboard the ship. Luigi was in his element and dragged Giuseppe into the throng. As they made their way through the market, the irresistible smell of mouthwatering food filled the air. An old man called out something that they couldn't understand, but they drew closer to his stall, anyway. He offered them each a bowl of prawn soup, and they savoured the tangy flavour.

"Not as good as the food at home, but better than what we get on the ship," Luigi said, lifting the bowl to his lips and draining the last of the liquid.

"*Si*. Definitely," Giuseppe agreed, handing his bowl back to the vendor. As he turned back towards the market, his eyes were immediately drawn to the vibrant hues of the rugs and clothes. He didn't want to return home empty-handed after so long away. He walked slowly past each stall, looking for the perfect gift for each member of his family. He came across a stall overflowing with a colourful assortment of trinkets, clothes, and utensils. After haggling with the vendor, he walked away with a scarf for Caterina, a fez for Lorenzo, a wooden bowl for his mother, and a copper cup for his father. He looked around for Luigi, but couldn't see him. Panic gripped him for a moment before reason took hold. Walking back the way he'd come, he turned a corner and burst out laughing. Luigi was lying back on a stack of large colourful pillows surrounded by a group of women and smoking from a shisha large enough for 6 people.

Luigi spotted him and waved him over. Giuseppe plonked on a pillow and took a long drag. He closed his eyes and blew smoke rings into the air while his whole body relaxed into the pillow. He knew it wasn't just the smoke that made him feel lightheaded. The would-be tourists were relishing their newfound freedom.

***

The Fassona were flying past the window as the car sped towards Rimissa. Instead of relaxing him, seeing the white cows grazing in the fields made Giuseppe tense. In a few short minutes, he would see his family for the first time in years. How much had they changed? How much had he changed? He was a different person from the naïve young man who had left to fight in Mussolini's war. He looked across at Luigi. So much had happened since the day they'd met on the ship bound for Australia. Their last journey together had taken almost two months. The ship's cramped quarters and uninspiring meals had become their new normal. The heat in the cabins sometimes became unbearable, and they took their blankets and pillows up on deck to sleep under the stars. When they arrived in Naples, they'd had to queue for hours outside the San Martino Accommodation Centre for processing, but it hadn't bothered Giuseppe. What difference did a few more hours make when he'd been gone for years?

As the car pulled off the road and onto the gravel driveway, the large sandstone farmhouse came into view. The tension in his body amplified. He hesitated before opening the car door. How would his family react? Would they be able to tell how much he'd been through? Or could he hide it all from them? He stood looking at his old life. The years away had changed him, but the farmhouse looked the same as it had the day he left. The wooden front door burst open, and his mother, Rosa, ran towards him, crying out his name. The commotion brought Caterina and Lorenzo out too, and they ran forward and embraced him. During the hug, he saw his father, Pietro, running over from the paddock. He almost felt like he couldn't breathe. Was this really happening, or was it a dream? Tears streamed down their faces, and they all talked at once. They stood holding each other for a long time before Pietro stood back and wiped his cheeks with both hands. Giuseppe's hand moved to his chest as he looked at each of his family members. A voice broke through his thoughts.
"*Salve*. I'm Luigi."
"*Ah, spiacente. Mamma, Papà, questo è il mio caro amico, Luigi,*" Giuseppe said as he grasped Luigi around the shoulders. With a warm smile, Rosa ushered them all into the house, showering the two returned men with attention.

Pietro sat in silence with both hands resting on the table in front of him. Giuseppe looked at his father's face. The lines on his forehead had multiplied and his eyes looked tired, but the message they conveyed was one that Giuseppe had longed for. The family didn't pry or ask questions of them. They allowed them to sit quietly as Rosa and Caterina prepared a light supper. Giuseppe felt a calmness come over him as he watched his mother and sister do the things they had always done. As soon as Rosa placed the bowl of gnocchi in front of him, he felt his mouth water at the tantalising scent. He and Luigi finished their food well before the others, their satisfied smiles evidence of their appetites. Giuseppe turned to his father.

"Pappa... there's so much I want to talk to you about. But first, tell me about what happened here?" When the ship pulled into Naples, Giuseppe, and Luigi noticed some buildings had been destroyed, and the damage was evident as they travelled through the countryside to Rimissa. The people, the buildings, and the landscape were all aggrieved. They got the feeling that it was still the same Italy, but it was a wounded Italy. Pietro confirmed their suspicions as he filled them in on news of the bombings and retaliation that had played out across the country. Luigi and Giuseppe listened in stunned silence.

"There is more," Pietro said, briefly putting a hand on Giuseppe's arm. "I'm sorry, but Mr Colombo is no longer with us. He tried to stand up to the soldiers when they invaded Rimissa, but he was killed by stray shrapnel." Giuseppe closed his eyes and bowed his head. He would have to pay his respects to his beloved English teacher. As Pietro and Lorenzo shared the details of the past few years, it became evident that few families had escaped tragedy. The elation that Giuseppe and Luigi felt at being back in Italy was contrasted by their despair at the devastation. The family spoke at length about what had happened to Rimissa and Italy but didn't enquire about Giuseppe and Luigi's experiences. Giuseppe saw Luigi yawn and rub his eyes.

"I think we should get some rest. I feel like I could sleep for a week," Giuseppe said, before showing Luigi to his room. Everyone in the house went to bed that night with full but heavy hearts.

***

Sitting on a flat rock in a paddock away from the house, Giuseppe ran his hands over the dog's head, rubbing behind its soft, fluffy ears. The Maremmano Sheepdog put its paws on Giuseppe's legs and laid its head in its master's lap. Giuseppe looked into the dog's dark eyes and smiled.

"Stop lazing about. Come and help me," Pietro said, pointing the stick he'd been walking with towards a broken fence further down the hill.

"Looks like our fun is over, Dante." Giuseppe gently eased the dog off his leg, then stood and stretched before following his father. He'd been back home for a few weeks. Some days, it felt as if he'd never left—he relished those days. It was the ones where he had flashbacks of what had happened during the war that he wasn't fond of.

He lifted the wooden pole into the hole and held it steady while his father filled it in and stamped the dirt down with his boot.

"I'm happy you're home," Pietro said, as he stamped his foot down one last time. "Your mother was beside herself." Giuseppe glanced at his father's face just in time to see the smirk. "She didn't have many letters from you. She worried so much. But then we got your letter about your marriage to Maggie. That was a good day. Full of happiness." The two men worked without looking at each other. "You miss her very much. Will you leave again? Will you go back to Australia?"

"*Si*. That was the plan." Pietro grunted and continued to dig. It had always been Giuseppe's plan to go back to Australia, but right now, he was enjoying being at home with his family. Dante barked a warning, and they looked up as Rosa approached.

"This came for you," she said, handing Giuseppe an envelope. He noticed the Colton Post Office postmark and Maggie's neat handwriting.

"I might take a break," he said, then made a beeline towards the rock up on the hill. He carefully unfolded the letter and brought it to his nose, breathing in Maggie's perfume.

Dear Giuseppe,

I miss you terribly. It's not the same without you here in our little home.

I've been speaking at length with Mum and Dad about our future. They weren't sure that you would be allowed back in Australia, so I told them there's only one thing for it. I'm coming to Italy! I bought a ticket with the money I had saved from the surgery, and Dad helped too. By the time you read this, I'll probably be on board the ship making my way to you.

I'm nervous about leaving. I've only ever been as far as Perth. But I want to do this. No, I need to do this. We should be together, and if that means me travelling all the way to Italy, then so be it. I hope your family will accept me. Please warn them of my arrival. I'm hoping you will be able to meet me in Naples when the ship docks.

I cannot wait to see you again.

Love always,

Maggie

When he finished, he read it again. He couldn't believe that Maggie would be so brave as to travel on her own. He ran down the hill, his smile stretched across his face as he called out to his parents.

"What it is, Giuseppe? You look like you'll burst," Rosa said.

"Maggie's coming here. She's probably on her way already." He hugged his mother before turning tail and running towards the house, calling over his shoulder, "I've got to tell Luigi."

As he approached the vegetable garden at the side of the house, he spotted Luigi and Caterina standing together. Caterina moved quickly to the side and handed Luigi the basket of vegetables.

"Guess what? Maggie's coming to Italy. She might even be on the ship right now," he said when he reached them.

"*Fantastico*! Will she stay here? In your room?" Caterina asked.

"I don't know, but at least she's coming. We'll sort everything else out later." Caterina let out a small laugh.

"You were never one for the finer details, *fratello*. But I'm happy for you. And I can't wait to meet my new *sorella*." Caterina hugged Giuseppe before nodding to Luigi and walking out of the garden. It was only then that Giuseppe stopped and thought about the scene that had been playing before him. He cocked his head and looked at Luigi, his eyebrows raised. Luigi looked down but couldn't hide his blush, then he held the basket between them. It was the giveaway Giuseppe needed.

"Ah! I'm right. You and Caterina, hey?" He elbowed his friend in the ribs.

"I... we weren't sure if you would be all right with it." Giuseppe had never seen Luigi so unsure of himself. The confident, often cocky, demeanour was gone and in its place stood a man who wanted nothing more than his blessing. Giuseppe knew what that felt like. He also knew that this was too good an opportunity to pass up. He squared his shoulders, puffed out his chest, and anchored a stern look on his face.

"I'm not sure I like this," he said, gesturing between Luigi and the house. Luigi furrowed his brow and swallowed.

"I'm sorry, *amico*. I know it's only been a month, but I like Caterina a lot," Luigi said, shifting from one foot to the other and looking from Giuseppe to the house. "Giuseppe, is this all right? If not, I'll leave the farm." Giuseppe raised both hands in surrender.

"*Caspeta*! It's all right. I was joking. I'm happy for you." He moved closer and held out his hand. Luigi grasped it, and the frown lines on his face disappeared. Giuseppe grinned and said, "I might be all right about it, but I wonder what Pappa and Mamma will think." Immediately, Luigi's face coloured, and Giuseppe burst out laughing before nudging him towards the house, intent on letting Caterina off the hook, too.

***

The warm summer days were already beginning to fade, but that didn't stop Giuseppe from rising early. He tiptoed to the kitchen and boiled a pot of water on the stove. Standing by the window, he gazed at the spot 70 yards away, where a small home was slowly taking shape. In the week since Maggie's letter arrived, he, along with Luigi, Lorenzo, Pietro, and their neighbour, Giorgio, had worked to build foundations, lay flooring, and erect walls. The building was slightly bigger than the old shack he and Maggie had shared at Jarrah Downs, and he'd made sure that it had a separate bedroom for privacy. He knew Maggie loved the homely feel of the shack, and he hoped to recreate it here on his own family's farm. One day, they'd build a large sandstone farmhouse like his parents, but for now, the petite wooden structure would have to do.

The corrugated iron for the roof had arrived at the warehouse in town. The beams needed to be raised, and the roof had to be fixed in place. He desperately wanted the house to be finished before Maggie arrived. He downed the rest of his coffee, grabbed a slice of the bread his mother had baked the day before, and then headed out the door. The old truck spluttered to life. As he sat, letting the engine warm up, it occurred to him that he hadn't ventured into town on his own since he'd been back. He felt a familiar tug in his stomach and marvelled at how something that was once so familiar now filled him with apprehension. With a few deep breaths, he prepared himself before reversing out onto the road.

"Young Giuseppe, I haven't seen you in a long time," the old man said as he pushed the large roller door across the front of the warehouse. Giuseppe greeted him and helped to heave the door open. "You're here for the iron, *si*? Your father told me you're home and you have an Australian wife. Why do you not marry a good Italian girl?" Giuseppe laughed and shrugged.

"It just didn't work out that way, Mr Vinci." Giuseppe felt his body tense in anticipation. Would he ask what happened during the war? What would he even reply to that question? The old man grunted and raised his hands in surrender, then turned towards the waiting supplies. After they had loaded the truck, Mr Vinci offered Giuseppe a drink. They sat quietly in the small staff kitchen, cups of coffee warming their hands. Vinci shifted in his seat so that he faced Giuseppe. Once again, Giuseppe's muscles tensed in anticipation.

"I'm an old man, and I have seen a lot in my time. Sometimes, in war, people do things they normally wouldn't do. It's not your fault. It's war. There's nothing else to be said, *capisci*?" The old man's eyes held a deep understanding. Giuseppe looked down at the cup in his hands and closed his eyes. He felt a hand squeeze his arm, and he looked up again.

"*Grazie*, Mr Vinci." The old man took the cup and deposited it in the sink. They walked in amiable silence to the truck, and Giuseppe waved as he drove off. On the drive home, he felt like a weight had been lifted. During the long nights at Marrinup, he'd often dreamt of coming back to his hometown and seeing familiar faces. But as the war drew to a close, he'd become apprehensive about his return. What would people ask? How would they react to him? What would he tell them? As he pulled into the driveway, he realised that in that brief conversation, Mr Vinci had released him from the pressure he'd put on himself.

Lorenzo, Luigi, and Pietro were already fixing the beams and rafters in place when Giuseppe pulled up next to the little house. They worked together to finish the rafters before lifting the lengths of iron off the truck and onto the roof. Giuseppe held a sheet up, waiting for Luigi to hammer in the nails, when the hammer flew past his head and almost dropped onto his foot. As the sheet slipped from his grasp, he dashed out of its path, narrowly avoiding being hit.

"*Fanculo*! Watch it!" he yelled up at Luigi, who was climbing down the ladder.

"*Spiacente*! Are you all right?" It was at that moment that Caterina came into Giuseppe's line of vision, holding a tray of meat, cheese, and bread.

"Well, that explains it," Giuseppe said, shaking his head. "I'd like to be here and not in the hospital when Maggie arrives. Concentrate, Luigi." He turned to Caterina. "You'd better stay inside if you're going to distract him this much." He laughed and slapped him on the back, then quieted when he saw the look on their faces.

"What do you mean by that?" Pietro asked him. Giuseppe looked from Luigi to Caterina, waiting for one of them to say something. There was no way around it now. He knew his father had picked up on his meaning, but Pietro's expression remained impassive. Luigi stepped forward with his hat in his hands. Looking at the ground, he told Pietro about his feelings for Caterina, who moved to stand next to him and take his hand. Giuseppe watched on, waiting for the burst of anger he knew his father would show. Caterina was the youngest, the only daughter, and the apple of her father's eye. It wasn't until he saw Pietro's eyes darting back and forth between Caterina and Luigi that he comprehended the similarities between Caterina and Maggie. He hoped his father would be more willing to accept the relationship than George Sleeman had been in the beginning.

"Welcome to the family," he said, putting an arm around Luigi and Caterina's shoulders. Giuseppe and Caterina exchanged confused glances before Giuseppe shrugged with his hands up. Perhaps their father was a changed man, too.

The four men continued working into the afternoon, and by 3 pm, they'd nailed on the final sheet of roofing. They stood back and admired the newly completed house.

"*Perfetto*," Giuseppe said. The others nodded in agreement. To Giuseppe, the little home represented a potential future. The question that he pondered as he walked inside and stood in what would be the bedroom was whether it would be enough to make Maggie stay in Italy.

Maggie lay back on the deck chair as the white clouds floated by, and the sea air filled her nostrils. A woman her mother's age walked past and smiled down at her, and Maggie felt a pang of homesickness. She remembered the look of anguish on her mother's face and the way her father's eyes had turned pink and watery before he had looked up towards the gangway.

"As hard as this is, I would rather you were happy than miserable. Even if it means you going to the other side of the world." Elizabeth had said as she hugged Maggie tightly and planted a kiss on her cheek.

"You be careful now. Not everyone is as friendly out there as they are in Colton," George had said. Maggie had exchanged a knowing look with her mother before making her way up the walkway and waving from the deck. She knew waving goodbye from the Fremantle docks had been hard for her parents, but she was grateful they'd been there to see her off.

She had been at sea for a few weeks, and the sound of waves against the bow had become a comforting soundtrack to her days. Her accommodations were pleasant enough, and she'd been delighted to discover her roommate was an Italian woman returning home after a few months with her aunty in Australia. Maria, who was 28, had chosen to remain unmarried and childless. Her vivaciousness reminded Maggie of Luigi's cheeky nature. Maggie turned her head to watch as Maria rose gracefully from the deck chair next to her. It was only 9 am, but Maria was already dressed in a tight-fitting red rayon sleeveless dress that stopped just above her knees, her face made up, and her signature red lipstick set in place. She went to the railing and flung her arms high, letting the wind pick up her long brown hair, and then she turned to look back at Maggie.

"Not long to go. We'll be in Italy soon," Maria said.

"Do you think Giuseppe would have received my letter by now? What if he isn't there to meet me in Naples?" Maggie bit her thumbnail. Maria sat back down next to her and pulled on her wide-brimmed black hat.

"If he's not, I'll take you to Rimissa myself," Maria declared.

"I couldn't ask you to do that," Maggie said. Maria shrugged.

"You didn't. I offered. Besides, it's been years since I was up that way." Maria sniffed the air. "I smell food. Let's go before the rush." Maggie felt herself being pulled to stand. "Here, you need a bit of this," Maria said, plucking her lipstick out of her brassiere and dabbing a small amount on Maggie's lower lip. She smacked her lips together and indicated for Maggie to do the same. It was the first time Maggie had worn lipstick in such a bold colour, and she felt quite scandalous. As they sauntered over the deck and into the dining room, she held herself higher, exuding a confidence that she didn't ordinarily possess.

The smell of hot coffee and toast hit them as the door opened. They sat at their usual table and were joined by a husband and wife from Switzerland and a man from Sicily. The man seemed quite enamoured with Maria, and Maggie watched, feigning nonchalance, but inwardly thrilled to be a spectator, as Maria flirted back. They had their fill and made their excuses before Maria discreetly exchanged a note with the prospective beau. They spent the rest of the day on deck, walking the length of the ship, playing cards with whoever was keen, or laying on deck chairs sunbathing and reading. Maggie was getting used to the daily routines of life aboard the ship, but she knew they would all change as soon as it docked in Naples.

"You're quiet tonight," Maria said as they sat at the small table near the entrance to their cabin. Maggie moved to the porthole to stare at the little patch of sky.

"I've been thinking about Giuseppe's family. I wonder how they'll react to me. I'm sure they would have wanted him to marry an Italian girl." Maria turned to her, eyes wide.

"Are you joking? They will love you. You're beautiful, smart, and kind. What parents wouldn't want that in a daughter-in-law?" Maria swatted her hand in front of her. "Don't even worry about it," she said. Maggie smiled. She hoped Maria was right. She would find out soon enough.

***

Passengers flocked to the deck, their excitement palpable, as the ship neared the harbour and Naples slowly revealed itself. The waterfront was lined with timeworn buildings, their vibrant colours contrasting against the blue water. Boats of all sizes were scattered across the port, and the hustle and bustle of people filled the air. Maria and Maggie waited as the vessel slowly docked. Maggie repeatedly scanned the crowd but couldn't see

Giuseppe amongst the waiting crowd. They disembarked and stood watching as families and friends loudly greeted each other. The noise and crowd set Maggie on edge, and her stomach churned. Maria clasped her hand and led her to the side to wait for the crowd to disperse. They lingered as the stevedores unpacked the luggage, and after pulling theirs from the large pile, Maggie sat on her suitcase and bit her nails.

The crowd slowly dwindled, and Maggie's fear grew with each passing minute. How would she get to Rimissa? Was Maria really willing to take her all the way there? She looked across at Maria, who was lazing on her own luggage, twirling her hair with one hand and chatting with a young stevedore. She didn't appear to be in a hurry to leave the almost deserted dock. Maggie looked back towards the ship. Maybe she'd made a mistake. Perhaps now that Giuseppe was home, he wanted nothing to do with her. Maybe she'd come all this way by mistake. She chewed her other thumbnail, then heard her name being shouted and turned to see Giuseppe jogging towards her. Her chest expanded, and she sprinted towards him. He picked her up and twirled with her in his arms, their laughter mingling with the sound of their kisses. Maggie felt herself lowered to the ground, but she didn't let go of his neck. She couldn't pull away, and neither could he.

"What took you so long?" Maria called. They reluctantly broke apart and walked over to where Maria was standing. Maggie made her introductions, recounting how they'd become fast friends during their time on the ship. "I thought I'd have to take her to Rimissa myself," Maria reproached. Giuseppe put a hand to his chest.

"*Spiacente*. I was held up, but it was worth it. Military Command has discharged me. I am officially a civilian again." He whooped and caught the attention of some dock workers, but he ignored their stares. "Nothing can ruin my day," he said as he put an arm around Maggie's shoulders. "I'm a free man, and my wife is in my arms again." Maggie leaned into him but was wary of the men watching their exchange.

"Well, we can't stand here all day," she said.

"You're right. Let's get out of here. You must try gelato." Maggie laughed but noticed Maria was busy arranging her bags.

"You're coming with us, aren't you?" Maggie asked her.

"*Si*, come. I need to thank you for being so good to Maggie," Giuseppe said. Maria looked towards the city and then back at the young couple.

"*Grazie*, but I think it's time for me to head home," she said, walking over and hugging Maggie. "I'm so glad your man came for you. You take care of yourself. Remember, you have my address if you ever need me." Maggie didn't know how to thank the woman who had been a big part of her first crossing of the seas. "Wait a minute," she said, running to her suitcase and yanking it open. She pulled out a silver broach in the shape of a horse and handed it to Maria. "Thank you for making my trip so memorable. I hope we'll meet again soon," she said as she gave it to her. Maria took it, then reached into her brasserie, pulled out her red lipstick and placed it in Maggie's hand.

"Here. Now, you can be just as bold on the outside as I know you are on the inside," she said. The two women hugged once more as Giuseppe grabbed Maggie's luggage. They wandered off the wharf and into the city for their first Italian meal together.

***

While Giuseppe drove, Maggie leaned comfortably on his shoulder. She watched the countryside change as they moved from the bustling port city of Naples to the outskirts of town and then on to farming land and eventually to Rimissa. Along the way, she could see the destruction caused by the Allies and the German Resistance. Homes and businesses were reduced to rubble, bridges had been hastily repaired, and the ground itself was torn apart by land mines. The destruction was interspersed with fields full of blooming sunflowers. The contrast was so sudden that when she first saw it, she thought it was a mirage.

Giuseppe drove slowly through Rimissa, pointing out the post office, the shop, and the church. It reminded her of the first time she'd taken Giuseppe into Colton. She saw Rimissa had not been spared from the war, but the people had begun to rebuild. New brick contrasted against the old stone to create a kaleidoscope of colour along the main street. She could feel Giuseppe watching her closely.

"How do you think your family will react when they see me?" she asked.

"Don't worry. They will love you," he assured her as she tried to wipe her increasingly sweaty palms down the sides of her skirt.

"It's strange being the one worrying about the family, *si*?" She smiled at him and then turned towards the window, waiting for his family farm to come into view. The home was exactly as she'd pictured it. A large stone building surrounded by fruit trees. She looked around at the expanse of land, noting the white cows and the field full of different vegetables. The small, newly built home near the front boundary sat in stark contrast to the older, established building.

Her feet had barely hit the ground before she felt her face squashed into a woman's bosom. As Giuseppe's mother hugged her tight, a stream of Italian words hit her ears, and the smell of pasta flared her nostrils. She looked across at Giuseppe and raised her eyebrows. He laughed and chided his mother before gently pulling them apart. She heard a yell as the front door opened, and Luigi and a young woman jogged over to them. Luigi hugged her and kissed her on both cheeks before introducing Caterina as Giuseppe's sister. Maggie could tell by the way he looked at her that there was something between them. She'd have to ask Giuseppe about it later. Luigi enquired about her travels and how her family was, and Maggie filled him in on news of the dismantling of the camp. She caught a dark look cross his face before he masked it with his usual grin.

"Come, come. We eat," Rosa said in broken English after some instruction from Giuseppe. Maggie nodded and joined them as they made their way over to the larger home.

The now-familiar smell of Spaghetti Bolognese filled the air, and Maggie's mouth watered. She hadn't realised how hungry she was. Caterina led her into the dining room, where a large table was laid out with huge bowls full of pasta. She locked eyes with

Giuseppe, and with a reassuring look from him, her nerves settled. As soon as she'd sat down, Caterina handed her a glass of wine and a large bowl. They all chinked glasses and the sound of "*saluti*" filled the air. Everyone began talking at once, but Maggie could only understand a word here or there. Whether it was the wine or the warm welcome, she sank into the chair, fully embracing the present moment.

When it looked as if everyone had finished, she stood and began to clear the table. Rosa and Caterina stood and put their hands on top of hers. "*Non, non. Lo faremo.*" Maggie raised her hands in defeat just as Giuseppe appeared at her side.

"Mamma and Caterina will do that. I want to show you something." He led her outside towards the small building. "It's not quite finished," he said. She looked at him in the fading light. He was different here. His demeanour had changed. He seemed younger somehow, and he was definitely happier. He opened the door and ushered her inside. The building, although recently constructed, managed to exude a sense of familiarity that instantly transported her back to the shack. Giuseppe had furnished it and began to decorate it in a similar fashion to their little home on Jarrah Downs. She circled the room, touching objects and looking at Giuseppe in wonder. On the mantle sat two wooden sheep statues that matched their nativity scene, which was safely stored in a box in the shack.

"What do you think?"

"It's wonderful," Maggie said, looking around. Giuseppe beamed and then shrugged.

"It's a start. We can build a bigger home later on when we need more room for a family." She turned to him. That was something they would have to discuss, but for now, she wanted nothing more than to spend some time alone with him. She walked into the bedroom and saw her suitcase sitting neatly in the corner. Giuseppe came up behind her and wrapped his hands around her middle, leaning down to nuzzle her neck. She turned in his arms and once more felt the world slip away.

***

Maggie opened her eyes and looked around the room. It took her a moment to process where she was. She peered at Giuseppe's sleeping form, the rhythm of his breath a slow, steady march. She gently peeled back the blankets and dressed quietly before creeping across the floorboards and out the front door. She closed it softly and looked across at the farmhouse. There was light and movement, but it didn't appear as though anyone had ventured outside yet. She took the opportunity to walk towards the paddocks on her right. The land was dotted with large grey rocks, and the hills which led down to the small stream running below provided views of surrounding farms. She walked further on and found a flat rock to sit on.

Watching the cows munch the green grass, she thought of home. There was some familiarity in being on a farm, but Jarrah Downs felt a million miles away. She looked back towards the smaller house. Was that her new home? Giuseppe had made it clear that he was expecting her to stay in Italy now that she was here. Her parents had asked if she would return, and in her heart, she thought she would, but now that she was here, she wondered if she felt differently. She wrapped her shawl tighter around her and sat, watching the sky lighten. By the time the sun had fully breached the horizon, she had decided to stay in Italy. She'd come all this way, and Giuseppe had spent years in Australia. It was her turn to make a sacrifice.

That afternoon in the farmhouse's kitchen, she stood off to the side and watched as Rosa and Caterina each sprinkled yeast over some water in the two large bowls on the wooden table. Rosa turned to her, gestured to the table and said, "Pizza." Maggie brought her fingers to her lips and kissed them in the way Giuseppe had taught her. Rosa and Caterina laughed before picking up their wooden spoons. "*Cucchiaio*," Caterina said, holding the spoon up to her. Grasping her meaning, Maggie responded with "spoon" before Caterina moved aside and gestured for Maggie to take over. Maggie watched as Rosa added olive oil, flour, and salt to the bowl before mixing it and then spreading it on the table to knead. Maggie did the same. While Rosa and Maggie kneaded the dough, Caterina moved around the kitchen, picking up random objects and calling their name in Italian. Maggie copied the words before saying them in English. After a few minutes, they put their dough back in the bowls to prove. Caterina grabbed a small book from the side table and then waved for Maggie to follow her outside.

They sat in cane chairs under the wisteria-covered pergola. Caterina held up the book she'd brought out and Maggie's mouth dropped open as she read the title—"Pidgin English for Italian Prisoners of War". Giuseppe must have brought it back from Australia. Did his family know what he'd gone through because of that book? Had he opened up to them at all about what had happened at Marrinup? Pushing aside the sadness that threatened her mood, Maggie opened the book and began to read, pointing out the words as she sounded them out. Caterina seemed to pick up the language much easier than Maggie did with Italian words. They read through a few pages but stopped when Rosa brought out a tray with three cups of coffee.

"Would you like to learn too?" Maggie asked Rosa, awkwardly indicating the book and her mouth. Rosa shook her head and said, "*No, no. Sono troppo vecchio.*"

"She says she's too old," Luigi said from the doorway.

"Oh, no. Please tell her she's not too old. I'm happy to teach her." Luigi translated, but Rosa just raised her hands in defeat. Luigi shrugged, and as Rosa turned her back to walk inside, he stepped closer to Caterina. Maggie watched him lean down and plant a quick kiss on her lips.

"How is Caterina going? I try to teach her, but my English isn't very good either."

"She's a fast learner. You'll be able to converse in Italian and English in no time," Maggie assured him. Satisfied with her answer, he gave Caterina another kiss and walked back towards the paddock, where they could see Giuseppe and Pietro making a pile of branches for the bonfire.

With her hands held out in front of her, Maggie could feel the bonfire warm her whole body. She looked up at the navy sky dotted with stars and a waxing moon. From her vantage point, she could see Caterina and Luigi to her left, with their chairs almost touching, while Giuseppe stood on her right, adding branches to the fire. She looked across the top of the flames to where Rosa and Pietro sat. Pietro gently pulled a blanket around Rosa's shoulders and when she looked up at him, Maggie saw the evidence of a lifetime of love in her eyes.

"*Vino*?" Lorenzo asked before filling her cup at her nod. She took another sip and felt it warm her from the inside. Her palate had grown accustomed to the red wine they often had after dinner. It still made her head spin though, and it did so as she got up and stood next to Giuseppe. She leaned into him, and he wrapped his arm around her waist. She couldn't help but smile. Giuseppe's parents, brother, and sister had welcomed her into their lives, and she felt like she'd been part of the family for years, not weeks. The language barrier rarely caused an issue, and with the younger ones taking the opportunity to learn each other's languages, it seemed to solidify her place among them.

She looked up at Giuseppe's face, and he beamed down at her. He loved her being here in Italy. He'd mentioned it almost every day. Her gaze travelled to the other faces around the bonfire and then landed deep in the flames. Until she stood at the edge of the fire, she'd felt like a visitor, not just to the country but to the Russo farm and family. Now, she felt in her heart a genuine sense of belonging. This felt like home.

***

"Hop in," Giuseppe called out from the truck window as it pulled to a stop in front of her.

"Where are we going?" she asked as she walked around to the passenger side.

"It's a surprise," he replied with a wink. She climbed in, and the truck swung into action, jostling them along the driveway and out onto the road.

"Let me guess, a picnic somewhere?" Maggie nudged the basket sitting between them.

"I can't hide anything from you, can I?" Giuseppe laughed. Maggie sat back, eager to watch the countryside. After the night of the bonfire, she'd confessed her feelings to Giuseppe, and they'd celebrated as only newlyweds could. The memory of it brought a blush to her cheeks.

Half an hour later, they pulled up in an open space near a large lake. Maggie took off her sandals and walked to the water. It was crystal clear near the sandy edge but gradually became darker the deeper it got. Mature fig and olive trees dotting the bank provided just the right amount of shade. Giuseppe laid the rug and beckoned her over. Rosa or Caterina had obviously prepared the food, but that didn't matter to Maggie. She savoured the chance to spend time alone with Giuseppe. They ate their way through cheese, olives, salami, and bread and washed it down with some white wine. Giuseppe let out a soft burp, and she gently berated him. They lay back on the rug, and she turned towards him and put her hand on his chest, watching it rise and fall with his breath.

"Time for a swim," he said after a few minutes, dragging her to her feet and towards the shoreline. They both stripped down to their underclothes and ran in. The water was brisk, and goose bumps covered her body as Giuseppe pulled her closer to him.

"This reminds me of our swims in the river at Jarrah Downs. Thank you for bringing me here."

"Anything for you." He leaned in and kissed her neck. She felt warm despite the coolness of the water.

Their date was over too quickly, and they were soon on their way home.

"I need to stop at the post office," Giuseppe said, as they passed through the town. Maggie waited in the truck while he went inside. She leaned her head back on the headrest and tilted it towards the afternoon sunshine streaming through the window. She almost drifted off to sleep and jumped when the truck door opened. Giuseppe sat and rifled through the cluster of envelopes.

"This one's for you." He handed her a letter with a Colton postmark.

"It must be from Mum," she said, putting it to her chest before ripping it open. Holding the letter, she felt an overwhelming wave of homesickness she hadn't anticipated. But when she examined the handwriting, she noticed it wasn't her mother's familiar loopy cursive but her father's abrupt all-capital script. Immediately, a lump lodged in her throat.

"What's wrong?"

"It's from my father." She looked for Giuseppe's reaction. He tried to keep his face composed.

"Do you want me to read it?" he asked. Maggie contemplated the offer before shaking her head.

"No, I should do it," she said. "It can't be good news, though."
Giuseppe nodded. She read silently. The letter was brief, just as
she expected. The contents shook her. She read the letter to
herself and then to Giuseppe. As they locked eyes, the shock on
his face mirrored hers, understanding passing between them.

Chapter 20
Giuseppe
Early 1947

Silence hung heavy in the air between them as they drove back to the farm. Both of them were lost in thought as they weighed the potential repercussions of the letter. When Maggie had scrunched her brow as soon as she opened the letter, Giuseppe knew it wasn't just her parents checking to see how she was faring so far from home. He'd watched as her mouth formed a perfect 'O', and her eyes blinked rapidly. After she'd read it to him, he felt himself have an almost identical reaction. Neither of them had expected the news, and he knew in an instant that it threatened to upheave their newly established happiness.

They walked inside and found Rosa and Caterina in the sitting room, mending clothes, deep in conversation. When they saw Giuseppe and Maggie, a hush fell over them.

"What's wrong? Something has happened. Is your father all right?" Rosa asked Giuseppe. He put his hands up and assured her that Pietro was all right and Lorenzo and Luigi were, too. Both women let out a collective sigh of relief. Rosa stood in front of Giuseppe and laid a hand on his arm. "What's wrong?" she asked again. Giuseppe looked over at Maggie. Concern crossed her face, and she wrung her hands in front of her.

"It's Elizabeth, Maggie's mother. She's very ill." Rosa embraced Maggie and rubbed her back, murmuring in Italian.

"What will you do?" Caterina enquired. "Will Maggie go back to

Australia? Will you go too?" Giuseppe shook his head slightly and shrugged. These questions had come to him on the drive home, but he didn't have answers to any of them.

"You know we'll support you, whatever you decide to do," Rosa said to them both before gently leading Maggie into Caterina's room and laying her on the bed. Although Maggie appeared worn out by the news, Giuseppe knew his mother and Caterina would look after her. He went in search of his father, Lorenzo, and Luigi, and found them in the shed, trying to repair a break in the plough's beam. Spotting him, they stopped work and listened as he relayed the news. The same questions shot at him. Again, he shook his head and shrugged.

"I don't know what to do," he said.

"Go back with her," Luigi responded.

"I know I should, but I don't know if I can go back there."

"What do you mean?" Lorenzo asked. "I'm sure they'll let you back in the country. These are special circumstances."

"It's not just that," Giuseppe said, looking back towards the house. Ever since Maggie had read the letter to him, he'd had a sinking feeling in the pit of his stomach. At first, he couldn't understand what it was, but the more he spoke about the possibility of returning to Australia, the more he understood what it might be. His eyes locked with Luigi's, and he saw the realisation slowly wash over him.

Luigi walked towards the shed door and ushered Giuseppe outside. They walked in silence for a few minutes and ended up near the flat rock. Luigi reached up and pushed on Giuseppe's shoulder, making him sit down before plonking himself next to him. They sat silently for a few moments, their gaze fixed on the gentle flow of the river below. Luigi was the first to speak.

"You can't let Marrinup win. You can't let Browning win. Maggie needs you. Elizabeth is her mother, and she's your family too," he said. Giuseppe knew he was right, but he couldn't shake this feeling that had settled inside him. Australia had been good to him in some ways; he'd found Maggie and made friends he knew he'd have for the rest of his life, but it had also been terrible. Sometimes, he woke in a sweat, feeling like the walls were closing in on him. He knew the war had changed him. His time in the detention cells, being locked up in the camp and being treated like a criminal had all affected him deeply. He couldn't bring himself to meet Luigi's gaze.

"Would you go back?" he asked as he picked at the sleeve of his shirt.

"In a heartbeat. There was a lot of bad, but there was also a lot of good, Giuseppe. You need to remember the good." Luigi picked up a handful of pebbles and jingled them in his palm. He picked one out and threw it as far as he could "Wristball on the oval." He threw another rock. "Playing cards in the mess." Another rock sailed away. "Drinking at the Dwellingup Pub. Watching you get married to your beautiful bride. Hans's schnapps. We had some good times with that." Slowly, Giuseppe felt his mood lift. He leaned down and picked up some rocks. He felt their weight, then hurled one as far as he could throw it.

"Meeting Maggie." He threw another. "The shack." And another. "The movie nights in the rec hall." He picked up another rock and

threw it hard. "Meeting my best friend and sharing it all with him."
He nudged Luigi on the arm. "*Grazie, amico.*" Luigi shrugged, but
couldn't hide his smile. They sat for a while and talked about what
they'd been through over the last few years, then made their way
back to the shed, both feeling lighter than they'd felt in a long
time.

Later that night, as Giuseppe lay in bed, he turned towards
Maggie. He'd brought dinner to her in the shack, but she hadn't
touched it. She had said little to him since she'd read the letter,
and he felt as if the news and its implications had created a space
between them. His talk with Luigi had helped him to decide what
his next move would be. Perhaps she was worried that he
wouldn't go back with her.
"George only paid for one ticket," he said as he moved closer to
her. "But you're not going alone." Maggie burst into tears. With a
gentle tug, he brought her close, and he could feel the softness of
her cheek as she burrowed into the crook of his neck.
"Dad says she's really unwell. But how sick is she? What if
she...?" She couldn't finish the sentence. He knew he should tell
her it would be all right, but he didn't know that for sure. He held
her as she cried.
"Whatever happens, I will be there." He knew it wasn't enough,
but it was all he could offer.

***

The guard rail was icy, and the deck was empty as Giuseppe
stood and watched the ship slice through the water. He'd left
Maggie sleeping in their cabin and ventured out into the cool

morning. This was his favourite time of the day—when the air on deck was crisp and calm, and he could savour the tranquillity before the other passengers started their day. He watched the colours on the horizon change as the sun slowly emerged. How many times had he crossed this ocean now? This crossing was almost at an end. They'd see their first glimpse of the Western Australian coast any day now. At least this voyage had been more comfortable than his previous trips. He and Maggie had a cabin to themselves. Their days were filled with leisurely pursuits, whether it was lounging by the pool or enjoying a meal with fellow passengers. It was a far cry from sharing a tiny cabin with three other men and eating pasta that had been cooked in milk instead of salty water.

He jumped when he felt hands curl around his waist.
"Not long to go now. I can't wait to see everyone. I wonder if Joan has had the baby yet." Maggie paused for a moment and then said, "I hope we've made it in time." She didn't need to elaborate. Giuseppe knew she was aching to see Elizabeth. As the ship got closer to Australia, he realised he'd begun to feel excited about returning to Jarrah Downs and seeing the Sleemans' familiar faces. This time, it would be different though, because this time he was officially free.

***

"Thanks, Dad," Maggie said as she jumped out of the car and sprinted towards the house, leaving Giuseppe and George to carry their bags. The ship had arrived mid-morning, and George had been waiting on the dock. Maggie had almost bowled him over while Giuseppe had simply smiled and offered his hand. Any awkwardness that he'd anticipated vanished as George pulled him close and patted him on the back. They'd talked non-stop during the long drive from Fremantle to the farm. George told them about how he'd helped Richard expand his farm, about the new workers they had hired, and about his new grandson. Giuseppe wondered if he deliberately excluded any mention of the war or what had happened to Marrinup.

Richard met them at the door, and Giuseppe noticed the bags under his eyes.
"Hello, Richard. Nice to see you again. I wish it was for a better reason." Richard embraced him.
"Welcome back, Joe... Sorry, I mean Giuseppe. That might take a bit to get used to." Giuseppe laughed and said, "I'll answer to either." Maggie came into the hallway carrying Richard and Joan's new baby over her shoulder. She turned and Giuseppe glimpsed his chubby face.
"Meet Joseph," she said with a massive grin on her face.
Giuseppe looked over at Richard, eyes wide.
"Yeah, mate. Joan and I wanted to name him after someone who we thought was courageous and honest, and Richard was already taken," he said with a wink. Giuseppe felt his heart swell.
"Well, don't just stand in the hallway, you lot. Come into the sitting room," Joan called. The group jostled themselves and the luggage into the room. Giuseppe hugged Joan and whispered, "Thank you. It is an honour," in her ear. She whispered back, "It was an easy decision."

"Would you like to hold him?" Maggie asked, and Giuseppe held out his arms. In that fleeting moment, as he looked down at the sleeping baby, he couldn't help but think of the baby they had lost. A bell tinkled, and they all looked toward the sound.

"That's Mum," Richard said.

"I'll go," Maggie volunteered.

"Come and get me when you're ready. I'd like to see her," Giuseppe said, as Maggie moved toward the door. She looked back with trembling lips and nodded.

Joan took Joseph and admonished George playfully for not offering Giuseppe a drink. George walked to the sideboard and poured them all a small brandy.

"I know it's not for a good reason, but welcome back," Richard said and chinked his glass with Giuseppe's. They discussed what had changed in Colton in the time Giuseppe had been gone and Giuseppe felt himself relax. Perhaps he'd been worried for nothing. Just as he finished his drink, Maggie returned and gestured for him to follow her.

They made their way down the hall towards the master bedroom, then Maggie stopped at the door.

"Prepare yourself. She's not the woman she once was," she said before leading him into the room. Giuseppe's breath caught as he took in the small figure in the large bed. Elizabeth had been average in height, but now she appeared childlike. Her face was sallow, and her skin a translucent grey.

"Please give us a minute, Maggie," she said. Maggie glanced at Giuseppe and he raised his eyebrows and watched her leave. He moved the chair closer to the bed and placed a hand on top of Elizabeth's. Her breathing was shallow, and she wheezed as she spoke. He leaned towards her.

"I'm sorry for how I treated you," she whispered. Giuseppe shook his head and began to rebuke her, but stopped when she squeezed his hand. "I can see you love Maggie. I should have seen it earlier. Promise me you'll always look after her." Giuseppe gave her his word. Satisfied, she laid back and closed her eyes. "Tell me about your home," she said. Giuseppe told her of the rolling hills and farmlands, the old buildings, and farmhouses, and the fields of grapevines and sunflowers. After a few moments, he sensed she was asleep, and he gently closed the door as he left the room.

***

The days passed slowly as they watched and waited, each taking turns to spend time with Elizabeth. Giuseppe could see the toll it was taking on the family, so he'd taken to doing the same chores that he had when he'd worked here. It felt good to be busy. He leaned over the railing and watched the brumbies eating the long grass. He felt a movement at his side and turned to see Richard standing with his hand on the top rail, silent tears streaming down his face. At that moment, Giuseppe knew Elizabeth had succumbed to her illness. He let out a long sigh and stood closer to Richard, putting a hand on his upper back. They stood staring at the brumbies, reminiscing about their time spent with Elizabeth and contemplating what the next few weeks and months would bring. When Giuseppe felt a full heaving sigh from Richard, he glanced at his face. Richard swallowed and nodded before turning back to the house. Giuseppe didn't move. The family needed time alone to come to terms with what had just happened.

He climbed over the fence, grabbing the rope that was dangling over a pole as he slid down into the long grass. He strode toward the largest brumby. Its brown hair tussled as it shook its head in his direction. He whispered softly as he approached, one arm outstretched and the other holding the looped rope out to the side. It seemed as if the horse sensed his need to connect. It didn't resist as his hand touched its nose and rubbed its head. He slid the rope over its neck, all the while whispering to ease both their nerves. He ran his hand along the length of the horse's head and shoulder before taking a quick glance underneath.
"I think you should be called Patrizio. What do you think?" The horse snorted, and Giuseppe laughed. "I'll take that as a yes." He led the brumby around in a wide circle. As they passed the fence closest to the shed, he noticed the ambulance pull up in the driveway, and he saw Maggie walk out of the house. Confusion clouded her expression, but as soon as her eyes locked with his, she moved towards him. He and Patrizio waited in the shade of the shed. Maggie climbed over the fence and jumped down into the long grass with a thud. When she reached him, she ran her hands along the brumby's nose, and then she seemed to melt into his arms. Giuseppe gently slid the rope from the brumby's neck with one hand while the other held her close. Once Patrizio was free, he trotted across the paddock, leaving them in their grief.
"She's gone. She's really gone."
"I know, *mi amore*." His arms wrapped around her shoulders, and

he kissed the top of her head. "*Poco in terra, molto in cielo.* She's in a better place now, and she's not in pain anymore." Maggie nodded and attempted to stifle her sobs. They stood facing the house, and Giuseppe noticed George and Doctor Mosely carrying a stretcher with Elizabeth's body covered in a white sheet down the steps. He pulled Maggie close to him so that she didn't feel like she had to witness it.

***

Giuseppe walked behind Maggie and the rest of the Sleeman family and took his place at the very end of the front row of the old church. He snuck a peek at the rest of the congregation. It looked as if the whole of Colton had turned out for the funeral. Every pew was packed with people in their Sunday best. Basking in the late morning light streaming from the stained glass window, Giuseppe felt lulled into quiet contemplation. He stood, knelt and sat when requested but spent most of the sermon wondering what this meant for his and Maggie's future. He had avoided any discussion with her about returning to Italy. She'd been so distraught at losing her mother that she'd spent days in bed, and when she was up and about, she had a lost look on her face. It pained him to see her like that, but he knew there was nothing he could do besides be there for her when she was ready to talk. Giuseppe felt Maggie squeeze his thigh as the priest led everyone in the final prayer.

Standing by the tree to the side of the churchyard, he watched as the mourners gave their condolences to the family. Maggie had wanted him to join them, but he said it didn't feel right. When he had glanced at George, he felt reassured by the nod of understanding that George had given him. The one silver lining of Elizabeth's death, if he could think that without seeming crass, was that his relationship with George had matured into one of acceptance and understanding. A cough nearby pulled him back to the churchyard, and he turned to see who it was. His breath caught, his stomach knotted, and he felt his shoulders curl inward. Out of his uniform, Officer Grady looked like any other mourner, but Giuseppe knew he'd recognise that face anywhere. He stood, his eyes fixed on Grady, waiting for him to break the silence. The other man extended his hand in greeting.

"It's nice to see you again, Giuseppe, although I wish it was on better terms. I was sorry to hear about Elizabeth's passing. My wife's in the CWA too." Giuseppe hesitated, then hooked his hand into Grady's and nodded, unsure of what to say. Grady turned to face the crowd. "Look," he said as he cleared his throat and shifted his hands to his pockets, "I want to apologise for what happened at Marrinup. We all did things we wouldn't do in our regular lives, but... well... that was the job. I was just doing what I was told." He heaved a sigh, obviously relieved at having lifted his burden. Giuseppe remained silent. Could he forgive and forget? Marrinup still haunted his dreams. He feared that what happened would always be a part of him, but as he looked at the man before him, he understood it would also be a part of Grady and the other guards, too. He thought once again that there were no winners in war. He watched the mourners gathered in front of them. Life was too short to live in the past. Holding a grudge would only eat away at him. He turned to face Grady and waited for him to do the same. Grady gulped and flinched as Giuseppe raised his hand to lay it on Grady's shoulder.

"It happened and we can't go back and change it. No matter how much we might want to. I accept your apology." He gently squeezed his shoulder, then turned and walked back to Maggie and the others.

***

"Jump up." Giuseppe heard Maggie call as she pulled on the reins and slowed Lily with a softly whispered, "Whoa". Giuseppe mounted the horse and perched his body close to Maggie's as Lily started trotting. The sun was low in the pink sky, but the air was still warm. He had always loved this time of day on Jarrah Downs. It felt like everyone, and everything, was taking a rest after a hard day's work. They were galloping through the paddocks, heading in a familiar direction. A smile crept across his face as the shack came into view.

"It's just like I remember it," he said as he jumped down and stepped aside to let Maggie settle Lily. They held each other's hand as he pushed open the door. Inside, the low light filtered through the windows. There was a layer of dust on every surface, but everything was exactly as it had been left. He watched as Maggie slowly made her way around the small room, first touching the table and then the bed frame. She'd brought him here for a reason. Since the funeral a few weeks ago, they'd avoided talk of the future. He knew he wasn't willing to return to Italy without her again. His instinct told him that Maggie wanted to stay, and this trip down memory lane was all but confirming his suspicions. This wasn't a conversation he wanted to have, but if he had to have it, he'd make it more enjoyable. He grabbed her waist, kissed her hard on the lips and manoeuvred her so that they both lay on the bed. A puff of dust rose as they settled, facing each other. He pushed a lock of hair behind her ear.

"You want to stay here, don't you, *mi amore*?"

"Would you hate me if I said yes? It's not that I don't like Italy or your home or family. In fact, I love them all. But I just want to be here. At least for now." He gently pulled her head to his chest and breathed in the scent of her hair.

"Of course, I will not hate you. We will stay, but you must promise that we will visit my family and perhaps even have them visit us here."

"Yes, of course. They'll definitely want to see us... and our baby." Giuseppe moved back so that he could look at Maggie's face. She wore the biggest grin, and his heart almost burst with happiness. A tear rolled down his cheek, and Maggie wiped it away. She didn't say anything else. She didn't need to.

Author's Note

The idea for this story was sparked by a trip my husband and I took to the ruins of the Marrinup prisoner-of-war camp approximately 4 kilometres west of Dwellingup, Western Australia. We spent an hour or two walking around the site, viewing what was left of the building foundations, and reading the information signs. I was struck by the fact that this camp was not too far from my hometown, yet I'd never heard of it. When I read about the prisoners working on farms, the story started to form.

My research and writing for this novel didn't start until much later, but as time passed, the story solidified in my mind. During my research, I came across conflicting facts about what went on at Marrinup and I had to make a choice which I would use. Below are the facts as I found them.

From July 1943 to August 1946, the No. 16 POW camp at Marrinup actively held prisoners. It functioned as the administrative centre for all prisoner-of-war operations in Western Australia and was staffed by officers of the Western Command. During its operation, it housed over 1600 German and Italian men—some had been captured during battles in India and Egypt, and others had been on board the HSK Kormoran when it sank in 1941.

The German men held at Marrinup worked as timber cutters, and the wood they collected warmed the homes of many Perth families. The Italian POWs worked as farmhands during the war, but they were forced to live on farms all over Western Australia rather than stay at the camp.

Doctor George Morel was appointed as a Delegate of the International Committee of the Red Cross in Australia and New Zealand. He was a Swiss citizen with a doctorate in economics who lived in Mittagong, New South Wales, before the outbreak of the war. He was tasked with inspecting the camp to ensure it complied with the rules of the Geneva Convention.

Other facts we can ascertain, either from the ruins themselves or from the accounts of prisoners and guards, are that:
- Garden beds shaped like card suits were constructed by a prisoner.
- Wristball was played at a nearby oval, and there are stories of a prisoner who had to promise not to escape before he was allowed out to play.
- The prisoners educated one another on words from their respective languages.
- Italian farmworkers were issued dictionaries in Pidgin English.

The Country Women's Association had chapters in many towns in the area. The women who were part of this amazing army of helpers knitted socks and balaclavas for the troops and held fundraising activities to provide for the guards at the camp.

While I have attempted to stick to the facts regarding life at camp as much as possible, I have taken liberties for the sake of the story. One is the incident with the Pidgin English book, which sent Giuseppe to the cooler.

The town of Colton is also fictional, but it is based on towns in the area such as Yarloop, Dwellingup, and Harvey. While Rimissa is a fictional town that draws inspiration from Italian towns in the region and their agricultural economies.

At the time of writing, the ruins of the No. 16 POW camp are still there. I recommend visiting the site and immersing yourself in the remnants of the Marrinup camp before nature claims it.

I hope you enjoyed reading Barbed Wire and Brumbies as much as I enjoyed researching and writing it. If so, please hop online and post a review!

Acknowledgements

I would like to express my deepest thanks to my family for their support. I know there were many days when I secluded myself in my office, staring at the computer. Thank you for giving me the time to pursue my passion projects.

To my husband, Neil, thanks for encouraging us to be an adventure family. If we hadn't visited Marrinup on one of our adventures, the idea for this story would never have ignited.

To my first readers—Mum, Lesley, and Abby, without your keen eyes, there would have been a few faux pas. Abby, I'm sure you're never going to let me forget the incident with the arm.

To the writing community, thank you for welcoming me into the fold.

To the readers, thank you for letting these characters into your imagination and your hearts.

Finally, to Logan, Abby, Stella, and Sophie, I hope with every fibre of my being that you follow your dreams.

About the Author

Alicia Hitchcock is a Western Australian writer with a love of history. She writes historical novels and contemporary fiction about strong female characters who overcome life's adversities. Her stories are filled with emotionally captivating drama, high-stakes tension, and heartfelt romance.

She is a member of the Australian Society of Authors, Romance Writers of Australia, and Writing WA. When she has some free time, she usually has a coffee in her hand and her nose in a book.

Visit her at aliciahitchcock.com